THE SHARP EDGE OF DEATH

Griff sensed, rather than saw, the Mexican on his left draw a knife from a long, slender sheath. But before he could react, Griff was struck by a ringing blow to his ear that sent him staggering along the bar. He recovered in time to block a kick aimed at his groin. Then he swatted away another fist and drove knuckles into a face that momentarily appeared in his line of hazy vision.

Two more men rushed at him and he picked up a chair. He smashed it against the chest of the nearest attacker and kept hold of one leg to use as a club. A bottle whistled past Griff's ear and he ducked instinctively.

Three more Mexicans came at him, faces ablaze with fury. Griff was in deep trouble—there were just too many of them. And that's when he saw the glint of the knife blade as it came slashing down at his neck!

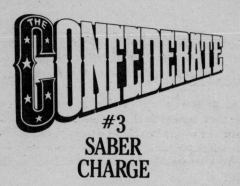

THE CONFEDERATE

#3
SABER CHARGE

FORREST A.
RANDOLPH

ZEBRA BOOKS
KENSINGTON PUBLISHING CORP.

*The author wishes to express special gratitude to Mark K.
Roberts for the valuable assistance he rendered in the
development and production of this book.*

FAR

ZEBRA BOOKS

are published by

Kensington Publishing Corp.
475 Park Avenue South
New York, N.Y. 10016

First printing: January 1985

Printed in the United States of America

This volume is dedicated with deep affection to Patrick E. Andrews, a longtime friend and fellow unreconstructed Rebel.

And here's to our Confederacy,
Strong we are and brave.
Like patriots of old we'll fight,
Our heritage to save.
And rather than submit to chains,
To fight, we do prefer.
Hoorah for the Bonnie Blue Flag,
That bears that single star!

PROLOGUE

Warm May sun brought a sweet perfume to the high plains. Wispy tendrils of vapor rose from the damp ground. The previous night's rain insured a humid day ahead. As he rode alongside Temple Ames, it made Griffin Stark think of a similar morning in late April, in the year 1863, along the Rappahannock River in far off Virginia. In a place called Fredericksburg . . .

. . . "That damned Yankee artillery is sure a caution, ain't it, major?" Sergeant Dunwittie remarked to Griffin Stark as they sat astride their matched grays on Marye's Heights, overlooking the ravaged town of Fredericksburg and the fields so hotly contested four months ago.

The Union forces had not pressed the attack since, yet they had not withdrawn. His confidence destroyed in General Burnside, President Lincoln had replaced him with Gen. Joseph Hooker. "Fighting Joe" Hooker had earned his name. He had a reputation as a skillful, hard-battling corps commander. He was also known as an ambitious officer and man, a troublemaker among the ranks of more conventional officers. After the long list of defeats by McClellan and Burnside, Mr. Lincoln felt more than willing to risk Hooker's shortcomings if Fighting Joe would, as Lincoln put it, "Go forward and give us victories."

Like McClellan before him, Hooker—who's reputation with the ladies would soon give the nation a new appellation for the ladies of· the night—began his command of the Army of the Potomac by demanding a buildup of troops and supplies. He earned the enmity of the officers by relieving all those who had served under Burnside.

A shrewd man, Hooker knew that the men saw their officers as figureheads. They stood for what the units did, *or failed to do.* In the minds of the simple men who filled the ranks, if the company, regiment, division, or corps got whipped, it was the fault of the officers. Hence, a general housecleaning was in order. And he established another thing. The constant bombardment of Confederate positions on the far· banks of the Rappahannock.

Not that the Yankees had been all that accurate. There had been some casualties, a few deaths. More had come from the weather: pneumonia and frostbite. Griff removed his stiff gray campaign hat and wiped at his brow.

"Sergeant," he declared. "They are more than a 'caution,' they're an outright aggravation. We'd best get moving. We have to swing wide of town and cross the river in that screen of trees to the west of here."

"Yes, sir."

Twenty minutes later, Griff and Dunwittie, along with Pvt. Daniel Harne, had crossed the Rappahannock and moved, unseen, behind Union lines.

"Notice those pole sheds," Griff remarked to his small patrol. He had taken the routine detail in the place of Lieutenant Monroe, not because it had been required, but for the exercise and to alleviate boredom. Perhaps being shot at by the Yankees would eliminate the state of ennui he had settled into since the frantic days at Fredericksburg in December of the previous year.

"Prob'ly stacked high with powder and shot," Dunwittie surmised.

"Yes. And only a few sentries," Griff observed, a plan forming in his fertile brain. "Keep those in mind for our return, sergeant. We, ah, might stir up a little excitement for the Yankees.''

Dunwittie beamed. *"Yes, sir!"* he enthused.

"Uh, Major Stark, sir,'' Harne drawled in a muted voice. "Over there, sir. I seen stuff like that up North oncst before.''

"What are they, Harne?''

"They's big wicker baskets, sir.''

"I can see that. What are they used for?''

Harne, pleased to be a source of information for once, instead of a dumb private in the rear rank, chose to expound on his knowledge instead of give a direct answer. "See them piles of colored cloth under the tarps? They's rubberized silk bags. Balloons is what they is. Hot air balloons. Those baskets git hooked up under them when they are full of hot air from a fire. Men can ride in 'em.''

"What would they be doing here? That sounds like some sort of circus stunt to me,'' Griff returned.

"Don't rightly know, sir. But the way it's all done up, I'd say they was fixin' to move 'em somewhere, an' soon.''

"How's that?''

"I was at this big exposition in Philadelphia. To use them balloons, the fellers had to stretch them out on the ground. These are all wrapped up tightlike. Same with the baskets. Looks like somethin' that's just come in and ain't been put where it's gonna be used.''

"Good thinking, Harne,'' Griff praised him. "What use would they be out here?'' Stark had asked the question to encourage logical thinking on the part of his men. He thought he knew the answer, but he wanted to see if they could come up with it, too.

"A feller can see fer a long ways from up there,'' Harne went on.

"Humm. What good would that do if he couldn't tell anyone on the ground about it?''

"He could drop notes,'' Harne suggested.

"If he had, uh, one of those, ah, wigwag fellers along,'' Dunwittie interposed, "he could send code by flags. Like they do in the navy.''

"That's an idea, sergeant. You didn't by any chance

happen to notice those jack-tars swaggering around over there, did you?"

"The ones with the striped shirts and floppy trousers?"

"The very men I mean, sergeant."

"I saw them, too, major," Harne remarked. "They was wearin' those sissy-lookin' hats with the big blue pompons on top."

"They're called 'signalmen,' I believe," Griff told his men. "So, we have balloons and signalmen on hand. I'd say ol' Fighting Joe was making ready to attack."

"Here at Fredericksburg again?"

"Most likely somewhere else. Some place we'd least expect. Oh, he might well send a diversionary force across to engage our troops on Marye's Heights and in the streets of town, but I'm willing to bet Hooker goes for some other objective."

"Like what, sir?"

Griff thought a moment. "Like the railroad tracks that helped Lee defeat Burnside and let Jackson keep the valley safe for a year and a half. With the bridges destroyed, rails torn up and locomotives blown apart, it would mean an end to rapid transportation for our troops."

"There's a rail yard and roundhouse at Chancellorsville," Dunwittie offered.

"Hummm," Griff mused. "A tempting target, if I'm right. But too easily defended and far behind our present lines. I think we had better get this all to Bobby Lee. We'll head back, now, sergeant."

"Yes, sir. Ah, sir, what about those powder stores?"

"Flip a coin, sergeant. Which might be more useful, blow up that powder or destroy these balloons before they can be moved?"

"Why, the balloons, of course."

"Right. And that requires a night approach and a lot of stealth. If we set off that powder, the Yankees will be alerted. Let's let it go for now. The volunteers who come over here to wreck the balloons can get it on the way out."

*　　*　　*

General Hooker looked with satisfaction on the officers around the map table in his commodious Sibley tent. He stroked his small beard and nodded in approval when the commander of the First Corps tapped a silver table knife on a little used ford of the Rappahannock.

"Precisely where we will cross. Our scouts report little enemy activity in that area. The Rebels think they own the south bank of the Rappahannock. It is our job to show them otherwise," Hooker declared pompously.

"How will we be able to affect absolute control, as the plan calls for, general? I mean, now that the balloons have been destroyed—"

Hooker glowered at his adjutant. "A minor matter, sir. Today is the twenty-ninth of April. Tomorrow our men will begin to march westward and affect crossings of the Rappahannock. By May first, we will be in the streets of Chancellorsville. My plans are perfect. May God have mercy on General Lee, for I will have none."

"Take your squadron west along the bank of the Rappahannock, major," Jeb Stuart told Griff the next morning. "Patrol as far as the mouth of the Rapidan. The Yankees have something brewing for certain and General Lee wants to know what it is. If you find no evidence of enemy activity, press on along the Rapidan to the bridge over the Chancellorsville Road."

The Rappahannock meanders leisurely southwestward from Fredericksburg. Maj. Griffin Stark took his command along its southern shore for a good six miles without spotting anything. Ahead by a couple of miles, the smaller Rapidan joined its mightier brother. The patrol, Griff thought, would be over before midmorning.

Another mile further on, he learned how mistaken he was.

"Yankees movin' along the opposite bank, major," sharp-eyed Sergeant Dunwittie informed him in a whisper.

"I, ah, I see them now, sergeant. How many do you

11

make it to be?"

"A regiment—maybe more. There's a clearing on that side, about a quarter mile up. We can get a better idea there."

Dunwittie's regiment turned out to be an entire division on the move. Behind it, came another and another. Seventy-five thousand Union soldiers, Griff later found out, had started out early that morning to reach fording places across both rivers. He sent a messenger back to Lee's headquarters and decided to press on.

Riding swiftly, the Confederate cavalry soon outdistanced the foot-slogging infantry division. Beyond the mouth of the Rapidan, Griff found more evidence of Union activity. Another division stood fast, its artillery train bogged down in a small stretch of marshy ground, where the Rappahannock made a big bend. Griff had crossed over and now rested his men and horses on Yankee territory. He moved forward with six troopers to attempt to overhear conversations among the enemy soldiers.

"How the hell's ol' 'Fuckin' Joe' expect us to get clear an' hell up to that bridge over the river with this kind of ground to cover?" a sweating artillery captain demanded of his subordinate.

"I wouldn't know, sir. But to do it by tomorrow is going to bust our guts."

"You can say that again." The captain paused and unbent from his hunched posture. He glanced at the land around him and then froze, eyes directed to a thin screen of brush and willow trees.

"I'll be damned. There's gray uniforms in those trees, Lieutenant Ashe." He quickly drew his revolver and fired a .44 ball into the thicket.

Across the short distance, a man grunted at the impact of hot lead on his shoulder and there came a Rebel yell.

"Christ!" Lieutenant Ashe exclaimed. "It's Jeb Stuart and his gray ghosts." He, too, drew his sidearm.

From behind the stand of trees, a bugel sounded and more Rebel yells filled the morning air. Thunderous hoofbeats rolled across the marshland and a swarm of Confderate cavalry swirled in among the mired cannon.

Artillerymen fell to the heavy balls of the Starr revolvers and deadly accurate fire of Pearson carbines. A horse screamed in agony and went down in its traces. Captain Turner and Lieutenant Ashe ran in among the thick of the fighting, attempting to rally their men.

"This way!" Lieutenant Simpson shouted to his troops. "Swing right. Head them off."

"Get between the artillery and that division up ahead," Griff ordered the company that rode with his squadron staff. "We'll have to hit and run."

Griff plowed into the middle of a wall of blue uniforms. A Springfield barked sharply at his side and he felt the sting of powder grains on his cheek. The ball clipped a crescent bit out of the brim of his hat. He turned that way and triggered off his Starr.

A Union soldier's face mushroomed red and he fell back on the trunions of a twelve pound Napoleon. Ahead Griff saw the silver bars of a Union captain and forced his powerful horse in that direction. As he did so, he turned in the saddle and shouted to Sergeant Dunwittie.

"Ten men to spike cannons, the rest ride down these gunners."

"Yes, sir."

A rifle ball moaned past Griff's ear and reflexively he ducked to the right. It saved his life as a .44 ball from Captain Turner's Remington 1860 Army split air where Griff's chin had been and smacked into the shoulder meat of a gray Confederate mount to the major's rear. Griff whipped his revolver to the left and slipped back the hammer.

When it fell, a round ball sped to the hollow in Turner's neck and popped a wet black hole there. Blood welled up and began to run as the Union officer's head snapped back, and he spilled onto the ground beside the corpses of many of his men.

"Pull back," a forward scout shouted as he rode pell-mell into the melee from his position ahead of the column of artillery. "Yankee infantry comin' on the double."

A metallic ring filled the air as Confederate cavalrymen drove brass spikes into the touch holes of Yankee cannon and broke them off with heavy mallets. They rammed the thick bases down the bores and seated them with a mighty swing.

Resistance had dwindled to a dozen artillerymen.

"Finish those cannon and let's get out of here. General Lee will want to know," Griff commanded.

A fast hour's ride brought them to the stately white farmhouse where Lee made his headquarters behind the defensive line at Fredericksburg. Strangely, the news Griff brought seemed to cheer the soft-voiced warrior.

"So Joe Hooker has decided to get off his duff," Robert E. Lee mused as he considered the map and the implications of Griff's scouting report, along with others. "About time. He's making for Chancellorsville. No doubt about that, gentlemen. Jubal," he turned to Gen. Jubal Early. "I'm going to leave you here with fifteen thousand men. Hold Fredericksburg. Hold it at all costs.

"Hooker is trying to turn my left flank. I intend to prevent that. I will take the remainder of the army and march at once for Chancellorsville. I cannot afford to have the right flank crumble behind me. Old friend, we've come a long way together. With God's grace, perhaps we will see this dreadful conflict ended this day." Lee blinked back the moisture in his eyes and addressed himself to Jeb Stuart.

"James, I want a forward screen of cavalry. Leave one squadron here to support Jubal, another to form an advance screen, and the rest will ride in the van."

"Yes, sir. Major Stark, your squadron will have the honor of leading the advance."

"Thank you, sir. Thank you, General Lee."

Griff had opportunity to recant his gratitude before the day ended. As the advance element of Lee's drive on Chancellorsville, Griff's men were first to encounter

Hooker's lead units.

"For God's sake!" Sergeant Dunwittie bellowed. "There's Yankees all around us."

"There's a whole division of blue bellies out ahead, major," the point man reported a moment later.

"Gentlemen," Griff told his officers unnecessarily. "We have found the enemy."

"More likely, they've found us," Lieutenant Monroe observed.

"We'll carry the battle to them, then," Griff decided.

In two minutes the air shivered with gunfire.

Rifles and muskets rattled and the crisp bark of carbines sounded over their ominous background. Clouds of powder smoke obscured the wide, bowl-shaped grassy field. Then the Union artillery unlimbered and opened up.

Charging gray horses folded their legs under their bodies and crashed to earth, catapulting their riders forward to be shredded by wicked sprays of cannister and grape. Union cavalry appeared and launched a counter-attack, sabres glittering in the bright sun of the last day of April. The Confederates met them with the shock of a battering ram.

Men wheeled their mounts, weapons flailing, revolvers spitting death in the dust and smoke of battle. Yankees screamed and died, while their counterparts fought tenaciously and gave up their lives with the same shouts of pain and horror. The forward observer's estimate had been correct, Griff surmised.

An entire division, he had encountered the previous day, with cavalry and artillery support, must have crossed the Rappahannock at a point northwest of Chancellorsville and advanced rapidly. To his amazement, he saw the Union troops digging in, rather than pressing forward. At least a regiment in strength, they quickly established a salient point and laid down withering fire while the remainder of the division withdrew slightly and formed a main line of resistance closer to town.

"Pull back," Griff commanded. "Sound *Officers' Call,*"

he told his trumpeter.

When the officers arrived at Griff's vantage point overlooking the Union emplacements, he gave them terse instructions. "We have to hold them here. Keep the pressure on, or that division will continue to advance. Why they stopped I don't know. Two companies to remain. The third will accompany me. General Lee must know of this at once."

"Chancellorsville has already fallen to the Union forces," General Lee told his staff meeting that night. "Our advance elements encountered them more than a mile outside town, to the west. Unaccountably, according to Major Stark, the enemy decided to entrench themselves there and await our pleasure. That is all well and good with me. I intend to attack."

"What!" several staff officers exclaimed. The combat unit commanders only grinned.

"Yes. I shall hold the line east of Chancellorsville with fewer than twenty thousand men. Thomas," he said to Stonewall Jackson. "Your corps strength is what?"

"Twenty-six thousand strong, general."

"Good. You will make a long march westward early tomorrow morning. Skirt Chancellorsville and then turn east and strike behind the Union right flank. I'm going to change Hooker's turning movement into an envelopment of his own right flank."

"Good Lord, general," Jubal Early exclaimed. "What you propose is to encircle an army twice the size of your own."

"With T. J. on our side, I predict it shall be done," Lee returned confidently.

In the darkness of pre-dawn, Jackson's men, with all but one squadron of cavalry, pulled out. Their course took them into wild tangles of bracken, hickory, and oak. Hoofs muffled with tow-sacks, the cavalry screened ahead

16

and to both sides. Within two hours, the outriders had become separated. Still Jackson pushed on. At last, Griffin Stark found himself, along with Sergeant Dunwittie and Private Harne, completely isolated from his command. They halted in a thicket of scrub oak.

"Where are they, major?" Dunwittie asked in a whisper.

"More to the point, sergeant, where are we?" Griff shot back.

"Uh, don't rightly know. But there's fires up ahead and I smell coffee and bacon. Figure the Yankees can't be too far away. If only we can break out of here and link up with the column, we'll have us a regular little tussle."

"What a hell of a place to fight a battle," Griff observed aloud.

CHAPTER ONE

"What a hell of a place to run into some unfriendly Blackfeet," Griffin Stark remarked as he and his companion halted briefly to gaze over the undulating terrain ahead.

"You ask this chile, *anyplace* is a hell of a spot to run into unfriendly Indians. What you been mullin' over so quiet like these past few miles?"

"I was thinking about the war."

"Were you now?" Ames's pale, nearly colorless gray eyes twinkled. He rubbed his bristly, ginger sideburns with one thumb and forefinger as he groped in a pocket of his buckskin shirt for his Catlin red clay pipe.

"Ya know," he went on in a calculating manner, "though this chile served as scout for that bunch of Confederates who wanted to go after the gold in Colorado, I didn't wear the uniform. That war's always interested me." He paused and peered at the sun, now well over the midday high. "We'd best be gettin' back to those engineer-type soljer boys. They might be map makers, but I allow as how they could easy get lost in these foothills. There's a passable Blackfoot village supposed to be around here within no more'n a day's ride. Unless some flatland pilgrims have been messin' in their stew pot, we should have a cordial welcome there.

"What say," Ames went on, changing the subject, "while we ride along the backtrail, you spin me some

19

yarns about the war?"

"I think I can oblige. My mind was on Chancellorsville. The country we went through yesterday made me think of it. When I look back on it, I'm certain that it was the most significant point in the whole war." Quickly Griff filled Temple in on the circumstances of the battle and the positions held by Union and Confederate forces on the evening of May first.

"The next morning, Jackson marched twelve miles westward, while Lee kept Hooker's seventy-three thousand men pinned to their trenches in front of Chancellorsville. When Jackson got into position and attacked at six that evening, Hooker's right flank collapsed completely . . ."

. . . "Look at 'em run!" young Lieutenant Monroe shouted.

Together with the other units of Griffin Stark's squadron, Monroe's company had dashed out of the screen of woods three miles from the western edge of Chancellorsville. The high, clumsy wagons of the Union baggage train offered little obstacle to the yelling Confederate cavalry. Hooker had relied so heavily on the shock of his initial advance that only a few pickets had been put out. Most of these fired but a single shot and ran toward the protection of the distant town and the deep concentration of troops beyond.

"Fire those wagons," Sergeant Dunwittie shouted from his position beside Griffin Stark. "Get 'em goin' good."

Behind the line of charging horsemen, Jackson's infantry came on the run. Rifles held at high port, they spilled a butternut-and-gray tide across the green fields. From hedgerows, Union marksman opened up with a crackle of musketry.

"To the left!" Griff commanded. "Get those Yankees in the hedges."

Beyond this scattered resistance, the fleeing sentries reached their own artillery park. Some officer had presence of mind to turn about two small, light field pieces and open fire. Large puffs of greasy powder smoke spewed from the muzzles, tinged orange by long tongues of flame.

Small geysers of earth rose where the roundshot struck. Then they came onward, rolling and bounding lazily across the turf like children's wind-driven balls. The illusion shattered when one struck the foreleg of a galloping cavalry mount.

Blood sprayed the air and the stricken animal shrieked in agony as it went down. The hapless rider flew from his saddle and crashed a shoulder and his neck into a fence post. It made a thick, meaty sound, like a butcher with a haunch of beef. The injured man kicked feebly and lay still. More fire came on them and Griff looked around to gauge how soon the infantry would be within range to engage the enemy.

"They're fallin' back, major," Captain McDade called out gleefully.

"I see that. Another five hundred yards and they will be in among those farm buildings. That could get dangerous." Griff took another look around. "Have the men close up. We have to pierce their defences and work in among them." He repeated his order to the trumpeter, who blew the proper signals.

"We're being attacked in the rear!" an agitated young lieutenant yelled at General Hooker.

"By whom? How?" Hooker looked up from the Chippendale table on which he had placed a map in the parlor of a spacious house in the center of Chancellorsville, which he had chosen as his headquarters.

"It's . . . it's, ah, Jackson, sir," the officer stammered.

"Thomas Jackson," Hooker said wonderingly. "That prissy school teacher, always reading his Bible, they say. How in hell did he get behind us?"

"I don't know, sir, but he's there all the same. A galloper came from the artillery park west of here. Major Drummond estimates two squadrons of cavalry acting as

21

advance to the infantry. He says it is no diversion. There's a full corps on the verge of overrunning his position."

"Send some troops. At once. Put a corps . . . two corps on the march."

"And what do we hold Lee with?" Hooker's adjutant inquired. "You've determined he has the superior force. Impossible as it seems, he's gotten this far. If this is just part of Jackson's corps, with some of Stuart's cavalry acting as a diversion, Lee will continue his attack. We could be caught in a pincer movement."

Hooker thought it over. Indecision gripped him. The news had badly shaken him. From outside the clatter of hoofs announced the arrival of more messengers. One knocked perfunctorily and hurried inside the parlor.

"Rebels attacking in force along our rear, general," he blurted out.

Artillery sounded in the distance, then the ring of bugles and the clash of arms. A shout went up from the direction of the trenches opposite Lee. In a brief second, a messenger panted into the room.

"Colonel Turner's compliments, sir, and Lee is attacking."

"You were right," Hooker said to his adjutant. "Better send, ah, two regiments for now. Let this situation develop a bit more before we over-commit."

"All hell's broken loose out there, general," Griffin Stark reported to Gen. T. J. Jackson. He saw the mild-mannered officer's frown and hastily apologized. "Sorry about the language, sir. But we've advanced over a mile already. Outstripped the infantry. The Yankees are falling back."

"Casualties, major?"

"We're taking a few. Less than expected, though. We're advancing so fast the enemy has no time for more than one volley, then they have to run for it."

Stonewall furrowed his brow with concentration and his full lips pushed in and out. "Go back to your men,

Major Stark. Ask them to hold their present position until the infantry catches up. And my compliments to Colonel Lowe on your way, sir. Inform him I expect to see his regiment in the lead when our soldiers reach the streets of Chancellorsville."

Griff gave a smart salute and hurried to his lathered mount.

The infantry had done a good job of closing the gap, he noted on the way back. Only now the right flank had come into a box formed by the Union cavalry guarding the exposed left of the Yankee line. Bugles sounded as Griff rode to a small rise where his battle flag flew brightly in the lowering sun.

"Yankee cavalry, major," Lieutenant Monroe informed him, pointing to where sabres flashed red-orange in the dying light of day.

"General Jackson wants us to hold here. Can we do it?"

"With a little luck, sir. Those boys seem determined to drive us out."

"Then we'll stop them, eh, lieutenant?" Griff hoped his jaunty confidence was not misdirected . . .

. . . "We held until nightfall," Griffin Stark went on, relating the events of Chancellorsville to Temple Ames. Griff's voice roughened. "That night, General Jackson came forward with some of his staff. They wanted to take a good look at the Yankee positions. They rode through our lines and stayed out for nearly an hour. When the general and his officers returned, a rookie who had been put on picket duty mistook them for a Union patrol. He . . . fired . . . and then . . . several more opened up. General Jackson was . . . seriously wounded." Griff's words came in a near whisper, choked with a grief he still felt.

"Uh, this chile knows the rest, Griff. Ol' Stonewall lingered on until the tenth of May, then he died. What was them last words of his?"

Griff cleared his throat. "The general had always been a truly pious man. He directed all his men to pray before battle and carried a Bible with him. He said, ah, 'Let us cross over the river and rest under the shade of the trees.'"

Temple blinked back the moisture in his eyes. "There's them green-stick soljer boys ahead. May as well make camp here fer the night."

"Good a place as any. I wonder, would the nez Percé trade with the Blackfeet?"

"Thinkin' about that boy o' yers, again, eh? Welp, near as this chile can figger, they might. Or again, they might not. We'll know when we reach the place."

After the evening meal, Temple Ames brought his Coffee Mill Sharps and hunkered down beside the fire. He took a sack of Arbuckle's from his possbles bag and poured beans into the open hatch in the buttstock. He held the device over a pot of boiling water and turned the handle. Savory coffee aroma filled the night air as the grounds fell into the water. He puffed on his Catlin pipe and nodded to Griff.

"What happened after Jackson got shot?"

"Everyone felt the loss terribly, of course. But Lee had learned that General Sedgwick had pushed Jubal Early out of Fredericksburg. He left Jeb Stuart in command at Chancellorsville. The next day we pushed Hooker hard enough he lost his nerve. The Yankees outnumbered us two to one. Lee took twenty thousand men and turned back on Sedgwick. Ran him right into town, while we kept nipping at Hooker. Once Hooker gave it up, his men did, too. By May the sixth, both parts of the Union army had been driven back across the Rappahannock. We lost twelve thousand, eight hundred men. The Yanks nearly twice that many. Worse, we lost Stonewall Jackson. Lee's only chance to win the war went with him."

"Interesting, Mr. Stark," a paunchy, graying officer remarked as he walked over to the fire. "I was at Fredericksburg, too. And at Chancellorsville. With the engineers. We put in the pontoon bridges."

"Your men acted with uncommon bravery, Major Gifford."

"Thank you. I've always been of the same opinion.

24

With Jackson gone, it became inevitable that Lee would lose in the end. Not to take anything away from Lee's generals, but of all of them, Jackson was the most inspired. He knew how to get men to give an ounce or two more than they believed they had in them. Outnumbered, out-supplied, it took that sort of leadership to keep the struggle going."

"It went on entirely too long," Griff said morosely.

"How do you mean?"

"What started off as a grand adventure in defense of States' Rights ended up in bitterness and enormous losses. What has come after has created a rift between North and South that may never heal."

"Uh, Reconstruction, you mean? I, ah, put in for duty in the West because of it. I could, uh, never inflict that sort of indignity upon a proud and admirable people."

"What the major means, Mr. Stark, is that though he fought for the Union, his family is from Kentucky," Captain Fairweather added as he came to partake of the coffee.

"He is right, of course," Gifford admitted. "You served with Stuart's cavalry, am I right?"

Griff nodded. "I commanded a squadron."

Gifford brightened. "The Grays, by God! I'm right, aren't I? You're the ones who turned George Meade's men."

"The same."

"What brings you out here, then?"

"Reconstruction. And my son's out there somewhere," Griff waved vaguely westward. "My wife died—was murdered by some of Sherman's men." There was hurt and challenge in Griff's tone.

"Can't say that I ever had any great love for Bill Sherman or his idea of how to fight a war," Gifford confessed. "How did your boy get here?"

"One of our slaves, uh, our servants, took him to my sister's place. After the war ended, she and her husband headed west. They took Jeremy along, naturally. Everyone around Riversend thought I had died in battle. Damned near did, at the Wilderness."

"Your brother-in-law and sister. They have a homestead somewhere around these parts?" Gifford made it sound as unlikely as it was.

"No. They were massacred by the Cheyenne. Attack on a wagon train. From what I have been able to put together, Jeremy fought the Indians ferociously. They took him with them."

"He's been living with the Cheyenne ever since?"

"Until recently, major."

"Call me Howard."

"All right, Howard. My given name is Griffin—Griff to those that know me. Anyway, Jeremy had been adopted by this war chief, Two Otters. The village was attacked by renegade Shoshone warriors. Jeremy was taken away with them. Later they traded him off to some Nez Percé for horses. That's what brought me out this far. I intend to get my son back."

"Have you had much luck in that direction?"

"Not so far. I'm hoping the Blackfeet can tell us something."

"We'll be at their village tomorrow," Gifford said. "Providing I can get these civilian surveyors we're wet-nursing to stir themselves early enough in the morning."

"Want this chile to put some gunpowder in their breakfast coffee?" Temple Ames suggested.

A chuckle rolled from Gifford's lips. "I'm well aware of your notorious antics, Coonstalker. It's one of the reasons I was anxious to engage you as a guide."

"Ain't nothin' wrong with a little tad of coarse-grain powder in yer coffee, Howard. It makes yer pecker stiff an' ya can send smoke signals with the blue farts."

"I also know about your penchant for tall tales," Gifford countered through another laugh. Major Gifford turned again to Griffin Stark. "Griff, how serious are you about tracking down your son?"

"It don't come any more serious than I am. I will find Jeremy if it is the last thing I do."

CHAPTER TWO

A light haze turned the Rocky Mountains a soft blue. Squirrels, chipmunks, and woodpeckers vied with each other to sound the alarm and saucily scold the short column of men who rode at ease through the thicker forest of pine and aspen. Here and there, the sun struck bright rays off the brass lens shades of surveyors' transits. At the head of the file, Major Gifford rode slumped in the saddle. Perspiration shone on his balding pate. Beyond him, over the next grade, Griffin Stark and Temple Ames paused to study the horizon.

"Smoke over there. Cook fires, I'd judge," Griff announced, pointing to their right front.

"Yep. Blackfoot village. I can make out the lodge poles on about ten tipis."

"Like hell you can," Griff chided.

"Sure's this chile is sittin' beside ya, you can count on it."

"Another hour will put us there."

"I reckon."

"I'll head back and tell Gifford."

Naked children of seven and eight ran giggling and shouting alongside the visitors when the column rode into the village an hour and a quarter later. Smaller youngsters hid shyly behind their mothers' legs and peeped out with wide, shoe-button eyes. The camp crier went ahead, announcing their arrival to all who could hear. Spotted

27

Elk, the civil chief of the Blackfoot village, greeted them in front of his lodge.

"What is this ma-map you make?" he inquired after the courtesies had been seen to.

"Marks on paper," Gifford explained through Temple Ames. "They tell where the mountains are, how high they reach, where the rivers run."

"Why do you need these things? We know where mountains are, where rivers go, we know deer and elk and bear. Do you make marks for these?"

"Ah, no, chief. The map is to show other people, who have never seen your land, what it looks like."

Spotted Elk's lower lips curled down in disdain. He waved a hand in a gesture of dismissal. "Land not flat. Not wiggly marks on paper. Trees tall, mountains big, water deep and cold. This is not my land."

"It's a representation," Gifford explained patiently.

Temple Ames had trouble with that word. He rendered it as a "ghost picture." That upset Spotted Elk.

"Ghost picture bad medicine." His eyes narrowed suspiciously. "You come to fight? Make picture, bring more men to kill my people?"

"No, Spotted Elk. Let me assure you of that. Men who understand the marks on the paper can tell by that how high your mountains are, how wide and deep the rivers, where there are passes through the range and valleys of rich grass."

A shrewd smile widened under Spotted Elk's hawk-beak of a nose. "Maybe then white men like our land more than where they live. Maybe then they come and take it way?"

"I certainly hope not," the major replied.

"It is always so. We make marks on paper the grandfather in Wash-in-ton call treaty. White men go away. Then come back with more pale-skinned ones to settle on the land they give us. Why is this so?"

"I'm afraid I can't help you on that. But *we* cause no harm, make no fights. We come in peace."

"Then you shall have peace for so long as you are in my village or on our hunting grounds. Tonight we will feast, talk, dance. You have the burning water?"

"Whiskey?" Gifford inquired rightly. "Well, I, ah, do happen to have a couple of bottles along. For medicinal purposes, you understand?"

Spotted Elk nodded enthusiastically. "Eat a lot, get sore belly, take medicine. It is good. Go now and make yourselves comfortable. We feast."

Griff and Temple chose to walk through the Blackfoot village. One small boy among the swarm that accompanied them on their promanade, whom Griff judged to be about the size of Jeremy, shyly reached out and took the former Confederate's hand. His companions giggled at this and made rude and suggestive gestures with their circled thumbs and forefingers and the thumb of the other hand. The youngster spat something at them in his language. Temple snorted in amusement as the boys ran off shouting and hooting with laughter.

"He said you were his friend. That if they didn't like it, they could go pull their peckers behind their lodges."

"I'll never understand the way the Indians raise their children. Doesn't that sort of, ah, thing effect the way they grow up?"

"'Course not. A stiff pecker's got no conscience. An' usin' it don't make ya grow up an idiot. You oughtta know that." Temple looked hard at Griff a second. "Now don't tell this chile," he went on, an unbelievable idea coming to him. "Don't tell me you never flogged yer tallywhacker when you were a little tad? By golly, I bet you never did!" he burst out in a fit of laughter.

They stopped near the horse herd. Small boys, in breechcloth and moccasins, like the one beside Griff, sat astride bareback creatures and worked their way through the grazing animals. The youngster—he'd given his name as Rabbit Nose—touched his chest and then waved toward the ponies as he jabbered in his musical tongue.

"He says he watches the big dogs—that's their word for horses—ever' three days."

"Good for him," Griff returned indifferently. Even so, he felt a warming toward the boy. Rabbit Nose's open

29

friendliness made Griff sad for want of Jeremy, yet in some manner partly made up for his son's continued absence from him. On the point of turning away, his eye caught a flash of white. Griff sucked in his breath and pointed.

"Over there. Ask Rabbit Nose if the Nez Percé have been here recently."

Temple complied and got a vague answer. "Says it ain't been soon an' it ain't been long ago."

"We'll have to look into it more with Chief Spotted Elk."

Bear Bull, the Blackfoot medicine man, wore his braids in front of his ears. Not yet tinged with gray, they hung like obsidian ropes; white, circular discs of fresh water clam shell and pounded brass worked into them so that his head appeared to ripple with light when he moved. His long, rock-jawed face had as yet to become seamed with the crags of age. He stood tall and proud, with a self-contained assurance. Atop his head, he wore the symbol of his office, a tightly wound, hornlike hair coil that protruded over his forehead from his forelock, with a dignity that would have been the envy of many Washington politicos.

As the ranking warriors gathered outside Spotted Elk's lodge to talk and gamble on the painted bone game prior to the feast, he appeared with his retinue of small boys and a teenage apprentice. His arms held rigidly before him, he bore the sacred pipe believed by his people to have been given to them long ago by the much feared and respected Thunder Spirit. He alone had custody of this great relic and it added to his power in matters secular as well as spiritual. He nodded with regal grace to acknowledge the visitors and bent low to enter the lodge.

"High mucky-muck," Temple observed. "This chile figgers we're in for the deluxe treatment. You know the trappin's fer smokin' a pipe, dontcha?"

"Yes," Griff answered lightly.

"Wal-l, the Blackfeet go about it a bit different. They starts to the north, then the east an' so on. Surprised others

30

don't, too. It's cause their worst weather comes from the north an' they reckon to make peace with those spirits first off."

"We'll probably have dog stew," Griff remarked with a slight twist of his lips.

"Count on it. An' buffala hump ribs, all sweet and juicy."

Griff brightened. "Now that I can go for."

Rabbit Nose still stood at Griff's side. He looked up with shining eyes at the tall white man and dreamed his private dreams of riding across the wide, flat lands to the east with this powerful warrior. He would watch the pony herd and tend to the fire each night and sleep warm and happy close by his new-found hero. When the white chief took a woman, he would crouch outside the lodge and keep warm at the cookfire embers. And, he promised himself, he would not feel envy or think mean thoughts. Suddenly his world brightened anew as the object of his fantasy discovered his presence and reached down to ruffle his hair.

"How do I get unglued from my companion here?" Griff asked Temple.

"When you go to the lodge where you'll be stayin' tonight, just give him a shove out the flap. Firm, but gentlelike. He'll get the message."

"Won't it offend someone in his family?"

"Naw. He's got other 'uncles' he can go sleep over at. You're just new an' they'll not expect you to know their customs."

"How do you mean?"

"Boys grow up with their uncles. Don't necessary mean blood kin, but usually a friend of the shaver's father. They learn how to use a bow, ride, care for horses, all that sort of thing from these uncles. Li'l Rabbit Nose here has decided to make you his uncle for the time being."

Unbidden, Griffin Stark's thoughts went to his own son. Would Jeremy be sleeping in the lodge of some Nes Percé uncle tonight? What would he learn tomorrow? His soul felt hard and dry, an ache spread in his chest. He

31

looked down at the Blackfoot child with new eyes. Surely there would be room in the lodge for one small boy.

The camp crier announced the feast. Those chosen as guests in the chief's lodge filed in, walked to the right and seated themselves according to a long-accepted custom. It left the places of honor for Griff, Temple, and the men of the survey party.

"First we smoke," Spotted Elk informed his guests.

From the decorated otter-skin envelope, Bear Bull produced the sacred pipe. Griff, and those other whites knowledgeable in the ways of the mighty horse-owning tribes, raised eyebrows. This would be a formal feast and official discussion of events important to the tribe. What was said and done would be binding on all present, so long as they gave allegiance to Spotted Elk.

When the pipe had gone its way around the circle, Bear Bull brought an antelope horn rest from the container and placed the sacred object on it, open end of the stem pointed north.

"There are men with us who come to gain knowledge of our lands. They say they come in peace. One of these I know. Our friend, He-Who-Stalks-Raccoon. He speaks straight. He says these are good men. To know something is to be better than before," Spotted Elk declared in a lengthy speech, which Temple Ames translated for the benefit of the white men.

"It is good that men seek to learn first, not to come, kill, waste game, and dirty the streams, having no knowledge of how the Earth Mother should be treated and what respect is due her children. We feast these men. We—" here he paused a moment and shrewdly eyed his principal warriors and sub-chiefs. "We welcome them. While they go about our land, they will carry a belt of peace wampum, white and blue beads to signify their tongues are straight and their hearts true. Let no man of our people harm them. Let no man of our people stand in their way. Let every village embrace them and let every lodge be open to them. I will send with them—" Spotted Elk turned now to Major Gifford.

"Five of my closest friends to act as guides and to herald their coming to our villages. Let all men honor this peace which we make here. I have spoken."

Mutters of approval went the rounds and Temple nodded sagely to Griff. "This chile ain't seen such an open-hearted welcome in nigh onto thirty years. These surveyor boys will be well cared for from now on. You can bet on that."

"When should I ask about the Nez Percé?"

"After we eat, no sense in hurryin' things."

The women brought food then. First, bowls of parched corn mush, pounded with wild garlic and cooked on a low fire of coals until quite thick. The second course came, the inevitable dog stew. This one had chunks of wild turnip, dried the previous summer, chilies, fresh shoots of wild onion, and pine nuts. Acorn cakes followed, to sop up the grease from smoking buffalo hump ribs, cooked to a pleasing redness inside and fiery hot from the coals.

When everyone had eaten their fill, belched prodigiously and eaten a bit more to show their host how well they thought of the food, Gifford got out a bottle of fine Pennsylvania rye and handed it to Spotted Elk. The chief drank deeply, smacked his lips in approval and passed the container along. Temple nodded to Griff.

"Among your horses," Griff remarked, attempting to sound casual, "I noticed a number of the spotted animals of the Nez Percé. Have you traded with them recently?"

Spotted Elk smiled broadly and nodded. "They come in the Moon of Falling Leaves. Bring many big dogs with the spots."

"Last fall," Griff mused aloud. They could be anywhere now. Spotted Elk continued to talk.

"They make good trades, like our women. They stay until ice breaks off of the river and snow goes away."

Energized by this bit of good fortune, Griff nearly stammered out his next question. "H-how long ago did they leave?"

"Five suns ago."

"Five days. Did they, ah, did they have a boy with them?

33

White hair, maybe in braids now?"

"Hunh!" Spotted Elk grunted. "They have two Cheyenne boys. One had white hair. He ride like wind. Sit horse like red-bug-that-bite."

"Hung on like a chigger," Temple added to clarify.

"How old was he?"

"I think, nine . . . ten summers. He have big shoulders, like you. Thick body, but not fat. Strong legs. His eyes were the eyes of the People."

"His mother was part Cherokee," Griff acknowledged.

"Not Cheyenne?"

"No. My son. How was this boy named?"

"He called himself Snow Rabbit."

"It's Jeremy!" Griff exclaimed in a near shout. "Thank you, Spotted Elk. I can't thank you enough."

"I have children," the chief responded. "I know a father's heart. One of my sons is of an age with this Cheyenne boy. They became friends. Now he sees you as a special friend. He is named Rabbit Nose."

"Wal-l, I'll be damned," Temple Ames put on the end of his translation.

"I think there *will* be room in that lodge for a small boy," Griff said in an aside. "Again, you have my deepest gratitude, Spotted Elk. When the Nez Percé left your village, which direction did they go?"

"To the big mountains. West, toward the land of their people."

"Major," Griff began, planning as he spoke. "You are in good hands with the Blackfeet. They will guide you. I'm going to have to leave you. I must find my son. I want Temple to come, if he will."

"But that would leave us without a white guide."

"You don't need one now," Temple snapped. "With that safe conduct pass from Chief Spotted Elk, an' some o' his boys to ride along, you got better than an army o' Griff's an' this chile could provide. Th' way this chile sees it, you done made maps of the way in here. You're goin' to make more on the way out to Or-e-gon. So, you can't get lost. If it's all the same with you, this chile is gonna amble

34

along with Griff here and see what comes of it."

"That's a windy speech for you, Coonstalker," Gifford stated, his lips twisted in a rueful grin. "There's no talking either of you out of it, I'm sure. All right, then. We depart in the morning. Our course is the same. At least accompany us until we come upon these Nez Percé you spoke of."

"Fair enough," Temple agreed. "'Cept for one thing. With all that peekin' through the glass an' map makin' you'd move too slow. We'll blaze the trail, mark water courses and such for you. But iffin we's to catch them Nez Percé, we have to make tracks."

"The faster, the better," Griff declared.

CHAPTER THREE

Strident notes belled from two trumpets. Crisply pro-
nounced Spanish words clicked like castinets as the
Mariachis sang and accompanied themselves on guitars.
The rapid-fire rattle of the song served to provide a
suitable mask for confidential conversation in addition to
entertainment. The cool interior of the high-ceilinged
adobe *cantina* off the main plaza of *Ciudad Juarez* had
emptied of all but four men. They sat at a round,
handmade wooden table. Small clay cups and a terra cotta
olla of tequila adorned the slightly uneven, unpainted
surface. Two of the men had the typical dark faces of
Indios. The other pair clearly showed their North
American origins.

"So. Now we can talk," a short, fat man with close-set
eyes and a weak chin declared. "Even the *cantinaro* has left
us." He wore a poorly fitted suit and the high, round-toed
boots of a military officer. "First, we should introduce our
associates. *Coronel* Breathwaite," he stumbled over the
English name. "I have the honor to present my strong
right arm, commander of my bodyguard regiment,
Coronel Ramon Jesus y Maria Cardoza."

"*Con mucho gusto*, Colonel," Col. Chester Breathwaite, late of the Confederate States Army, responded in
wretchedly accented Spanish.

"*Equalmente, Coronel*," Cardoza replied oilily.

Cardoza, unlike his superior, was a big man. His heavy

37

shoulders drooped slightly but did not distract from the feral power he exuded. Clean-shaven, he wore a small, thin mustache on the precise center of his long, Indian upper lip. Although thirty-seven, he appeared younger, his skin holding a healthy glow from much outdoor living and his keen black eyes focusing sharply, in a disconcerting manner, on anyone he encountered. He fixed Arthur Treadwell with a disdainful, unfocused gaze and then returned his perusal to Breathwaite.

Chester Breathwaite cleared his throat to ease the strain he felt and introduced his companion in turn. "Gen. Emilio Santos, Colonel Cardoza, I have the honor to present the senior vice-president of the consortium, *Señor* Arthur Treadwell."

"Charmed," Arthur breathed out languidly.

General Santos gaped. Ramon Cardoza sniggered. To hide his irritation over Arthur Treadwell's effeminate manner, Chester Breathwaite took a big gulp from a clay cup of tequila. He nearly strangled over the strong, fiery liquor. He recovered himself with a gasp and spoke, his voice at first a hollow, breathy exhalation.

"General Santos, the purpose of our meeting is to inform you of the consortium's decision. It is my pleasure to announce that my efforts on your behalf have been successful. The Federated Rail Consortium has agreed to provide necessary financing to advance your efforts on behalf of the people of Mexico."

"We will get the guns?" Cardoza interrupted.

"Oh, yes," Breathwaite answered coolly. "And much more. Caisson-loads of ammunition for your cannon," he began listing. "Money to pay your soldiers."

General Santos gave him a surprised look with his close-set eyes.

"Naturally you don't expect the government to keep on paying your wages when you make the break official. So, who then would you go to?"

"Excellent," the diminutive officer declared. One hand went to his face and he trailed a finger lightly over the circular scar, caused by a bullet that passed through both cheeks. He had obtained the wound honorably, fighting the French only a few years before.

"Juarez is not a leader," Santos went on. "He is a brilliant strategist, his words inspire millions, he can demand and get loyalty from millions more. Yet he is not the sort of leader Mexico needs at this time."

"You, ah, see yourself as more suitable to this task, general?" Arthur Treadwell drawled.

"I . . . or someone like me. I do this only for the good of Mexico."

Arthur made a weak gesture, flipping his wrist as though shooing a fly. "That is why your soldiers are looting the ranchos, banks, and businesses all over the state of Guanajuato?"

"It is the rich!" Santos declared vehemently. "Always we have the rich with us, taking our sustenance, grinding the people into poverty and despair. *They* sided with Maxmillian. *They* are the true enemy of the people. Juarez has betrayed us, surrounded himself with rich men who make laws that benefit only them and use the army only to despoil the *peones* and leave misery where there could be plenty."

"Juarez promised to give the land to the people," Cardoza interjected. "Only five million hecaters have so far been divided up. Now Juarez and his rich advisors are devising legal means to take that back from the *peones* who received it in the first place."

"What's wrong with being rich?" Arthur inquired in a peevish tone. "The men of the consortium are wealthy beyond your wildest imaginings."

"*Si.* But they do not contrive to place a yoke around the necks of the Mexican people," Santos shot back.

"Oh, *of course not.*" Arthur sneered in such a manner that Breathwaite wanted to strangle him.

"To, ah, return to our discussion," General Santos intoned. "Our needs are simple. You have covered three of them: rifles, shot, and powder for the cannon, money to pay the soldiers. What else can this consortium of yours provide?"

"Recruits. Many disaffected soldiers from the Confederacy and the Union have drifted west. They have precipitated along the border in Texas, New Mexico Territory, even Arizona."

"Riffraff," Santos dismissed.

"They are trained soldiers, combat experienced. They will not run like a rabbit when the first shot is fired." Breathwaite saw the unconscious tightening of Santos's eyes and knew he had hit upon a sore point. Inwardly he prided himself and pushed for his first concession. "Promise them a bit of the loot and I can have them delivered to you by the hundreds."

"An interesting proposition," Cardoza interposed. "One we will think upon. What else do you have?"

"Information," Breathwaite told him. "Inside information, purchased at great price from trustworthy minions of the Juarez regime. We can tell you where and when to move to be most effective against Benito Juarez and also— which is more important—where not to be. You will know, almost before Juarez himself, what his troops are doing to counter your little, ah, *coup d'etat.*"

General Santos bellowed with laughter. "You amaze me, *Coronel.* With scheming, crafty minds like yours, why did the Confederacy lose?"

Arthur Treadwell snorted disdainfully. "We were too busy lining our own nests. What's the good of war unless one can profit by it?"

"For once," Santos said in rapid Spanish, "your friend has said something intelligent. We, of course, find it necessary to, ah, obtain this feathering along the way. How else can we meet the expenses of such a grand undertaking?"

"*Como sí, como no?*" Breathwaite exclaimed, pleased with his rapidly increasing facility in the foreign tongue.

"What did he say?" Arthur demanded, his own scanty knowledge of the language insufficient to follow the exchange.

"That you made a brilliant observation. He's little more than a bandit, after all. You know that as well as I. He admitted to taking a bit along the way."

"Thank Heaven for that. God, if we had come across an idealist, none of this would work."

"Juarez is the idealist. An impractical philosophy for a politician. No, Juarez won't be around much longer. And when he is gone—"

"When can we expect delivery of the first, ah, consignment?" General Santos interrupted.

"Why, ah, Mr. Treadwell and I will be leaving for Guanajuato within the week. We bring along a chest of gold pesos and following us will be a wagon train with ammunition, rifles, and tack for your horses."

"A pleasure doing business with you, *Coronel*. Only . . . tell me? What is it that your consortium expects to get out of all this?"

Breathwaite reddened unconsciously and cleared his throat. Arthur took a cautious sip of his tequila and made a circular flip of his wrist to signal the mariachis to begin playing again.

"That must be obvious to one with the perspicacity you possess. The consortium would naturally expect exclusive import and export privileges. And, ah, perhaps the opportunity to revise and regulate your banking system?"

Santos howled with laughter. He struck his knee with an open palm, gulped down two fingers of tequila and poured more. "You are truly a man after my own heart. If one is to steal, why not steal big, *no*?"

"We, ah, understand each other, then, *mí general?*"

"Like brothers." Santos's black eyes glittered like hard slivers of obsidian, boring into Breathwaite's brain as though to seek out his deepest secrets. "Better than brothers," he amended. "Like two thieves in the night, eh?"

"*Touché,*" Arthur put in, recognizing the words the general spoke.

"Arthur," Breathwaite growled.

Since the fiasco of the attempted land grab in Montana and Wyoming, Arthur had been in bad graces with the consortium. Unbeknownst to him, he had been sent along with Breathwaite so that the former colonel could keep an eye on the aberrant son of the Treadwell clan. As principal members of the Federated Rail Consortium, Arthur's brother Albert had determined that his maimed sibling would not become an embarrassment to the financial empire or the family. Deprived of all but two inches of his manhood by a swift slash of Griffin Stark's sabre, Arthur's life had become a torment to himself and to Albert. His recent unnatural tastes in sexual experiments had not improved the situation. Breathwaite considered all this, took another sip of tequila and bit into a slice of lime.

"We must be going now," Santos announced, rising. "It is a long journey back to the state of Guanajuato. It is—how you say?—a thousand miles from here. We leave by stage in the morning. I would recommend the same transportation to you. In Chihuahua, you can take the train on to Aguascalientes and another stage to the city of Guanajuato."

"Have a good night's rest, general." Breathwaite dismissed the two Mexicans. After they departed he turned a scowl on Arthur. "You nearly overplayed our hand, you simpleton. Do you think these men are stupid or insensitive? Goad them so far and you'll find a stiletto between your ribs."

"Oh, come now, colonel. Aren't you being over-dramatic? After all, we do represent the consortium. That is a great deal more power than those garlic eaters have ever dreamed of having."

"It doesn't make you bulletproof or immune to a knife. On a one-to-one basis, I'll take that fellow Cardoza over you any time, Arthur. He's a killer. You are a pussycat by comparison."

"Don't be nasty. I might complain to my brother."

"Who do you think put you here, in my charge?"

"*I* . . . in *your* charge? Hardly, my dear fellow."

Resigned, Chester Breathwaite growled. "Watch what you say and do. That's my final warning."

"Ta-ta, Chester, my good man."

A small boy came to the tableside. He studied the two *gringos* and spoke at last to the younger one, his English heavily accented, his finger pointed at Arthur's crotch. "You wan' poot it in my seester? She good fawk. Real tight. On'y five pesos."

"Go away, you little wretch," Arthur snarled.

The youngster studied the weak curl of Arthur's lips, the dainty gestures and sugary voice. "Maybe you wan' poot it in me, *no*? You like leetle boys better, *no*?"

"Get out of here you hideous monster!" Arthur shrieked. He hurled a half-filled cup of tequila after the boy as he hastily departed. What frightened Arthur most was that he had felt his groin twitch and found himself enjoying the possibility of the lad's last, lewd suggestion.

CHAPTER FOUR

"What are we going to do?" The vivacious young woman who asked that question paced about the cramped space of her brother's office. Green eyes ablaze, she stopped abruptly to face the desk, gave her level, horsewoman's shoulders a significant toss and stamped one small foot in vexation. She placed her tightly clenched fists at the juncture of her narrow waist and flaring hips and waited for some reply.

"We haven't heard from Griff in some time. There's no telling where he might be."

"Oh, Damien, you must do something. I . . . I get so mad, I could go after them myself." Her long, glossy black locks swayed with the vehemence of her words.

"There's not much we can do. I can't get a furlough from the army. Griff's . . . out there somewhere." Damien Carmichael made a vague gesture with one hand, indicating the whole of the frontier beyond the small cantonment he commanded in the heart of Montana. At last he rose, came around the desk and held his sister at arm's length.

"I've done what I can, Jen. I was up half of last night, writing letters. I included all we learned about the consortium's plans to move into Mexico. I sent them to Griff, care of every military post I could think of where he might show up. Even a few that seemed off the track. All we can do now is wait. If he decides to act, he'll write us."

"We haven't heard from him since he left," Jennifer Carmichael protested.

Damien's brown eyes softened as he looked at his sister. His full lips drooped in sympathy as he studied the concern that lined her petite, heart-shaped face. He let only a second go by before he replied.

"There isn't exactly daily mail service out here, Jen. You know that."

"I miss him so. And I worry about him. Out there with all those wild savages. Sometimes, I wish his son had never been born. Then Griff wouldn't be out chasing after him like this." Jennifer suddenly realized what she had said. She went pale and a stricken expression creased her face. One small hand darted to her mouth.

"Oh . . . oh, God, I don't mean that. That's a horrible thing to say. Jeremy means everything to Griff."

"More even than you?"

"I . . . no. I don't think so. Only a boy of ten, without mother or father, alone among the Indians. It must be so awful for him. From what Griff said before he left here last summer, Jeremy had found a home among the Cheyenne, only to lose it again. We would make a good family, Damien. Of that I'm sure. I love Griff and I could easily come to love his son. It's this waiting, not knowing, not sure, even, if Griff or Jeremy are alive or dead."

"He's all right. Griff can take care of himself. And he has Temple Ames along. Together they make a formidable pair. Whatever has happened to Jeremy, they'll find out. Have a sip of port and get that frown off your forehead, Jen. We'll hear from Griff soon. I feel it."

Sunlight filtered through the aspens, making dappled spots on the rumps of the horses, much like those of the illusive Nez Percé ponies they sought. Griffin Stark and Temple Ames had followed the trail for five days in a slightly southward direction into Shoshoni country. They sat on the ground now, around a small fire, tended by a Shoshoni sheep herder. Griff listened patiently while Temple translated the answer to his question.

"He says they were here two days. Left with the sun yesterday."

"We're getting closer. We can catch up by tomorrow some time."

"Reckon we can." Ames frowned slightly. "He told one other thing. The Nez Percé didn't have no kids with 'em."

An ice dagger of pain ripped through Griff's heart, pierced his throat. His voice came out a strangled croak. "What?"

"Weren't no little ones, of any description."

"Where did they go then? When?"

"That we'll have to find out when we catch up."

Shortly after noon the next day, Griff and Temple rode down into a meadow where the Nez Percé grazed their few remaining horses as they slowly worked their way toward their home in Idaho. Griff had spotted them first and made himself known before he and Temple rode down to the wary traders. He and Temple received a friendly, if cautious, welcome. To his surprise, one of the Nez Percé spoke English and two of them could get along in Lakota.

"We're looking for a boy," Griff began after the formalities. "About so high, dressed as a Cheyenne. He has white hair."

"You seek Snow Rabbit, then?" a trader who had called himself Terrance Raven Claw answered.

"He *was* with you! Is that right?"

"Yes. Bear Heart took him as a son. His friend, Beaver Tail, became Joshuah Lame Horse's boy."

"Where are they now?"

"Oh, they go away long time now."

"When? Where did they go?"

"To the land of the Snakes and Utes. Go to see the Navaho. Maybe go to see the Big Water where the sun drowns before they come home to our people. Big adventure. Boys much happy for this."

Griff frowned before asking another question. "You said the boys were happy at the prospect of all that travel? Are you sure?"

"Oh, yes. They have nice ponies, good Appaloosa blood. Want to race wind, see strange people. They go to south seven days past. Take ponies to trade. Bring much silver and blue stone to our people." A mischievous light filled Raven Claw's eyes. "Maybe boys find Mexican girls to pokey-pokey. First time, big fun, that right, no?"

"Jeremy is only *ten years old*," Griff protested in the wounded tone of a father. Then he reconsidered. He hadn't been all that much older himself that magical first time. "Then we have to head south," he told Temple.

"Reckon as how we do. This chile ain't never seen beyond the big tradin' center at Santa Fe. This is makin' up as how we'll have us an ad-venture of our own."

"You will stay and take meat with us tonight?" Raven Claw inquired politely.

Ames shrugged as he translated. Griff made quick answer. "Might as well. As many miles as we have between it won't make all that much difference."

Albert Treadwell leaned back in the hammock and sighed with lazy pleasure. He had taken a few well-deserved days off from his busy New York office to come here to the family plantation on the coast of Maryland. He accepted a frosty pewter tumbler of mint julip from the white-coated darkie who had brought it on a silver tray. A long sip and he let his thoughts roam.

Always a mistake, unless suitably lulled by other enterprises, he found himself contemplating Damien and Jennifer Carmichael. But most of all . . . Griffin Stark.

His enmity toward Griffin Stark went far beyond his earliest involvement in the consortium. As he thought of it, the malformed bones and withered tendons in his maimed left hand cramped with pain. It had been a bright Saturday morning in early June, in the year 1857. Damien Carmichael and Griffin Stark had just returned from graduation at West Point. There had been a fox hunt that day. At the stirrup cup, Griffin Stark had insulted him. Insulted him in a manner that cut like a knife and demanded instant revenge . . .

* * *

. . . Large oaks and stately beech trees shaded the greensward, spacious drive, and stable yard of Oaklawn Plantation. Young people in brightly colored riding habits mingled with the older huntsmen. Uniformed servants circulated with trays of julips and hot toddies, stout barley beer and ruby-tinted crystal glasses of port. Gradually most of the youthful guests gathered around Damien Carmichael and Griffin Stark.

Albert felt that this was a bit too much tribute to be paid to a foreigner from Georgia. This was a gathering for Marylanders. Stark was decidedly out of place. He decided to deflate the blown-up popinjay.

"Well . . . see who's here," Albert Treadwell drawled as he walked toward where Griffin Stark held an impromptu court. "With the notorious Griffin Stark on this hunt, I might as well not even chase that bushy-tailed creature. The way I heard it, they had him *teaching* marksmanship at the Point."

"Not *teaching*," Stark mimicked Albert's tone of voice. "Coaching."

"Isn't it really all one and the same?" Albert had asked in a bored tone that brought a few quiet snickers from his close friends.

"But you *will* be riding out with us, won't you, Albert?" Stark had asked him in a tone Albert was soon to learn to be wary of.

"Oh, yes, of course I will, dear boy. Wouldn't miss it for the world."

"Will you be riding English . . . or sidesaddle?"

Tinkling laughter from the ladies hurt most of all. Even those young blades whom he considered a part of his circle joined in the merriment of the insult at his expense. Darkly, Albert had vowed revenge. And he nearly had it, too.

More by design than chance, Albert managed to put himself in the path of Griffin Stark's headlong chase after the wily red fox. In his left hand, he clutched a melon-sized rock. Albert felt the white flecks of foam that formed at the corners of his mouth and his heart beat with excited expectation as he kneed his mount forward at the man he so hated. Suddenly, to Albert's horror, Griffin Stark had turned, saw him and reacted swifter and far more deadly than he had anticipated.

Stark's hand dropped to the polished walnut grips of his Perry breech-loading percussion pistol. It was one of a pair he carried in saddle holsters slung over the pommel. As Albert pressed in close, intent on smashing the skull of this impudent outlander, Stark drew the big .52-calibre single-shot weapon and thumbed back the hammer. Albert's mouth sagged and his eyes showed a lot of white as the sights steadied on his body. Then the muzzle moved slightly and Stark touched the light trigger.

A flat roar of exploding black powder bounced off the trees and startled birds from their early morning perches. Albert felt a powerful blow to his left hand. Chips of shattered stone cut his cheeks and sprayed outward an instant before the dull throb turned to incredible pain. The rock had disappeared and, in its place, he saw a grisly hole and a welling flow of blood. Numbness settled in as he uttered a shriek of agony and reeled in the saddle.

Still propelled by the force of the bullet, Albert fell into the matted vegetation at the side of the trail.

"You . . . you ruined me!" he wailed as he tightly clutched his wrist in an attempt to staunch the flow of crimson that pumped from both sides of his hand. "My hand! Oh my God, my hand. I'll never use it again!" Despite his determination and the goading of pain, Albert paled and his eyes began to roll up in their sockets.

Unrelenting, Stark looked down on him without pity. "*You* attacked me, remember? You're a coward, Albert. Any *gentleman* would have challenged me at the hunt breakfast. Here, let me help you," he concluded as he swung from his mount.

Stung by the harsh words and his own shame, Albert cringed away from the offered assistance. His humiliation had not ended. Reason abandoned him as his inner fear overrode his common sense and need of aid. "K-keep away f-from me. Y-you'll try to finish the job," he whined, heedless of the importance of salvaging some face. "I know it. I—"

"Suit yourself, Albert," Griffin replied coldly. "But don't come asking for satisfaction later on. For my own part, I've already settled the matter. For yours . . . your conduct doesn't deserve the courtesy extended to a gentleman."

A moment later, Damien Carmichael had ridden up. He saw Griffin dismounted, though he didn't at first see Albert on the ground. His strong young voice rang through the woods.

"What's this? Don't tell me you've bagged that fox already?"

"No," Stark had replied, "only a civet cat."

Albert's hand had never healed properly. It remained scarred and drawn into a predatory claw by damaged tendons and missing bone. The incident put a black pool of hatred for Griffin Stark deep in Albert's heart . . .

. . . The unfortunate incident with Griffin Stark had nothing to do with the consortium's decision to order his extermination, however. That had come during the war. A courier for the consortium, bearing funds in gold for the continued operation of some Southern members of the internationally connected organization, had been intercepted by Rebel cavalry. Thinking him a Yankee spy, they had taken him to their headquarters.

There he had been interrogated by Griffin Stark. Under forceful questioning, he had broken. To prevent himself from being hanged as a spy, he had revealed a great deal about the consortium, without naming the organization. He gave names, though it remained doubtful if Stark had remembered them. He referred to certain involvements of the consortium in enterprises in the South, which later proved to add to the disaster of defeat. Only small pieces of a large puzzle. Yet, with the information overheard by Jennifer and that accidently obtained or otherwise at the disposal of Damien Carmichael, it became enough to expose the consortium. Then, their network of inter-locking companies, banks, and newspapers would be exposed. That would prevent the ultimate takeover of the entire country. Many of their activities, Albert was fully aware, could only be considered criminal.

They bought politicians, judges, and military officers in the fields of uniform and equipment procurement and armaments. They used terror tactics where needed to obtain title to land legitimately owned by others. The consortium, through front men and false companies, had conspired with others to gain control of mills and mines, farms and factories. Not the least, they never shied from the use of murder to obtain their ends. Because he held buried in his memory the identities of key consortium personnel, of banks and companies owned or controlled by the consortium, Griffin Stark had to die. The sweet revenge it would give him made the proposition even more savory to Albert Treadwell. Purged of his dark thoughts, Albert roused himself.

He swung his legs out of the hammock and called out to his servant. "Stevens, another julip, please."

"Yassuh, Mistah Treadwell."

He'd have another, dress for dinner and drive the trap into town for some seafood. His agents had lost track of Griffin Stark. No matter. They would find him sooner or later. And then . . . and then . . . Albert and his tragic unmanned brother, Arthur, would have their vengeance.

Lying under the stars, Griffin Stark let his mind drift back over the long, trying years. A large chunk of his memory, nearly six months in fact, consisted of nothing but a blank. A swirling miasma of unclear images, blackness, and pain. He knew from what he had been told later, that he lay for weeks on end, consumed with fever, delirious and unresponsive.

He had been seriously wounded during the final, fateful days of the Battle of the Wilderness. His left thigh bone had been shattered by a rifle ball. Right shoulder dislocated and a bullet lodged deep inside. His forearm had been broken below the elbow on one side by another ball. His bloody, unconscious form had been found on the field and taken to a Yankee surgical tent. There he had been recognized by his close friend, Damien Carmichael, then a major in the Union army. Although a Southerner himself, Damien had stayed by the Yankee side. He used his position to spirit Griff away to the Carmichael townhouse in the small Maryland town of Sunderland.

There, or so Jennifer Carmichael and Damien had told him later, he fared no better than at the tender mercies of the Yankee meat cutters. Except for one vital thing. He kept his leg and arm. Not without penalty, though. The fever raged, infection and swelling spread and the sickly odor of rotting flesh filled the small room where he lay in alternating spells of deathlike coma and thrashing delirium. He would have died, or at best been a cripple, had not the Carmichaels remained steadfast. At the most extreme moment, Jennifer had prevailed upon a learned doctor, a student of surgery in Europe before the war, who agreed, under protest, to perform a radical new operating procedure.

It had worked, Griff recalled with gratitude. Only an occasional twinge remained to remind him of the wasting and decay his body had endured. It had not always been like that. Long weeks went by before any noticeable improvement could be observed in the patient. Often near despair, Jenny held on. She prayed and changed supporting bandages and held Griff's head in her lap to feed him thin soup. At last he rallied.

Some of his first clear moments were his saddest. Not long after he became able to sit upright and feed himself, question Jennifer about what had happened over the long months of his illness, the bells of the town pealed cheerfully. The war had ended. Lee had surrendered at Appomattox. Griff's cause for living, his whole way of life came to a sad and untimely end. The slaves were free, courtesy of Mr. Lincoln. He had no way of operating his plantation, Riversend. Worse, he had not heard from his wife and child in nearly a year. His continual concern over this added a further burden of grief to Jennifer. Over the weeks of his malady and his long recuperation, she had fallen deeply in love with him.

When neither propriety nor fierce determination could

contain her emotions longer, she at last confided that love. Still, the state of his family and their safety came foremost in Griff's mind. Jennifer agreed to accompany him to Georgia.

There they found the burned-out ruins of Riversend Plantation, but no sign of his wife or child. A long search ensued. Not until Griff encountered a former family slave did he learn the dreadful truth.

His heart burst and tears ran unashamedly as he learned of his wife's brutal murder at the hands of a gang of Sherman's Bummers. Only her courageous action in killing one and wounding another of the uniformed slime had prevented her from rape. It had brought, instead, a quick death. His son had gone to his sister's home and from there into the West eventually to be lost among the anonymous lodges of the Cheyenne. All that remained to Griff was his burning desire to be reunited with the boy and his raging grief over Bobby Jean.

Partly from that grief, partly in frustration and in confused emotion, Griff made love to Jennifer Carmichael. It happened one dark night on a road in South Carolina, a short distance across the line from Georgia. Almost desperately he found himself burning with passion and unable to refrain from taking the lovely girl who offered herself as salve for his wounded heart and troubled mind. For her own part, Jennifer came to him in the fulfillment of a dream. From that day their love grew, blossomed, and waited only the bliss of fruition.

Would it ever happen, he thought sadly, lying on a bed of pine boughs in the Rocky Mountains, camped among Nez Percé traders. Jennifer waited far away at Damien's current command, a small outpost in Montana. Jeremy, the son he had not seen in four years, was believed to be headed south in the company of itinerant traders. Could he ever draw the strings of his sundered life together? Would he ever know happiness with Jennifer and Jeremy in a home of their own? Though it pained him deeply, he pondered the unanswerable questions until at last the oblivion of sleep overtook him.

CHAPTER FIVE

Frightful screeches came from the steel tires of the coach wheels as the conveyance swayed over stony ruts in the narrow road. Every few yards, the vehicle tilted precariously as it rose on a rock impossible to avoid and dropped on the other side with bone-jarring violence. Thirteen people had been crammed into the interior, normally designed to hold eleven. Arthur Treadwell endured the torment with grim silence. Frequently he put a linen handkerchief to his nose to filter the dust that boiled up constantly. Abruptly the road changed, grew wider and, if possible, more rocky. As consolation, the dust ceased.

Relieved of this discomfort, Arthur spoke for the first time. "Surely there is a better way than this?"

"We could have purchased horses in Aguascalientes," Chester Breathwaite replied mildly. "Though I've been given to understand that traveling this country alone can be somewhat hazardous. Bandits, you know," he added with a sardonic smile.

"Like the one we are going to meet?" The coach lurched as it picked up speed on a downhill run. "Good God!"

Breathwaite peered from the side window. "We'll be there in no time, now. I can see the shaft-heads of several mines on the hillsides ahead."

Guanajuato, when they got there, proved to be a city of ups and downs. Though it seemed that no matter how long one walked upward, or where one turned, there was always another hill to climb. The streets, if they could be called that, turned out to be little more than alleyways and narrow warrens reminiscent of rat trails through a trash midden. Vehicular traffic had been entirely banned from the center of the city during daylight hours. Consequently, no one hurried anywhere.

"And no one seems inclined to," Arthur observed when Breathwaite pointed this out to him. "Where are we staying?" Arthur puffed out as his legs churned in unaccustomed effort and his lungs reacted to the high altitude.

"The Posada Sante Fe. It's been a hostelry since the Spanish ruled here. General Santos made the arrangements. It is supposed to be around the next corner, right on a big garden."

"Oh, yes. The *Jardin de la Union*. When do we meet with Santos?"

"After we settle in. Our luggage is being taken to the hotel."

A few moments before, they had passed a tall, forbidding building of native stone. Many persons stood about, gazing raptly at the upper story and the cornices. At the corners, bronze plaques celebrated something, though too far from the street below to read the inscriptions. Arthur jerked his head in that direction.

"What was that big building we passed? The general's headquarters?"

"No. They call it the Alhondiga. It was supposed to be a granary, but the Spaniards used it as a fortress during the uprising that brought independence to Mexico. Those hooks under the cornices are where the Spanish impaled the heads of the leaders of the revolt: Hidalgo, Allende, Aldama, and Jimenez. One of the gentlemen on the coach told me about it. He said that the heads hugn there for ten years."

Arthur paled slightly. "Ghastly. What would happen it Santos's little revolt failed?"

"Something very similar, I suppose," Breathwaite returned in an offhand manner.

"We . . . ah, certainly don't intend to stay here long enough for that to happen, do we?"

"Of course not, Arthur." They rounded a corner. "Ah, there is the garden, down below us."

Everywhere there appeared grinding poverty, despite the output of the rich silver mines. The people had the hollow faces of hunger and moved about listlessly. General Santos had already extended his absolute authority over the city and the state government. So far, the representatives of the consortium knew, he had somehow managed to keep this intelligence from the Juaristas in Mexico City. To hold his rebellion together until financing could come from the consortium, Santos had instituted crushing taxes, even upon the poor. Despite this, brightly colored posters adorned street lamp poles and building fronts.

"What's all of this about?" Arthur inquired, waving a hand at one of the placards.

"A *faria*. A sort of carnival and country market, I suppose you could call it. You read enough Spanish to understand, Arthur."

"Uh . . . yes," he began tentatively. "What is this about three runnings?"

"Oh, you mean the *Corridas de Toros*. The running of the bulls. The bullfight, my boy. There are to be three formal bullfights and a festival for amateurs to test their skills. Want to try your hand?"

"God no. Everything in this country seems so . . . so violent."

"They are a violent people. Indians and Spaniards. Not much to chose between them, I say."

Together, Arthur and Breathwaite entered the hotel. It was cool and dim inside. They went to their rooms and found their luggage waiting.

"How did they get this here ahead of us?" Arthur called through the open door between their quarters.

"Must know a shorter way. I get the feeling our directions were by way of a grand tour of the town."

"I'll change and we can go to see Santos."

"Good idea, Arthur. That road left us in a rather

disreputable state."

A short, stocky sergeant ushered Arthur and his companion into the presence of General Santos with only a minimal delay. Santos, resplendent in a uniform of green tunic, white trousers, and a wide red sash, rose to greet them.

"Welcome, *amigos*. I trust you had a safe journey?"

"Yes, General Santos," the former Confederate colonel replied. "A bit dusty and rough from Aguascalientes on, though."

"Regrettable. The government set upon a big program of building railroads. The tunnels are not complete, or we would have better communications with the outside world. Take seats, please."

"General, we saw the supplies safely on their way in carters' wagons from Leon," Chester Breathwaite began once he had made himself comfortable.

"Good. Good. That was my first concern. As to the, uh, gold? It is adequately protected?"

"You can rest assured of that, general. Those rough looking, ah, *soldiers* you had waiting for the gold nearly scared us out of a week's growth," Arthur inserted.

Santos gave him a thin smile. "Your Spanish is improving, *Señor* Treadwell. That is also good. There are bandits in these mountains, *Señores*. It is necessary to have the toughest, most reliable types of men for such important missions as escorting the gold."

"And what if they decided to throw in with some of these bandits?" Arthur asked lazily.

"Oh, that would never happen, *Señor* Treadwell." Santos gave him an icy smile. "My men know that should they be tempted to such an enterprise, I would have them hunted down to the last man and killed. Ever so slowly."

Arthur swallowed hard. "I . . . see. Now then, the consortium has a small list of requirements. Ah . . . shall we call them conditions? Not many, you understand, general. Nor are they harsh."

"Please go on."

"First of all, the disbursement of the money is to be under our supervision. Or that of other representatives of the consortium."

"Understood." Santos's small eyes glittered and his voice came out tight with strain.

"Secondly, the small arms will be put in the hands of your most experienced troops. Older weapons, or those needing repair before use in combat, are to go to your local recruits."

Santos relaxed slightly. "A sensible requirement. Naturally the best arms should be in the hands of the best troops."

"Thirdly, the European banks who have advanced the funds would like written agreements now to insure their privileged position in your future government's treasury as well as commitments to the exclusivity of trade."

"That, ah, might be a bit difficult to accomplish at this time," Santos said evasively. "I must consult with my associates. I am not alone in this, you know."

"Oh, I think you are, general," Arthur advanced in a brittle tone. "I think you are entirely alone in this little revolt. The next king of Mexico, eh?"

Deep red suffused Santos's flat, Indian face. Spittal flew when he shouted in rage, rising from his heavy, gold-inlaid colonial period armchair. "I do this for the people! I am fighting to liberate the oppressed peasants from the crushing yoke of the rich and the cruel system of the *hidalgos*. You toy with your life to insult me so, *Señor*."

"General, please!" Chester Breathwaite interrupted. "He meant nothing insulting. Arthur is young. The young are also idealists. His heart, as are those of all members of the consortium, is behind your noble cause. In his dream of perfection, he only visualizes the fears that any man might see." He paused and glowered at Arthur.

It had been a mistake to let Arthur handle any diplomatic endeavor so fraught with danger as this, Breathwaite realized too late. Santos might be a hill bandit-turned-general, but he still had all the primitive blood lust of his ancestors and the power to indulge it at his whim. Relief washed over his cramped chest as he saw Santos relax and produce a smile.

"You are right. I forget. My own idealism, as you put it,

59

sometimes blinds me to what others might see in my efforts. It is good to be reminded. Have no fear, *Señor* Treadwell, I have no designs on an emperor's crown. I am a republican through and through. I greatly admire your General Washington, and the great emancipator, *Señor* Lincoln, is fast becoming a national hero in Mexico. Let us take a bit of tequila and allay our consciences." Santos walked to a sideboard and personally poured three small crystal glasses of the faintly amber liquor.

"Since you are to stay to supervise the distribution of the money, you will be here for our *faria*, no? I think you will enjoy it very much. Guanajato is second in population only to the capital in *Ciudad Mexico*. That makes for a lot of celebrating. Now. Are there any more conditions?"

"Only one. That of secrecy. At no time are you or any of your confidants to make known the involvement of the consortium in your proposed revolt against the Juaristas."

"Agreed. Most heartily agreed, *Señor* Treadwell." Santos produced a rueful smile. "If some of the zealots among those in opposition to Juarez were to know of our, ah, connection, they would have my head. *Mexico por Mexicanos*! That is the rallying cry. We fought hard to oust Maxmillian and the French. The people want nothing more of foreign intervention. So it will be our little secret, eh?"

Before they left Santos's office, the general assigned Colonel Cardoza to introduce Arthur Treadwell and Chester Breathwaite to the nightlife of Guanajuato. He informed the two Americans he would meet them at their hotel a little before sundown.

The trio had dinner in a lavishly furnished restaurant that belied the poverty of the people. Strolling musicians entertained and the inner courtyard where they dined smelled fragrant from the blossoms of bougainvillea, lemon, and orange. Afterward, over brandy and cigars, Cardoza suggested a bit more robust entertainment.

"I know this excellent *putaria*," he enthused. "The girls are most skillful in all sorts of ways to delight a man. You will find it, I am sure, most pleasant."

Arthur declined, pleading fatigue from the journey. Breathwaite, a gleam in his eyes, accepted readily. He and Cardoza accompanied Arthur to the Posada Santa Fe, where Breathwaite retrieved a small leather valise before continuing on to the bawdy house.

"I see that one catches your eye," Cardoza remarked a few moments after they entered the establishment. He nodded toward a shapely young woman, more a girl, who leaned against a small lemonwood bar. "She is a good choice. Very, ah, acrobatic."

Without another word, Chester Breathwaite walked to a place beside the girl. "I am most interested in making your acquaintance," he said politely in Spanish. "I am called Chester."

"I am called Consuelo. You are interested in a . . . night of entertainment? Or perhaps only a brief visit to my room, *Señor?*"

Breathwaite could not restrain reaching out one hand to lightly cup a small, firm young breast. "I would greatly like a night of such bliss as your, er, eyes promise, *Señorita.* Unfortunately I haven't that much time."

"Well then, let us not waste what you have."

Financial arrangements were made with the madam. Breathwaite followed Consuelo up a narrow, spiral staircase of wrought iron in one corner of the large room where the girls congregated with their potential customers. He carried with him his small leather bag. The young prostitute opened a flimsy door and ushered him into a dimly lit cubical.

A short candle flickering in a clay dish sat in front of a plaster statue of the Virgin of Guadalupe. Next to it a rosery hung on a wooden peg driven into the adobe wall. A tiny, circular window, framed in colorful tile, with an iron grillwork, had been set high in the wall and had no covering. Through it, Breathwaite could make out the faint twinkle of stars. The bed sagged, long abused by the energetic calling of the room's occupant. The head and foot were of brass. A lattice of leather strips provided a platform for the mattress. Consuelo crossed to it and

61

turned back the covers. Then she swiftly, expertly disrobed.

Breathwaite marveled at the compact symmetry of her body. Almost a child, her small, upthrust breasts, their areolas dark, nipples virginally pink, jutted proudly from a thin chest, no more developed than that of a child. Her torso arrowed to a tiny waist, where her hips flared only slightly. Barefoot, her feet and hands added to the illusion of extreme youth. Suddenly aroused, his thick, engorged manhood strained painfully against his trousers. Chester Breathwaite sucked in his breath and hurriedly removed his coat, shoes, and trousers.

"Let me," Consuelo urged him.

With deft fingers the child-woman undid the buttons of his shirt and slipped it off his body. Again she went to the pearl-shell fasteners of his longjohns and peeled him out of them so that his throbbing penis swung upward in anticipation. Not the largest she had seen, Consuelo observed clinically, but ample for the occasion. She reached for it and her client snorted like a bull.

"*Ay que quapo!*" she exclaimed.

Breathwaite reached to the small table where he had lain his valise and opened it with trembling fingers. He brought out a black leather hood, which he slipped over his head, pliable gloves of the same material, that he fitted on his hand, and an unusual diaperlike garment with a hole in the front which he directed the girl to put on him.

"There. Let me step into it. That's it. Good girl. Now draw it up. Yes, higher. Now stick my sack through it. Yes . . . yes. Oh, that's good."

"What about your—"

"Leave him in there. Make him work for his fun," Breathwaite snapped. "Now, girl, get on your knees. That's it. Call me Daddy while you lick. Lick me hard, you bad little girl."

"Y-yes, D-daddy."

"Oooh. Good. Sooo good. Lick me. Lick me!" Chester Breathwaite cried as he reached into the valise again. This time he brought out the whip.

CHAPTER SIX

"That's gunshots," Griffin Stark declared as he listened to a distant roll of muted thunder.

"Yep," Temple Ames agreed. "'Bout two ridges over, by the way this chile figgers. These here Sangre de Christo Mountains can fool a feller. We'd best push on."

As they rode through the rugged terrain of northern New Mexico Territory, Griffin Stark marveled at the land. Tall pines, briskly running streams, and lush undergrowth gave way from time to time to the stark flora of a desert, only to come back after a rugged climb to a still higher plateau. The shots grew louder and more persistent as they advanced.

"You figure it's Indians?"

"Yep. Of one sort or another."

"Fighting among themselves?" Griff asked further. "Like those Utes and Shoshone we came on?"

"Nope. Too much gunfire. They's pickin' on white folks."

"We'd better hurry."

Temple put out a restraining hand. "Mebbe not. No tellin' how many we'd be ridin' down on."

"They might kill those whites," Griff protested.

"Could be they'd kill us, too."

Griff won the argument by spurring his mount forward into a gallop. Temple Ames, cursing his companion's impetuosity, flailed after him.

Atop the second rise, they looked down on a rutty trail that wound around the bases of several towering mountains in a generally southward direction. Three large freight wagons had formed into a rough triangle, teams unhitched and in the center. From under and inside the thick-walled vehicles spurts of smoke appeared, laced with brightness. A second later, the crackling reports of rifles reached their ears.

Around the wagons, objects of the heavy fire, rode some twenty-five Indians. They wore incredibly long loincloths, that flew in the wind of their galloping maneuver. High moccasins, boots really, came nearly to their knees and their long hair was not braided in the manner of plains' tribes, but hung loose, flapping in the breeze, restrained only by wide headbands of ragged cloth.

"Never seen Indians like those," Griff commented as he unlimbered his shiny new Model '68 Winchester Henry.

"Reckon as how they might be Apaches. Fiercest red devils anywhere," Temple suggested. "Ten of 'em is likened to be more deadly fighters than thirty Sioux. Fight best on foot is what this chile has heard."

"Looks like that's what they're making ready to do now."

The number of horsemen had decreased. Beyond a scrim of stunted smoke trees, Griff made out a young boy holding the reins of the abandoned mounts. He counted roughly thirteen.

"We'll wait until they all get off their ponies. While we do, we ride around where we can hit at that half-growned one in the brush."

"Good idea," Griff agreed. "We can spook their mounts and ride down on them like a whole company of cavalry."

"That shines. Then 'Paches won't know what hit 'em."

Cautiously they moved their mounts from one spot of concealment to the next, while the Apaches formed up to attack the helpless wagons.

"Damnit, Jake, they're slitherin' through them weeds

like snakes," one grizzled teamster, who served as camp cook, hollered over to the train boss.

"I know it, Sy. Keep an eye on the bastards. Looks like they aim to come from all directions."

"There's only six o' us left," another wagon driver remarked. "How we gonna hold 'em off?"

"Piss on 'em for all I care," Jake responded. "Make every shot count. Don't open up until you have a clear sight on the red devils." Jake took a cautious peek over the high side of his wagon and watched the Apaches advance. He felt at his waist to count the number of rounds he had left. Not enough, he thought resignedly.

"How you fellers fixed for ammo?"

"Not so good, Jake," Sy lamented. "Put my last spare cylinder in my Dragoon. Got maybe a dozen rounds for the Spencer."

The other four teamsters made similar reports.

It had never seemed darker to Jake Peterson.

Fire and smoke spat from a ring some fifty yards from the wagons, the tall grass ripping apart with the passage of hot lead. A dozen Apaches rose from their prone advance and ran headlong for the beseiged men. Their sharp yips and howls echoed off the nearby slopes.

A split second later, two rifles barked with deadly authority from the hillside above a small stand of smoke trees. A pair of warriors stopped running and plowed dirt with their short, hooked, ugly beaks.

"Yeeeeee-aaaaaah-hoooooo!"

Chills rippled down Jake Peterson's spine. He had heard that yell far too many times. Twice at Bull Run, throughout the valley and at Fredericksburg and Chancellorsville. And many more after that. He knew it only too well, but wondered how a Rebel army had gotten into New Mexico Territory in 1870. He took quick aim and shot an Apache who had come within ten yards of the wagons. Then he looked up and saw two men riding headlong down the slope, firing as they came.

Horses scattered from the wispy hiding place among the smoke trees and an Apache boy of thirteen or so staggered into the open, his chest ripped apart by a .44 slug. He fell before he made ten steps.

"Pour it on!" Jake shouted to his men. "There's help on the way!" Never in his life had he believed he would be glad to see Rebel soldiers charging his direction.

"We caught 'em with their britches down!" Temple shouted as he rode beside Griff.

Griff had tied his reins together, cavalry style, and dropped them over his saddle horn. That left both hands free to fire his repeating rifle and steer his horse by his knees. Battle trained, through time and patience, by Griff, Boots performed like a seasoned veteran. He cut left and right at the command of knee pressure, swirving to make a poorer target, while not an ear twitched at the explosive detonation of the Winchester so close to his head. A third, fourth, then a fifth Apache went down kicking in the dirt as the galloping horsemen drew nearer.

Now Griff saw increased activity and better accuracy from the beleagered wagon drivers, accounting for the next three casualties. Apaches sprang up from all points of the compass, caught by surprise. Griff threw back his head and let go another Rebel yell.

Fierce fighters though they might be, the Apaches held a superstitious dread of the unknown. This band had never before heard the unearthly keening of that formidable war cry. In an instant, while their brothers fell around them, the survivors broke and ran.

Several, with stouter hearts than their comrades, stopped to turn and fire at the unexpected help. Lead screamed off rocks and one fat slug cracked through the air close enough to Griff's head that he felt its hot breath on his cheek. A second later, pain exploded in his right thigh as an arrow buried deep in the meat.

Seemingly from nowhere, almost on top of horse and rider, a slender young Apache warrior sprang up from the tall grass and let fly a second missile that moaned past Griff's shoulder, clipping buckskin and human flesh on the way. Instantly, Griff swung downward with his rifle barrel, smashing it into the crown of the brave's skull.

Bone collapsed under the force of the blow. The Apache's knees buckled and fell away, twisting. The combined motion of the galloping horse and the turning warrior wrenched the rifle from Griff's hand. Quickly he drew his revolver, using it left-handed, as was his nature, while his right sought the basketlike hilt of his special sabre.

Highly honed steel whispered free of the leather scabbard and flashed upward in the afternoon sun. With a swish, it swung down on the dying hostile. The keen edge bit into bone and muscle at the base of his neck and severed his head clean off his body. Geysers of blood spouted into the air as Griff rode by. He wheeled Boots to the right and looked around the field of battle.

None of the enemy remained to contest it.

"By dang it, Johnny Reb, you saved our asses, sure as I'm borned," Jake called out happily from atop his wagon. "The name's Jake Peterson. Late of the Twenty-third Ohio Volunteer Infantry. An' it's God's truth that I've never been so happy to see a person in my life."

Griff grinned at the spew of words. He decided to have a bit of fun. "Major Griffin Stark, of Jeb Stuart's cavalry, Army of Northern Virginia, at your service, suh." He swept his hat from his head in a familiar gesture of his former commander and swung it low as he executed a stiff bow.

Jake's jaw dropped. "Lord agoshin! Yer that big, yellin' bastard that put a hole twixt the eyes of Sergeant Mayhew at Fredericksberg. I was standin' right beside him when the Reb cavalry hit us from the flank."

"Sorry I hadn't time to make your acquaintance at our first encounter, suh. The pleasure is mine, now suh."

Suddenly Jake burst out laughing. "An' mine, sure's Hell's hot. Looks like I can be of service to you, though. That arrawh's gotta come out."

"I'd be obliged. This is my friend, Temple Ames."

"Howdee-do," Jake returned. "Couple o' you boys help

the major offin his horse. Get the likker from the chuck box. I got some powerful carvin' to do."

"This chile can take care of it if ye like," Temple offered. "Reckon they's been more'n a hundred arrows cut out by these hands."

"You got me there, Mr. Ames. Carve ahead," Jake offered. "You boys have any particular plans?"

"No. We're, ah, looking for some Nez Percé horse traders. They have two boys with them. One has white hair," Griff informed the teamsters, while two of their number eased him from the saddle and sat him down where Temple indicated.

"Ain't seen nobody like that," Jake answered for the rest. "We're on the road to Santa Fe. Iffin you've nothin' else to do, might as well throw in with us. Be a might bit safer with them Apaches up here. Lord, you'd think they would stay down in the desert."

"This used to be their hunting grounds," Temple commented as he produced a smooth stone and began to hone his big bowie knife.

"Ain't no more. This is *civilized*. Oncst you get that done, Mr. Ames, we'd best make some tracks. Camp along about dark. That way we might keep our hair."

"Call me Coonstalker," Temple returned. "This chile aint' ever 'Mistered' unless somebody wants somethin' off me that ain't for the givin' up."

"Fair enough, Coonstalker. What do you boys say then?"

"We might as well go on to Santa Fe. From what Temple tells me, there's a lot of hose trading done there." Griff winced as Temple grabbed the shaft and neatly cut through the wooden arrow.

It might also make good sense, he decided, to ride a wagon for a while, instead of a horse.

CHAPTER SEVEN

What a strange language these *Tua* people have, Jeremy Stark thought to himself. It was even more musical than that of the Nez Percé. Worse, he couldn't understand a word. He sat in the sun with his Cheyenne friend, Beaver Tail, in a circle of *Tua* boys. Bare shoulders touching on all sides, they engaged in a game using paint-daubed sticks, the rules of which Jeremy barely understood. Despite this, he had never felt so alone in his life. Around them towered the two and three storied structures of the Taos Pueblo.

"You won, Snow Rabbit," Beaver Tail told Jeremy in Cheyenne. "Pick up the turqouise pieces they bet and throw again."

Jeremy complied with an overwhelming sense of indifference. The polished blue stones, carved in the shapes of animals, birds, and fish, represented considerable wealth for a boy of only ten years. Especially among the tribes of the north who did not possess much of the treasured gem. At that particular moment, he missed his home in the Cheyenne camp with Two Otters and Rainbow.

One of the boys who had lost heavily spoke up in the musical Taos language. "Let's go play in the water. It is too hot to sit here."

Several others readily agreed.

Everyone jumped up and ran toward the shallow creek

that meandered through the Pueblo grounds. The laughing boys stripped off moccasins and loincloths and leaped, shouting shrilly, into the chilled mountain water. These boys, Jeremy soon observed, did not know how to swim. Not like he did, or Beaver Tail. They had no water deep enough to learn in. It felt cool, though, and that was what really counted. For the time being, his lonely thoughts went away.

Bear Heart and Joshua Lame Deer sat in the shade created by a two story building. Around them squatted men of the Pueblo. Over their shoulders, Bear Heart saw the boys start up from their game and run toward the creek. The white braids of his adopted son, Snow Rabbit, soon took the lead. It gave him a good feeling.

He had made a mistake in leaving his oldest son at the village. He missed the boy almost from the first day trailing east with their large herd of horses for trade. Then, in the last summer, when he had obtained the white-haired Cheyenne child, he knew again a father's pride.

Snow Rabbit worked hard, rode like a Nez Percé and had clear, keen eyesight and sharp ears. Unlike some boys, he made no noise when he walked through the forest and he didn't jabber constantly like many. Yes, Bear Heart considered, he had good fortune in this choice of a new son. The trading had gone well since Snow Rabbit had come to them. Although the men of the mud lodges talked down the ponies, their eyes betrayed how much they wanted them. He and Lame Deer would take back many bags of the blue beads and shiny necklaces for the women. When the trading had ended, he mused, they would have light burdens.

They might go further south, to the land of the Mexicans. The men of Taos talked of how the Mexican soldiers prided themselves on owning fine horses. They could show theirs off, make arrangements to bring more the next summer.

Or they might go to the big water, he went on planning.

70

Many white men lived in that country. It would be good to see it and travel to their homes through the gentle valleys where food abounded.

"We will take your horses," a *Tua* man announced suddenly. "Although the price you ask is too great. We will give you . . ." his voice trailed off as the bargainer weighed a reduced amount of turquoise and silver.

Jeremy Stark lay atop his buffalo robe on the flat roof of a three story pueblo. The light, warm blanket woven by the women of the Pueblo did not cover him. Heat from the sun still radiated from the mud blocks of the structure and provided all the comfort he wanted. The cool night air of the mountains tickled across his bare flesh as he gazed upward at the stars. As they marched across the sky, his thoughts drifted with them, fixed on his family. His real mother and father, not his Cheyenne parents.

He remembered little of his father. And that recollection was from when he was four years old. He was tall, Jeremy mused. Almost the tallest man he had ever seen. With curly blond hair and eyes of the same wild gray that the small pond behind Riversend reflected on a rainy day. He smiled a lot, of that Jeremy was certain. And his voice boomed when he spoke. He wore gray: a long gray coat with lots of shiny brass buttons and trousers with a yellow stripe down the outside seam. He had a gold star on each side of his high, straight collar. Impressions of his mother remained far more vivid.

Her name had been Bobby Jean. But he had always called her Mommy, or Mother when he had been bad. She was the most beautiful woman in the world. She loved him and would always hug and kiss him before sending him off to bed. He knew how she had died, too. He could still clearly see that day when the ugly men came up on horses. They wore blue. "Yankee Color," it was called around Riversend. Two of them had no shirts and their dirty, sweat-stained longjohn tops showed above their trousers. They said something that Mommy didn't like and she took

71

out the gun his father had given her. There was a lot of shooting and he began to cry.

He cried so hard he thought his heart would come up his throat and out his mouth. The men did something bad to Daphne and killed Caesar and two other slaves, then they set fire to everything. Jeremy had never cried again like he did that day. Through the watery wall of his tears he watched his home and all the buildings of Riversend go up in flames. The slaves ran away, those still alive. After the men left, his nurse, Daphne, came to him and soothed his sorrow. She shamed some of the field hands into coming back.

They dug graves for Caesar, Cicero, and Pliny, then, off in that little grove of trees Mommy loved so much, they dug another one for her. After it had turned dark, Daphne had taken him to his Aunt Julie's house. He had liked it there, at first. Then his Uncle Evan had come home from the war. One of his hands was gone and he complained about everything. Within a few months, Uncle Evan had sold his land, loaded his blacksmithing tools and small forge into two wagons and the family had moved north and west, to a place called Illinois.

Jeremy hadn't liked it in Illinois. So when Uncle Evan moved on again, it suited him fine. He and his cousin played together along the way, until she sickened and died of a fever. After that the Tuckers moved constantly. In every town, it seemed to him, Jeremy had only begun to make friends, when Uncle Evan would say things had to be better further on. Off they would go and the loneliness of that life burned deeper into Jeremy's heart.

They stayed longest in Broken Bow. There Jeremy had gotten along well with the town boys. They taught him to cuss and to smoke cornsilk cigarettes and all about what made girls different from boys. He'd also learned to swim. But then, as usual, Uncle Evan decided things weren't going right and it would be better further along. Just before his eighth birthday, they left for some place called Oregon.

On the way, the Indians had come along and attacked

the wagon train that they had joined. They killed Uncle Evan and Aunt Julie. Instead of being scared like he had been as a little kid, Jeremy had gotten mad. He fought, shooting two Indians with his little squirrel rifle. Only wounded, they thought it funny and took the short-barreled .31 calibre Pennsylvania away from him. He thought they would kill him, too, but they did not.

One big, laughing warrior had come to him and poked and prodded Jeremy's chest with a stiff finger. He said something to the others and they laughed. Then the big Indian had pulled out a knife. He cut away Jeremy's shirt and longjohns and left him bare to the waist. The gathered warriors nodded and muttered their approval. The big man, Two Otters, Jeremy learned later, took Jeremy with him on his horse. Later there had been an argument with a white man.

Two Otters won and took Jeremy home with him. In broken English, Two Otters informed Jeremy he was to be the Cheyenne's son. At first he hated that. Although he had a quick mind and a good ear for languages and soon learned the Cheyenne tongue, he refused to speak it. Then, gradually, he made friends with Beaver Tail. The two boys sided together against the taunts of the older lads. Jeremy began to speak Cheyenne. He helped Beaver Tail learn to swim better and the boy asked him to become his brother.

The knife hadn't hurt at all when Beaver Tail cut Jeremy's thumb. Beaver Tail licked the blood from the wound and handed the blade to Jeremy.

"Cut mine," Jeremy remembered Beaver Tail telling him, "and lick the wound. Then we press them together and we are brothers."

From that day on, Jeremy had dressed, talked, and thought as a Cheyenne boy. Until the Snakes had come to raid the village. He fought them and even killed one. It had been awful when Two Otters made him scalp his victim. But he got over it and felt pride to see the small circle of skin with its long tuft of hair hanging from the buttstock of his Pennsylvania rifle. He was the youngest boy in the village to take a scalp and, technically if not physically, become a full-fledged warrior. Two Otters even let him wear an eagle feather.

Then the Shoshone had come back and killed Two Otters. They stole Beaver Tail and him away. A week later the renegades had traded him and his friend off to the Nez Percé for much needed horses. It took Jeremy no time at all to decide that he could be every bit as good a Nez Percé as he had been a Cheyenne. Particularly after his adopted father, Bear Heart, had given him a beautiful Appaloosa pony of his very own. A scuffle of footsteps interrupted Jeremy's reflections.

Beaver Tail came scuttling across the roof and lay down beside Jeremy on the buffalo robe. "I've been listening to Bear Heart and Joshua talk. We are leaving tomorrow."

"Where do we go?"

"Past a village called Santa Fe and on to the place where the Mexicans live. Then we go west to the big water. Bear Heart said it would be funny to watch you and me try to swim in the salty waves of the 'Lake that Goes to the Sun.' That's another name for the big water."

"Is . . . is it a long way?" Jeremy's voice sounded vague and disappointed.

"Oh, yes. It will take all summer to get there. Why? Don't you want to go?"

"I . . . well, I miss our village and Rainbow's good corn mush."

Beaver Tail mussed Jeremy's white hair. "Don't be a baby."

"I'm not a baby," Jeremy protested.

"No, Snow Rabbit. You have taken a scalp, killed three men. I have killed, too. We are warriors and warriors must like adventure."

"Al-all right. And I'll laugh at you, too, when you try to swim in the salty waves."

Giggling, the two friends wrestled in boyish exuberance for a few minutes before falling to sleep under the black velvet dome of sky.

CHAPTER EIGHT

Griffin Stark found Santa Fe to be a town of reds and browns.

Red adobe bricks formed most of the houses and commercial buildings. Many of which were plastered over with a stucco made of crushed red rock and shiny bits of mica and quartz, so that they dazzled in the sunlight. Where the red clay soil had given out, a light buff material, colored like coffee with thick cream in it, had been used. The few trees and shrubs were confined to inner court-yards of the high-walled houses. These gardens provided the only relief from the unrelenting sameness of the high altitude desert terrain. Despite the country's forbidding nature, the streets of Santa Fe swarmed with people.

Ranch hands, called *vaqueros*, swaggered along the narrow streets around the central plaza, their broad-brimmed, high crowned sombreros like so many parasols. Barefoot children of Spanish, Indian, and Anglo an-cestory—and every imaginable combination thereof—ran shouting in play on the hard-packed ground of the *Plaza de Armas*, where a few stunted trees struggled to survive.

Along one winding alleyway, small balconies with wrought-iron banisters overhung the walkway. Upon them, ladies of dubious virtue draped themselves on white-painted chairs and called out provocatively to potential customers below. At Griff's insistence, Temple agreed to rooms in the large hotel on the plaza. There they could enjoy an honest bed for the first time in three months.

"I'm for a bath and a shave," Griff told his companion as he rubbed his bristly chin. "Then we can look for the livestock yard. Maybe those Nez Percé are here, or have been. We'll learn something anyway."

"This chile don't cotton to hot water in a tin tub. It weakens a man. Iffin I can find a good, cold stream, I'll scrape off the trail dust. But a shave . . . now that's a luxury long overdue."

Every room in the hotel had a door that opened onto the lush green, inner courtyard and windows that gave a view of the plaza or the distant mountains. On the continuous, second floor balcony, Griff paused at the entrance to his quarters.

"I'll meet you down there by the fountain in about ten minutes. We can find us a barber."

Fragrant odors from charcoal cooking fires, grilling meat and pungent chili peppers, onions, and garlic swirled around their heads as Griff and Temple walked diagonally across the plaza where a hand-lettered sign in bright red announced *Barberia Santa Cruz*.

"This chile's stomach just done a flipflop," Temple announced as he sniffed the air.

"We'll eat after we clean up."

"An' wet our whistles a bit? This chile's plumb near forgot the taste of whiskey."

"We'll have a few," Griff agreed. "But I want to get to the corrals."

"*Buenas tardes, Señores*," a smiling fat man greeted them as they entered the shop. He wore white and obsidian eyes sparkled with welcome from his broad, leather-dark face.

"Howdy," Temple allowed. "We need our chins scraped and some of these ducktails clipped back a bit."

"*Inmediatamente, Señores*," the barber went on, switching with facility from Spanish to English. "Please to sit down."

"I'd like a bath, too," Griff added.

"In the back, *Señor*. After the shave, I will have my first

76

son bring hot water."

Hair trimmed and whiskers removed, Griff stepped through a hanging bead curtain into the cool back room of the barbershop. A large tin hip tub stood in the center of a plank floor, bleached white from the splashes of years of bathers. Griff removed his smelly trail clothes and put them on a chair. From a small satchel he carried, he took out fresh garments and arranged them on hooks set in one wall. The back door opened and a boy of eleven or twelve entered, struggling with two huge wooden buckets of steaming water.

He dumped them into the tub and added cold until satisfied with the temperature. Then he turned and addressed Griff. His voice held only a slight flavor and lilt of Spanish accent.

"I will scrub your back and pour your rinse, *Señor*. The bath is two bits." Suddenly his eyes widened when he looked at the ugly, puckered scars on Griff's left thigh, chest, right elbow, and shoulder. Then he saw the fresh wound, made by an Apache arrow. *"Dios mio!"* he exclaimed.

"I was in the war. Got shot up a bit."

"And the others, *Señor*?"

"An Apache arrow. That happened on the trail in here."

"Y-you are a fortunate man, *Señor*," the lad stammered. "To still be alive. I have seen men hurt less in an affair of honor who died."

"You've seen a lot in a few years, boy," Griff replied. "And you're right, I'm damned lucky to be here. Do you have soap?"

"Uh, oh, yes. Over there. I will get it for you."

Fifteen minutes later, Griff stepped out onto the street, smelling faintly of lavender soap and bay rum. The boy, whose name was Pepito as he had told Griff, had folded away the dirty clothes while Griff lathered himself. Then Pepito applied a stiff-bristled brush on Griff's back and rubbed the damaged shoulder with surprising tenderness. During the bath he had dragged the story of the Indian fight out of a reluctant Griff. Pepito had then insisted on

77

the bay rum rubdown, offering it on the house. Unaccustomed to such adulation, Griff felt somewhat uncomfortable and decided not to mention it to Temple. Right then, a ribbing was something he could do without.

"Belly thinks this chile's had his throat cut," Temple growled.

"We'll eat. Pick a place."

They had thinly sliced beef, called *carne asada*, grilled over a bed of charcoal, onions roasted on the same fire, and a bowl of soupy beans. With it came a fiery relish of chopped tomatoes, chili peppers, and onions. A seemingly endless supply of hot corn cakes, which their waitress called *tortillas*, came in a wicker basket, covered by a towel. At Temple's suggestion they washed it down with tall, slender glasses of deep amber beer.

"Think that will hold you?" Griff asked as Temple belched loudly, slapped his swollen stomach and rose from the table.

"Till I can get a real meal. Let's sashay on down to the corrals."

No one had seen or heard of any Nez Percé horse traders at the Santa Fe stockyards. A few head of scrawny cattle filled one pen, sleek post horses for the stage line pranced in another. A third held some shaggy mountain ponies who quarreled over the fence with a dozen mules. All of the buyers Griff questioned expressed a hope that the Indian horse breeders would show up. They could get top dollar for those handsome animals, they unanimously agreed. Disappointed, Griff turned aside and they started back toward the hotel.

"What about a couple of snorts?" Temple urged, eyes twinkling.

"All right, Temple. We'll find a quiet place and do some considering."

Ames snorted. "If we can, you mean. Ever'body around here seems hell-bent on whoopin' it up, no matter the time of day."

The cantina they entered was nearly pitch black in contrast to the bright sunlight outside. Griff dimly made out a line of men at the bar and more seated around small tables. Blinking, he steered his way to an empty spot and took a chair.

"Could we have gotten ahead of them?" Griff asked as Temple settled opposite him.

"Might. If they stopped a lot to trade. Sure didn't use the same trail we took."

Long minutes passed as they continued their speculative conversation. After a while, when no one had come to take their order, Griff got the distinct impression they were being ignored by the barkeep. Griff came to his feet and crossed to the bar.

"Two glasses and a bottle of your best whiskey, please," he ordered.

The saloonkeeper blinked at him with dark, smoldering eyes and turned away as though he had never been addressed. Griff slapped his hand on the mahogany.

"I ordered a bottle of whiskey, Mister."

With a swift move for a man so fat, the barman spun around. Yellowed stumps of teeth showed under a full mustache in an ugly snarl. *"No comprendo inglés, gringo."*

The man on Griff's right sniggered. The ex-Confederate felt a hand on his shoulder and turned quickly. He looked at a long, ratlike face, with a thin wisp of black hair framing the mouth and close-set, beady black eyes glittering with hate.

"You have come in the wrong place. This is a cantina for real men, not for a *gringo carbrón* like yourself. You an' your frien' should leave before something unfortunate happens."

"I like it here. I think we'll stay for a drink or two. Bartender, *I want that bottle,*" Griff demanded in a cold voice, never taking his eyes from the man who sought to intimidate him.

Griff sensed, rather than saw, the movement when the sniggering bar patron drew a knife from the long, slender sheath inside his belt. Instantly, Griff drove his left elbow back into the man's solar plexus.

Breath whooshed out and the knife clattered musically on the glazed, red tile floor blocks. Then Griff snapped the same arm forward, the fist closed and rock hard. It caught his first opponent high on the chest and staggered his slight frame backward. That gave Griff time to spin and backhand the knife wielder, knocking a spray of saliva and blood from thick lips that stretched in a distorted droop from the force of the blow.

"Yowie!" Temple Ames yelled from deep in his leathery lungs. "Haaa-hooo!"

Although well up in his fifties, Temple had the appearance and bearing of a man fifteen years younger. He fought with all the same energy. Griff caught a glimpse of his companion, standing on their table. He had one swarthy head in the crook of his left arm, holding the unfortunate man off the ground by brute force, while he battered the face of a second. Then a ringing blow to Griff's ear sent him staggering along the bar.

He regained himself in time to block a kick aimed at his groin. He swatted away another fist and drove knuckles into a face that momentarily appeared in his line of hazy vision. Two more men rushed at him and he picked up a chair. He smashed it against the chest of the nearest attacker and kept hold of one leg to use as a club. A bottle whisked past Griff's ear and he ducked instinctively.

Three more Mexicans came at him, faces pinched in fury: One reached for a wide-bladed bowie knife at his waist. Before he could close his fingers around the hilt, Griff broke his arm with a solid smash from the table leg. The injured man howled and reeled away from the fracas. Griff pummeled the next man with a series of short, hard right jabs, while batting at his legs with the table leg. In a quick sideward glance, Griff saw Temple leap off of the table onto the back of the third patron who struggled to get in close enough to smash a bottle over Griff's head. To the other side, Griff caught swift movement.

Grunting with effort, the pudgy bartender ran at Griff with a big wooden mallet upraised. He swung and yelped with pain when Griff bobbed backward. The cudgel missed its target and smashed into the bartop. Griff clamped his blunt, powerful fingers over the barman's face and gave him a mighty shove.

A bellow of rage came from the fellow as he hurtled backward and crashed into the glass rows of his stock in trade. Liquor, shelving, and barkeep cascaded into a heap on the floor. Griff made out faint shouts from outside and the shrill of distant whistles. He forgot them, though, as he ducked a hamlike fist and slipped in under to work a solid tattoo of lefts and rights against an iron-hard midriff.

Grunting, the man absorbed Griff's blows while a broad grin spread on his face. "You are a regular gamecock, *Señor*. I like a man with spirit."

"Then why are we fighting?" Griff grunted out.

"Porque no? It is for the fun, eh?"

Then he swung a huge fist that sent Griff sprawling over a table. The flimsy legs gave way and the ex-Confederate found himself amid a forest of churning bodies as a general free-for-all broke out. Everyone started to punch up whoever came close and the original cause of the set-to was completely forgotten.

Suddenly the town constables charged in the door. Griff leaped back from a hastily swung knife slash and kicked his attacker in the crotch. Red-faced, the man went down howling in pain, both hands clasped to his aching testicles.

With all the methodical precision of farmers in their fields, the lawmen began wielding their nightsticks like scythes, downing the combatants indifferently. When one came close and sized Griff up for a smack alongside his head, he wisely rolled with the blow and let his shoulder absorb most of the force. He hit the floor and lay still.

A few minutes later, the march to jail began.

Eleven men, including Griffin Stark and Temple Ames, stood in a long, bedraggled line before the tall, imposing redwood bench in the Territorial Court. The judge, a portly, gray-haired man in a black robe, leaned forward

81

and studied the faces of the miscreants.

"As I understand it, we still have to establish who took the first swing and who it was he poked. Is that right, Mr. Prosecutor?"

"Yes, your honor."

"Well then, why haven't you gotten on with it?"

"No one will tell me anything, Your Honor. Not a one of the prisoners will cooperate."

City Magistrate Julio Mendoza looked sharply at the prosecutor. "Now why is that, do you suppose?"

"Well, ah, Your Honor, most of the defendants are, ah, related in one way or another."

"Including two of my cousins I see here, is that what you mean?"

"Uh, yes, Your Honor."

The judge glowered at the far end of the line, where the rat-faced knife artist and an equally skinny, hollow-cheeked Mexican stood looking sheepish. The jurist cleared his throat and wiped his lips on a linen handkerchief.

"I ought to lock you all away where they'll have to send you sunlight and air by freight wagon. Ramon, Lupe," he admonished his cousins. "What the hell are you doing getting in a brawl like that?"

"We, uh, that is, ah, Don Julio, it was a *pinche gringo*. You understand that, *no?*"

"As a matter of fact, I don't. Which of you are the *Norteños* who so unwisely tangled with my *compañeros?* A, ah, *Señor* Ames and *Señor* Stark?"

"I'm Griffin Stark, Your Honor," Griff acknowledged as he stepped forward.

"An' this chile be Ames," Temple added as he moved out of line.

"The fine for fighting in a public place is ten dollars, in gold," Judge Julio Mendoza announced, eyes narrowing. "If you cannot pay it, you will do twenty days in jail."

"*Por Dios!*" Ramon Aparicio exclaimed.

"*Primo . . .* cousin," the judge repeated in a sorrowful tone. "Such an outburst is an insult to the court. You do

82

not wish for another fine to be added to this, do you?''

"*No, Señor Juez.*"

"Thank you, Ramon. Now, then, as I said, the fine is ten dollars. In this present action, however, we are faced with a problem. Since none of you will point a finger at the guilty parties, we do not know who actually participated in the fight. Therefore I am forced to dismiss the case for lack of evidence."

A collective sigh of relief whispered along the file of men. The judge rapped his gavel lightly and continued.

"Now that that is out of the way, tell me, please? Why is it that none of you would accuse any of the others?" He rose and removed his robe to signify that this conversation was off the record.

"Ah, well, you see, Julio," Ramon began. "Last night, in the *carcel*, we got to talking with these *gringos*. We learn that they are good men. Men like ourselves, who have fought Indians and scouted for the army."

"*Sí, primo,*" Lupe injected. "And farmed land, raised cattle. They do not come to take. They are only looking for a child."

"What is this?" the judge asked sharply.

"My son, Your Honor," Griff explained. "It's a long story. He was taken from a wagon train by the Cheyenne, then Shoshone warriors took him from the Cheyenne camp. Now he is with some Nez Percé horse traders we thought might have come to Santa Fe."

"*Hijo de la chingada!* Son of a bitch!" Judge Mendoza exclaimed. "This sounds like one of those fanciful *novelas* my wife is always reading. How old is this boy of yours?"

"Ten, Your Honor."

Mendoza frowned. "He was taken how long ago?"

"Two years."

"You know, don't you? Captives that young often chose to live the rest of their lives as Indians. Your son may not be willing to come back to you."

"I've heard that before, Your Honor. Even so, I want the chance to see him, to talk with him. His mother was killed shortly before the end of the war. He and I are the only

83

family each other has."

"You are a brave and determined man, *Señor* Stark." Judge Mendoza's face took on a puzzled expression. "Somehow your name seems familiar to me. Though the reason escapes me at the moment."

"I've never been to Santa Fe before. We came down here from the Dakota Territory."

"Ah-ha! That is it. The *commandante* at the small army post outside town has a letter for a Mr. Griffin Stark. It, too, is from the Dakota Territory."

"Damien," Griff said in an aside to Temple.

"Very well," the judge dismissed. "Since you are all of the same mind, return to the jail, pick up your belongings and you are free to go. And . . . good luck, *Señor* Stark."

"Stark . . . Stark . . . yes, here it is," a young corporal clerk muttered as he thumbed through a file folder of sealed letters. "Griffin Stark."

"That's me. Thank you. And thanks to your commanding officer."

"You're welcome, sir. Since it's from a Captain Carmichael, it's like army business anyhow."

"More or less." Griff turned from the desk and walked out onto the low-roofed porch that fronted the adobe headquarters building. Temple Ames looked at him, expectantly.

"It's from Damien, right enough."

"Wonder what's so important for him to write this way?"

"We'll soon see." Griff opened the letter and began to read aloud.

Dear Friend Stark, it began. *I have sent copies of this letter to every military outpost I thought you might have a remote chance of visiting. Through sources close to Washinton, I have learned that the consortium is mixing into the unrest in Mexico. Several of the generals there are not in accord with the Juarez government. One in particular, a General Emilio Santos, is reported to have taken power in the state of Guanajuato. The consortium is supposed to be backing him financially and with arms. Among agents of the consortium believed to be in Guana- juato at this time is Colonel Chester Breathwaite. I can't blame you if you wish to continue the search for Jeremy at this time. However, old friend, I am sure your desire to bring Breathwaite to justice is as intense as mine. If you decide to pursue Breathwaite, please write me before you leave the country. Jennifer sends her love and I my very best wishes. Your friend, Damien Carmichael.*

"Damn!" Temple swore. "Right when we was gettin' close to the li'l nipper."

A frown deeply creased Griff's brow. He shared Temple's opinion. Yet this promised a chance to even scores with Chester Breathwaite and learn, perhaps, why it was the consortium wanted him and the Carmichaels dead. Jeremy, Jeremy, he thought sadly, where have those savages taken you now?

"The trail is as cold now as before we knew he was in Two Otter's camp," Griff reasoned aloud. "We know where Breathwaite is. I want his hide on my barn door. For all we know, Jeremy and the Nez Percé might be on their way to the Idaho country and their home lodges."

"Then we oughtta be headin' north, not south."

Griff gave it only brief, but painful, thought. "No. No, we're going to Mexico after Chester Breathwaite."

CHAPTER NINE

Arthur Treadwell gazed out the tall, broad glazed window of his office at the gray haze that obscured Staten and Governor's Islands. A small rain squall scudded across New York Harbor. Ships from around the world brought their commerce here and the dregs of Europe emptied out onto the shores to find new homes in a land of promise.

Promise, bah! Only for those who were shrewd enough and tough enough to seize what they wanted and hold onto it. Fodder for the mines and mills and foundries of a nation that would soon be entirely in the control of the consortium, Arthur thought with lustful avarice. That's what these immigrants represented. Before long the vast range and farmlands of the Far West would have to be consolidated into a few consortium-owned cooperatives of thousands of sections each. Only enough acres to feed the people of the country, Arthur cautioned himself. No need wasting valuable space that would provide housing for workers and their dependents. Then factories could be built and the resources ripped from the ground to produce products for sale in Europe and throughout the world to fill the always hungry coffers of the consortium members. If he could believe Breathwaite's report, they might add another country to the list of those under the iron will of the FRC. Arthur's eyes slid to the neat stack of papers that lay squarely in the center of his uncluttered desk.

Chester Breathwaite had found his forté, dealing with

military minds. Corruptible military minds, Arthur reminded himself. The former colonel ought to be at home there. The supplies had arrived in good condition. He even had a note of gratitude from General Santos attached to the signed agreements and the observations of his agent in Guanajuato.

The enterprise seemed to prosper. The big question remained. Would Santos be able to hold everyone in line and successfully execute his overthrow of Juarez? After that, well, Breathwaite knew what to do.

"We go to the land of Sonora," Bear Heart explained to Jeremy and Beaver Tail. "There are soldiers there called 'Lancers,' who will pay much money for our beautiful horses. To get there we must go through what the white men call Arizona Territory. It is the land of the Apaches and we must be careful. They hate everyone but their own kind."

"Why do we not go straight south and then turn west into this Sonora?" Jeremy inquired, still enjoying the freedom to question afforded Indian children, after his years living under the dictum, "Children are to be seen and not heard."

"The year grows longer. If we are to be through the mountain passes and into the golden land of the big water before the snows come, we can spare no time."

"This way saves us five suns on our journey," Joshua Lame Deer added.

Images of soon seeing the big water and swimming among tall waves that they had been told could knock them down appealed to the boys and they rode along this new course happily, without further question. No signs told them when they crossed over into Arizona, but they soon learned that their passing had been noted. Avarice glinted in the dark eyes that watched them sit astride their spotted-rump ponies. Polished metal disks caught the light of the sun and flashed unseen messages across the mesas.

On the third day in Arizona Territory, the ground seemed to sprout bronze-skinned Indians in long breech-cloths and high-topped moccasins. They rose, streaming dust from their muscular backs and brought weapons to the ready.

"Apaches!" Bear Heart cried out. "Show them how the Nez Percé fight!"

The hammer fell on a percussion cap and Jeremy's .31 squirrel rifle boomed into the heat-laden desert air. An Apache clasped a hand to his right breast, an inch below the nipple, and tried to staunch the flow of blood from the wound Jeremy had given him.

Surrounded by so many enemies, Jeremy wisely put his rifle aside in its thong sling and reached for his bow. To his left, Beaver Tail's bowstring twanged and an arrow flew toward a grinning enemy who advanced at a run.

It caught him in the thigh and he tumbled on the ground, howling in fury. Only three Apaches had firearms and their shots had gone wild. They desired to spare the horses if at all possible and yet end this encounter quickly. They rushed forward with knives, tomahawks, and stone war clubs.

The nearest warrior leaped at Bear Heart and found himself impaled on a short Nez Percé war lance. Gagging in a fountain of his own blood, the Apache clasped both hands around the rough wooden shaft and fell backward, nearly unseating the Nez Percé. Jeremy's small war club made a meaty smack as he smashed it down on the wounded brave's skull.

The Apache let go of Bear Heart's lance and fell away as the Nez Percé kicked his mount in an effort to outrun their attackers. Jeremy followed suit, turned backward, guiding with his bare knees, as he discharged another feathered projectile at a howling warrior. He gave a yip of victory when the arrow lodged in the running Apache's belly. More of the stocky, ugly desert fighters appeared, closing the net on their victims in the age-old manner their people had used to run down wild game. They yelped and hooted as they ran in two overlapping fan-shaped lines.

This placed twice the number of warriors in front of the fleeing Nez Percé and the two boys. Beaver Tail fired an arrow and reached for another. A thrown knife swished past his head and bounced on the hard, stony ground. Joshua Lame Deer plunged his lance into the knife thrower's chest.

A shriek of agony came from the dying Apache's lips. He staggered away into the desert a few steps, then stiffened and fell rigidly into a clump of cactus. His body registered no pain, though.

Jeremy suddenly found two mounted Apaches racing directly toward him on converging course. No time to nock another arrow. He jabbed at one's face with the tip of his bow and grabbed his knife in his left hand. As the warrior jerked backward to dodge the bow's threat, Jeremy rode in close and slashed across the man's stomach.

Red lips pealed back from the wound and the Apache's intestines spilled out in purplish coils that glistened with moisture in the harsh sunlight. The disemboweled warrior reeled on his pony's back, then pitched to one side. To his embarrassment and shame, Jeremy found he was crying. An icy lump of fear knotted his stomach and his nostrils quivered at the raw scent of human blood. His left arm dripped gore from his enemy from wrist to elbow. His shrill boy's voice rose in a warcry and he drummed heels into his spotted-rump mount's ribs.

Even as he leaped forward, the other Apache who had charged him drew in close. His tomahawk flashed in the brassy sunlight. Then it bit into vulnerable, silky bronze skin along Jeremy's ribs. Hot waves of pain radiated from the wound, and Jeremy could not silence the anguished cry that tore out of his throat. Blood ran in a sheet down his side.

When he looked down, he could see the yellow-white covering of three ribs, where a flap of skin flopped loosely at his side. A great weakness washed over him and he stared helplessly as the Apache raised his arm for another swing that the beleagured boy knew would split his skull.

The next instant the warrior snapped forward against

his mount's neck. A Cheyenne arrow, with its red ring design, quivered in the center of his back. Beyond him, Beaver Tail raised his bow in salute and kicked out at an Apache who attempted to drag him from the saddle. Suddenly Bear Heart was beside his adopted son.

"You are hurt, Snow Rabbit."

"No, Father. Only a little cut. I can still fight."

"Pull off and use that rifle of yours. You shoot left-handed, that is good. First, let me bind that wound."

Bear Heart used his loincloth, the only strip of material readily available. Naked, he rode off to break a path for Jeremy to follow. "Hurry, Snow Rabbit," he called back to the boy. "Your rifle will turn the tide."

A cloud of dust rose around the struggling forces. Jeremy sat on a low knoll thirty yards from where his friend and the Nez Percé fought a losing battle with the Apaches. Swiftly, as he bit his lower lip to keep from crying out at the pain, Jeremy loaded powder, patch, and ball. He put the accurate little piece to his shoulder and eared back the hammer.

The Pennsylvania rifle exploded. An Apache fell dead. Jeremy reloaded.

Another shot. Another dead Apache. Oily sweat ran nearly as thickly as blood down the stocky little boy's body as he rammed home a third round.

His shot went low, smashing into the groin of his Apache target.

With a howl of utter agony, the wounded man fell and began to roll on the ground. In the same instant, Jeremy realized the warrior he shot had been the leader of this small war party. One of the braves came to the writhing chief and bent low. He rose with a look of horror on his face as he held one of the wounded chief's testicles between two fingers. He hooted a signal to the other warriors and they ran off a ways into the desert.

"We must ride for it," Bear Heart declared. "They are after our ponies."

"I . . . I feel awfully weak, Father," Jeremy told him.

"Come. Ride with me, then. We will lead your pony."

He sat Jeremy in front of him on the padded Nez Percé saddle and the small party jumped their mounts to a gallop.

Relentlessly the Apaches followed, trotting afoot far behind or ranging alongside on their horses. With equal resolution, the blood continued to flow from Jeremy's wound. He turned a sickly yellow-green under his deeply bronzed skin and his eyes rolled in their sockets.

"He won't live long if we don't stop," a worried Bear Heart told Joshua Lame Deer.

"Up ahead there," the Nez Percé advised his friend. He pointed to a cluster of rocks.

Among the scattered boulders, the small party made their stand.

Twice more the Apaches attempted to reach them. Each time the two Northern warriors and the Cheyenne boy fought them off with expert use of the bow. Losses mounted for the attackers. Jeremy lay on the sandy ground. He moaned and cried out with each screaming attack by the Apache warriors. The changed situation allowed the Nez Percé to use their rifles.

The long range weapons began to take a bigger toll. Then an ululating wail went up from the Apaches and they turned away from their intended victims. On the shoulders of four of them, they bore the dead body of their leader.

"It is over," Bear Heart announced.

Quickly he and his friend Joshua Lame Deer set about tending Jeremy's wound. "There is a rabbit out there somewhere," Bear Heart told Beaver Tail. Go and kill it and bring me the intestines."

While the small Cheyenne boy set out on his task, Bear Heart took a pouch of moss and pounded berries from his sash and opened it. He removed his loincloth from the wound and covered his nakedness. Then he set about washing the gaping slash with water from an elk bladder canteen. Jeremy flinched away in his semiconsciousness and called out in Cheyenne for his mother and father.

Joshua felt the child's brow and shook his head. "He

grows hot."

"He fought bravely," Bear Heart replied. "Let me pack the cut."

Jeremy's mouth sagged open and Bear Heart put powdered aconite root into the boy's mouth and dribbled a thin stream of water after it.

"Drink. Drink this, my son," he urged.

Reflexively, Jeremy swallowed. The powerful narcotic put him to sleep.

Beaver Tail returned with the rabbit intestines.

"Wash them and cut them in long, thin strips, like string," Bear Heart instructed.

When the Cheyenne lad had completed the assignment, Bear Heart reached into another pouch at his waist and drew out a bone needle used for repairing moccasins. With it he began to sew shut the long flap of skin that hung down from the wound over Jeremy's ribs.

"We have done all we can," Bear Heart announced when the crude surgery had been completed. "Now it is up to the Great Spirit."

"Really, Arthur, you must be aware of what the consortium intends for Mexico," Chester Breathwaite told Arthur Treadwell over a sumptuous luncheon on the balcony of their hotel, overlooking the teeming streets of Guanajuato.

"Certainly. I'm quite familiar with the plan not to stop with Santos."

"So right. He is a crass, vulgar mestizo bandit. He belongs in the hills robbing poor villages. Certainly not one to be trusted running a country."

"What I don't know is why he was chosen to finance, instead of one of the other dissident generals."

"Because his is so *stupid*. He will never realize our true purpose. The Mexicans are a hot-headed, emotional people. Once Santos and the other generals depose Juarez, many of them will remember that they once shouted the name of Benito Juarez from the rooftops and marched barefoot in his ragtag army to expel the French. Even in his disgrace, they will see him as a hero."

"So," Arthur said through a nasty smile. "We let Santos dispose of Juarez and his close followers. The blame will fall on them. The people will become discontent again. All the while, the consortium continues to pump money into a likely successor. Am I right so far?"

"Exactly to the point, Arthur. Let's see if you can carry out the rest of the scene. After the execution of Juarez and his cabinet, what happens?"

"We cut off the money flow into Mexico. The consortium ceases to export Mexican goods and the economy fails. The people become discontent. Then, the recruit supply to the rebel generals dries up and then . . . and then . . ."

"The consortium steps into rectify the horrible situation. Since no blame can fall to us for the murder of Juarez and the overthrow of his government, we will be welcomed as the new 'saviors of Mexico.' Our agents and their front men will do in Santos and the other rebel generals and turn Mexico into a docile and obedient slave state, run by the consortium."

"Administered along the lines laid down by Marx, I suppose."

"Naturally, my boy. He established excellent guides for turning people into cattle and getting the most out of them before they died of overwork or old age."

"Then, before long, Mexico will be ours and we can begin to milk it of all that gold and silver in these mountains."

"Absolutely. Count on it, Arthur. You will become the Silver King of Central Mexico."

CHAPTER TEN

A dazzling sun beat down on the muddy-green water of the Rio Grande, called the *Rio Bravo del Norte* on this side of the border, in Ciudad Juarez, Mexico. Anglos and Mexicans stood around the small pole corrals haggling over the price of cattle and horses. On the fringe, Griffin Stark and Temple Ames discussed the probable virtues, or lack of them, of a half dozen burros brought out for their inspection.

"Never had any run-in with these little donkeys," Temple told Griff. "Figger they's not much different than mules. Stubborn, smart an' 'bout as much trouble as they are use."

"To cross that desert, we have to carry everything with us. It would be a good idea to have spare mounts, too," Griff insisted. "These little animals are supposed to need less water than horses or mules."

"Wonder if they speak English?" Temple asked more in seriousness than sarcasm.

"We'll find that out, I suppose. They are supposed to carry over three hundred pounds each. What with grain for six animals, our spare water and food, they'll have a full load. I'd like to take more. But I learned in Stuart's cavalry that there's a point at which the number of bellies you have to fill exceeds the weight carrying advantages. Unless you use wagons, of course."

"An' we ain't got time for that. So, we get two of these

95

critters. Then we load up the supplies and head out in the mornin', right?"

"There is a train from Chihuahua City going south to a place called Aguascalientes. We can ride to there."

"What do we do once we get to this Guanajuato?" ·

"I've been thinking on that on the way here," Griff admitted. "So far, I have no idea how to go about dealing with Breathwaite. Learning French at the Academy, as well as the Latin I got beforehand, I've been able to read and make some sense out of their newspapers. One story said that a rumor had it that the governor of Guanajuato had been arrested by General Santos. If that's the case, then all law is in his hands and we won't have much of a chance to appeal to the authorities to arrest Breathwaite and hold him for us. We'll have to go there, have a look around and then decide what to do."

Temple grinned. "Sorta like scoutin' Injuns."

"Or riding advance screen for Bobby Lee."

A small, skinny man in worn, but meticulously clean clothes approached. "*Señores*, I am called Paco Ramirez. I understand that you are preparing to journey to Chihuahua. Myself and my partner, Hernando Castro are likewise making that trip. We have gone many times and know the road well. If you would be interested, we would be happy to accompany you."

Griff studied the short man with interest. He appeared to be in his mid-twenties, stringy muscles indicated an unsuspected strength. He had a narrow face and shifty eyes and his breath had a sour odor that Griff could not identify. As first impressions went, this Paco Ramirez didn't add up to much.

What he said, though, made sense. They were strangers in a strange land. At least Ramirez spoke English. It would be useful to have a guide on this stage of their journey. More so when they got far into the interior mountains of Mexico. Griff glanced at Temple, who wrinkled his nose and shrugged his shoulders.

"It would break the monotony for Hernan' and I and provide you with someone who knows the way,"

Paco added.

"We leave in the morning," Griff told him, deciding. "Can you be ready by then?"

"Oh, *sí*. We could leave yet today if you wished."

"Fine, then. I am Griffin Stark and this is Temple Ames. We are staying at the Posada del Sol. Be there an hour before sunrise."

"*Sí, Señor*. We shall be ready."

Guitar strings vibrated to the haunting music of a wild gypsy dance. Clouds of smoke hung in the air of the low-ceilinged Juarez cantina where Griff and Temple had stopped to take a drink in the late afternoon. The billows floated lazily until the dancing girl's abandoned performance tore them to shreds and sent the broken wisps gyrating toward the small windows high in the walls. With a frenzy of strumming, the music ended and the girl bowed low, her head only three feet from Griff's table.

"That senor-ita's got eyes for you, Griff," Temple said behind his hand, his attention fixed on the lithe, muscular legs exposed fleetingly through the ruffled slit in the dancer's dress.

"Uh, what? I was thinking about what those Indians from the Taos Pueblo told us before we left Santa Fe. If the Nez Percé and their horses are really going into Mexico, chances are we might get a line on Jeremy."

"It's a big country, Griff. More land than people. Nothin' says we can't try, though. Now, like this chile said, that there gal has the hots for you. Man'd be a fool not to take advantage of that."

"I'm not so sure."

"Well, I be."

A moment later, the girl joined them at their table. "You will buy a drink for Luisa?"

Despite his preoccupation, Griff felt a stirring in his loins. It had been a long time since he had enjoyed the company of a woman. This dark, satiny beauty had hauntingly good looks and wore a fragrance that moved him to the depths. He smiled and signaled the bartender.

When the drink had been set before her, Luisa tucked the small wooden coin that came with it into the top of her low bodice. Then she looked directly into Griff's gray eyes.

"I am not a *puta*. I do not—how you say—sleep with the men who buy me drinks. I am a *bailarina*, a dancer."

"But for me?" Griff heard himself say in a voice that croaked.

"*Ah*! For you it is different. You are handsome, you are strong. Yet, you have a look about you of tragedy and loneliness. It cries out to my woman's heart."

Despite his determination to press on with the pursuit of Chester Breathwaite, Griff felt his chest tighten and his groin swell as he asked her, "Where shall we go?"

"I have a room near here. A small pension house. I will wait for you outside."

"I'll be there, Luisa."

"How are you called?"

"My name is Griff."

"*Bueno*. In ten minutes time, Griff?"

They walked at a slow pace, though Griff's heart raced. He held her gently by one elbow and supported her weight over the uneven cobbles. A small key opened the low, narrow door to her dwelling. Inside, Luisa lighted a lamp. She raised her arms and they disappeared beind her back.

In a twinkling, she peeled out of her dance costume, a colorful, flouncy dress with short puff sleeves and many attached ruffled petticoats, done in green, white, and red, the colors of Mexico. When it rustled to the floor, she stepped out of it. For all his past experience with women, Griff gaped.

Large, firm breasts jutted out from her heaving chest, the swelling nipples barely covered by a plain camisole that hung from those tempting pinnacles straight downward past her flat belly and ending at mid-thigh. He yearned to discover what delights it concealed. She stepped to him and, with fumbling fingers that proved her declaration that she was not a prostitute, helped him disrobe. Then she stepped back to admire his long, muscular frame, with its network of scars and blemishes. A slightly mocking smile curved her lips.

"*Dios mio!*" she exclaimed as she gazed at his pulsing maleness. "Had I known you were so . . . so . . ."

Griff's aching need swelled in his loins, radiated through his body. Shaken by his sudden passion he reached out to the girl.

"So magnificent!" she completed her remark. "Hurry. Hury. Touch me there. Ah, yes, and there . ... higher. Aaah."

Griff directed her to the bed and eased her back on it. He slid between her outstretched legs and felt the fire of her womanly treasure as he touched it with his rigid phallus. Slowly, tremblingly, he entered her. Her musky scent rose in waves that dizzied his head and his heart pounded as he willed himself to take his time. Her legs and arms entwined him, urging him deeper.

"*Ah . . . ay . . . ay!*" Luisa keened as Griff penetrated to her very core.

"It is wise, *Señor* Stark, to pause for siesta through the heat of afternoon," Paco advised.

The two Americans and their Mexican companions had been traveling roughly due south for six hours. They stopped at noon to rest the animals and eat a light meal of cold dried meat and a small melon purchased outside Juarez. Now, as the remains were disposed of and implements stored in one large hide envelope of a packsaddle, the short, skinny Mexican enlarged on his explanation.

"The sun does not set until late out here. We rest until four o'clock and then ride on until darkness."

"It's your country," Griff agreed.

"But first, *Señor*, a little something for our digestion." Paco went to his sway-backed horse and produced four small green bottles from a saddlebag. He removed the corks and handed the containers around. "*Pulque,*" he explained and Griff knew the source of the sour odor that came on the two men's breath.

Griff took a swallow and nearly spat it out. Unlike any beverage he had ever encountered, the pulque had a raw, bitter aftertaste, every bit as bad as its initial assault on his palate. Temple made a face and Griff wanted to laugh when the former mountain man gave the drink an apt name.

"Panther piss."

When the quartet had consumed the odorous potion, Paco withdrew with Hernando to the shade of a paloverde tree. They spread blankets, tipped their large sombreros over their eyes and drifted off. A few minutes later, Griff and Temple did likewise. Fatigued by his amorous, nightlong encounter with the lovely Luisa, Griff sank into a deep, soundless sleep. A short distance away, Temple snored and sweated through the burning heat of midday. An hour went by before Hernando spoke in a whisper to his friend.

"I say we kill them now, take what is of value and return to Juarez."

"Too many people knew we left together. It would not be wise, *amigo*."

"Then, what—"

"We will wait. What is wrong with going to Chihuahua? Who knows what we might find there?"

"But we have never been to Chihuahua before, Paco."

"*No es importa.* There is no hurry."

"*Este señor Stark me cae gordo.*"

"He gives me a pain, too, Hernan. But they are *gringos*, so they are rich. Think of the loot we will have when we do kill and rob them."

The next two and a half days went well. At Griff's urging, they made an easy forty miles by sunset each night. Chihuahua lay only two more days away. As the four men settled down for the siesta, Griff noted huge billows of peculiar-colored clouds building to the southwest, some ten miles.

"Look at those," he said to Temple.

"Don't look like no storm clouds this chile has ever

100

seen," Ames observed.

"They are dust clouds, *señores*. A sand storm. *Muy malo*," Paco informed them. "It would be best," he went on, thinking fast to take advantage of the situation, "if we found some sort of shelter. There is supposed to be a water hole a short ways to the west of us, with rocks and a big cave where we will be safe."

"In the direction of the storm?" Griff asked doubtfully.

"It is, unfortunately, the only choice we have. We must hurry."

As Griff and Temple went to their horses, Paco turned to Hernando and gave him a big wink, his thin lips turned down into an arc to match the thin, scraggly strands of his mustache.

They had gone a good two miles to the west, Griff estimated. Still no sign of this supposed oasis. In that time the storm had moved very close to them. Strong gusts that preceded the tumult whipped up unexpectedly and scoured their flesh with bits of sharp-edged sand. Boots shied nervously and Griff urged him on.

"I'm going to push ahead a little. The burros are slowing us down," Griff told Paco.

"It is no use, *Señor*. Maybe we should turn back."

"No. If that water hole is out here, we'll find it."

Inwardly Paco delighted at this suggestion. It would be much easier to overpower these big *gringos* if they could once be separated. He shrugged his shoulders and made a show of considering Griff's remark.

"It is as you say, *Señor*. I would look a little more to the south, perhaps."

Griff rode off, seeking the fictional shelter Paco had invented. Behind him, Paco and Hernando moved closer to Temple Ames.

With the swiftness of a rattler's strike, the sandstorm howled around Griffin Stark as he rode southwest on Boots. The wind roared and his face smarted from hundreds of tiny grains that slashed his skin as the fury of

101

the tempest turned daylight into night in a world of moving sand.

Grit filled his mouth, eyes, and ears. Tears ran in a futile attempt to wash away the offending matter that smarted like a million grains of red pepper. Particles invaded the same places on his mount. Boots snorted and his dark hide twitched in discomfort. Wisely, Griff dismounted and wet a kerchief from his canteen.

It turned to instant mud in the whirl of stinging bits. Even so, he covered Boots's mouth and nose with it and slowly turned around. Back to the stygian bluster, he took long, elaborate steps in an attempt to retrace his course. The errant wind tugged at his hat and set his sleeves and trouser legs to flapping. He could feel the sand making a thick crust in the hairs on his neck. Only the faintest of light, a feeble sun, showed through the half-mile high cloud that enclosed him. Random currents of turbulent air jerked him first one way, then the other. Griff began to stagger, then to lose his tenuous grasp on his direction. Still the cataclysm buffeted him.

A hundred creeping yards further on, Griff tripped over the thick trunk of a fallen saguaro cactus. Its pipe organ arms speared him painfully with dozens of sharp spines. Griff stifled a groan and forced himself to his knees. The effort of battling the storm proved too much. He could go no further. Panting with exertion, the many thorns in his legs making a miniature hell of each movement, Griff crawled to Boots's side. He grasped the stirrup bow with the desperation a drowning man uses on a rope.

All his energy had been drained by the rampaging winds and suffocating sand. No matter how hard he tried, he could not pull himself upright. Gasping in tormented surrender, he sagged back to the ground.

Only dimly, and after a long time, did Griff note any lightening along the western limits of the tumult. Imperceptably the wind abated. Heavier particles rained down out of the whirling miasma above him. Then lighter material began to fall. At last, through his grime-filled eyes, Griff saw the bright blue of a peaceful sky. He coughed and spat out a gritty mixture of mucous and sand. Inside his head, the storm still seemed to howl its fury. He moaned and reached feebly for his canteen.

With the desperation of a thirst-crazed man, Griff gulped down a long stream. He gagged and nearly spit it up, swallowed raggedly and took in more. His chest heaved, lungs tingling with the sweet aroma of fresh, dust-free air. Gradually his strength returned. He stood, body stinging anew with the prickle of the cactus spines. Griff bit his lip in determination and swung into the saddle.

Weakness swept over him like a gray fog. He swayed in the stirrups and forced himself to strain upward, not to slump and perhaps fall asleep as he rode. An hour's zigzag search had still not located any sign of Temple Ames and the two Mexicans.

Griff continued to seek them, widening the sideways jinks he took off the estimated course of his outward journey. The terrain had altered radically. Three long, nearly white lines of sand dunes existed where he could swear none had been before. Giant saguaro, that had towered over them, now lay buried to their upper arm branches. Clumps of occatilla had been uprooted. Elsewhere the land had been swept and scoured to a faceless plain.

At last he came across some smudged hoofprints. He studied their shape and the direction of the thrown sand. The animals had been moving toward the road to Chihuahua. He raced in that direction for half a mile and saw a huddled form lying on the desert floor some three hundred yards ahead. Cautiously, though quickly, he closed in.

Temple Ames lay on his side, blood slowly seeping from a sand-crusted cut along the side of his head. Griff dismounted and hurried to his side. Ames moaned as Griff gently rolled him over. His eyes moved behind the closed lids and he coughed feebly. Griff returned to Boots and got his canteen. He knelt on the burning ground and slowly dribbled the clear liquid onto Temple's lips.

With a sputter and sudden lurch, Temple Ames came

out of his stupor, arms flailing. "Ya thievin' bastards!" he shouted. Then his eyes slowly focused on Griffin Stark.

"Uh, Griff. This chile figgered you was a goner. Them thievin' Mezkins jumped me. Were nigh onto endin' this chile's time on earth. The storm hit an' they got scarit, the way I reckon it. They'd hit me oncst, and gathered up the pack animals. That runty one, Paco, came over and whacked me again alongside the head with the butt of his quirt. Musta had lead in it."

"He sure laid you open. How long ago?"

Temple peered at the sun. "No way of figgerin' it. That storm fowled up this chile's time sense. Oooh," he groaned as he placed both hands to his throbbing skull. "They lambasted me a good one. This chile can't wait until he gets his hands on them slippery bastards."

"No matter. It's a hell of a way to Chihuahua. We have to get moving."

"There's only one horse."

"That's why we have to make tracks."

"We could die out here," Temple stated their problem simply.

CHAPTER ELEVEN

Through habit established by the privations he had to endure during the last years of the war, with the Army of Northern Virginia, Griffin Stark always provided ample supplies on his own mount. As the blazing sun slanted down the western sky, lengthening their shadows and bringing some relief from the blistering heat of midday, he made an inventory.

"Two canteens. Damned glad for that. A small tin of sugar, a bag of beans, one of venison jerky, a pound of that dry shredded meat we got in Juarez, uh, *machaca* I think they called it. And in this saddlebag, ten pounds of oats for Boots. We'll have to walk, lead my horse."

"Dang it. That makes the two days to Chihuahua more'n a week."

"Maybe not. There's bound to be someone out here. A ranch or town. We had better start. It will be close to sundown by the time we get back to the road."

"Think those fellers will be layin' for us?" Temple asked, a gleam of anticipation in his eyes.

"No. They got most of what they wanted. Probably figure the desert will do for us. How's your head?"

"Feels like this chile stuck it in a nest of hornets. Right now I could even go for some of that pulque to numb it a bit."

"You'll have to make do with water . . . and little of that."

* * *

"Mí general," an excited young lieutenant blurted as he entered Emilio Santos's office and saluted. "Our troops have encountered resistance in Silao. The *alcalde* has risen the people against them. There have been casualties."

"How many?"

"The messenger said seven men killed. Captain Gomez has barricaded his troops in the church on the plaza. He asks for a relief column."

"He shall have it then. Send Colonel Cardoza to me, also Major Jimenez and Captain Rojas."

Ten minutes later, the three officers stood tensely in front of the general's desk. Santos quickly explained the situation to them. He concluded with terse instructions.

"We must send a relief column for Captain Gomez. Two companies. Those with the new weapons our *gringo* friends provided. I want a lesson made of Silao. This is the sort of operation you like, my friend," he remarked to Colonel Cardoza.

"Take the town. Loot it, rape a few women, shoot the instigators. If you cannot find them, execute a dozen or so men on general principles. Major Jimenez, see that the necessary supplies are made ready. Captain Rojas, your company will have the honor of leading the assault."

"Muchisimis gracias, mí general," the lean, saturnine captain responded oilily. Unconsciously he ran long, spatulate fingers through his straight, slicked-back raven hair. His full lips curled upward as he contemplated his own brand of delights he could indulge at Silao. His mouth assumed a *V* shape that reminded Santos of that of a praying mantis.

"The assault company will be on horseback. The second company is to run. And I mean, run to Silao and be prepared to swing into position to the west of town to block off any escape. The second wave will attack ten minutes after the first. Questions?"

"Are we to kill everyone?" Cardoza inquired.

"No. Exterminate the men if you will. Leave the women and children alive to tell others what it means to defy my orders."

"Very good, *mi general.*"

A moment later, Arthur Treadwell sauntered into the general's office. "I heard that some small village has risen against your, ah, benign rule, General Santos," Arthur drawled.

"That is correct," Santos acknowledged, tight-lipped with fury that this *gringo* should know so soon and so much about his momentary setback.

"Ummm. I see. Well then, if you don't mind, I should like to accompany anyone you send to rectify the situation. I might find it amusing. Also it will give the consortium a firsthand account of your profifiency. Something that will count heavily, I assure you."

"Very well, *Señor* Treadwell. You may go with Captain Rojas and his company. They lead the assault. And, ah, Rojas, bring Gomez to me. He should have been aware of the situation building there and taken the appropriate steps to prevent it. You should have pacified the area by two days from now, Colonel Cardoza. Gomez will be a private by nightfall of that day, provided I don't decide to shoot him for incompetence. That is all. Put your orders into action."

Damien Carmichael sat at his desk, brooding over the two letters in front of him. Griff had received his letter in Santa Fe and decided to go after Breathwaite. All well and good. Damien wished, fervently, that he had knowledge of the contents of the second missive in advance and been able to contact Griff directly, before his friend went off into a foreign country.

More bad news. That's what the second message contained. News of Santos's uprising had reached Mexico City. President Juarez was known as a kind man who readily forgave former enemies and embraced all, Indian, *mestizo*, and *hildago* alike. But he was death on those who would openly revolt. Damien's sources informed him that Juarez would soon order a punitive expedition to be launched against Santos. It looked to him like Griffin

Stark would be caught in the middle. A foreigner bearing arms during a revolt; and in the area contested by both sides. It could, Damien considered, cost Griff his life.

"Damien! Damien, look," the voice of his sister interrupted Damien's thoughts. "Corporal Munson brought me this. It came in the mail. A letter from Griff."

"Yes, Jen, I had one, too," her brother told her in a tone of caution.

Always well-atuned to Damien's subtle nuances, Jennifer tensed at the sound of his voice and lowered her hand. "What is it, Damien?"

The elder Carmichael sighed heavily and indicated his own letters. "I'm afraid Griff is headed for a dangerous situation. The Mexican government is going to do something about Santos's revolt. If Chester Breathwaite runs true to form, he will slip away into the night and leave his protegee holding the bag. That might put Griff between the two opposing factions."

"But, surely . . ." Jennifer began, her voice trailing off as the realization of what that could mean for Griff penetrated. "Oh, Damien! What can we do?"

Damien shook his head. "Nothing, I'm afraid. We have no way of contacting Griff. I can send word, privately, to Benito Juarez, explain about Griff and his search for Breathwaite. If only . . . if it can only reach Mexico City in time."

"Please, Damien. Please do everything you can. I'm so afraid for Griff."

Damien put an arm around his sister's shoulders. "I understand, Jen. I'm troubled, too. I'll send the message by telegraph. At least we can be sure of it reaching the Mexican border before the end of the day, today."

"Bless you, dear brother. I think I'm going to cry."

"No you're not. You're too tough for that." Damien cleared his throat. "Have you given any thought to returning to Maryland?"

Jennifer looked up, stricken. "I never contemplated such a move. Why, Griff is out here, looking for his son. I want to be near him. To have what time we can together. If he would have let me, I would have gone along this time."

"I know you would. If it hadn't been for Griff's hard-headed, common sense, you probably could have managed it. Truth is, Jen, that it would be better for all concerned if you did go back home."

"No!" the spirited young woman flared. "I can't do that. I won't."

"Then at least consider returning to St. Jo. The open frontier like this is no place for a lady. No place for any woman, for that matter. It's dangerous, dirty and there's nothing in the world for you to do."

"That's not so. The experience I received during the war has proven its worth more than once. You have no doctor. The men detailed to deal with wounds and care for the sick are ignorant of the simplest procedures of a hospital or surgery. As long as I can provide that knowledge and can work along with the men, I can be of use. And, I'll be closer to Griff, too."

"You're even more stubborn that when you were a little girl, I'll say that for you," Damien allowed through a grin. "But Griff is more than a thousand miles from us right now. Well into Mexico I would assume. He would rest easier, and I know for certain I would, if you were to return to St. Joseph."

"I'll not think of it."

"Jen . . ." Damien drawled a warning.

Tears appeared in Jennifer's green eyes and she angrily batted a small fist at them. "I *will not* cry!" she blurted out. Unwilling to continue an argument she felt on the verge of losing, she whirled with a rustle of petticoats and started for the door.

"What's for supper tonight?" Damien called after her.

"Shoe leather for you, Mr. Meanie," she taunted, reverting for a moment to a favorite childhood threat she used on her big brother to get her way.

Stars shone brightly down over the high Montana plains that night. Her evening chores done in the kitchen of the quarters used by her brother, Jennifer Carmichael climbed the crude sod-block stairway to the roof. She brought with her a light-weight chair with cane back and bottom. She seated it where she could watch the southern sky and arranged her skirts around her, chastely covering her ankles, though the darkness prevented any display of immodesty. She leaned back and thought of Griffin Stark.

Jennifer had been madly in love with him from the age of eight. Well, at least smitten, she admitted. At ten, when he and her brother had been graduated from the Military Academy at West Point, her body already burned with the juices of emerging womanhood and her infatuation turned into genuine love. Then tragedy struck. Griff was to marry. And a Georgia girl at that.

Her brother tried to explain. Griff and Bobby Jean had known each other since childhood, had grown up together and, within the confines of the mores of the anti-bellum South, courted in their teens. They had been in love for more years than Jennifer had been alive. It meant nothing to her. In a tearful meeting with Griff, she had poured out her unrequited love. Her heart ached as he talked to her as though she were a little girl. She resolved to do something about that.

Carefully, she pointed out to him that girls only a bit older than she, and some her own age, were already married. Girls of twelve and thirteen, some only eleven, bore strong, healthy children to the men they had married. He countered with a remark that this was a thing of the past. He pointed out that proper Southern girls didn't marry until they had completed finishing school and been "turned out." Among their social class, sixteen wasn't even considered an old maid anymore. Only Northern trash and poor whites of the Southern mountains seriously thought of marrying and giving babies to girls so young. Shamelessly she pleaded with him to wait for her. She would grow up real fast. Why, within two, no more than three years, they could have a home of their own and children to make them happy. Jennifer's face flamed with the recollection of it, though none were present to see her embarrassment.

Somehow he had talked her out of it. Had even gotten

her to agree to accompany her brother to Georgia and to attend the wedding. Her heart had broken and she cried piteously as Griff and Bobby Jean had become one. Then Jeremy Stark had been born. The thought of Griffin Stark's baby boy made her heart swell to the breaking point. It was almost as if Jeremy were her own child. She wanted to hold the baby, cuddle him. After that, the war came and Griff's life became fraught with danger.

All through the horrible conflict, Jennifer prayed for Griff's safety as she grew into an attractive and desirable young woman. Sternly, she rejected all suiters, secure in her own mind that some day Griff would see her for what she was and love her. When she became his nurse, after the frightful wounds he had taken, her spirit blossomed anew. She overflowed with love as she tended his fever-wracked body, washed him and fed him when he roused enough to take food. When he came near to dying, she thought she would, too. Through her strong intervention, and that of Damien, a doctor had been persuaded to perform the operation necessary to save Griff's leg and arm.

After that, he mended well. Each day of his improvement brought new happiness to Jennifer Carmichael. She thought now of the long months before he had been able to walk with the aid of two canes. All through that terrible time, he had no word of his wife or child, or of the condition of his plantation in Georgia. When he became strong enough, he determined to go out to learn for himself.

Jennifer accompanied him, shared his grief as he discovered the destruction of the plantation buildings and the murder of his wife. They had endured much together. Then, one night, the insults of some arrogant Reconstruction Army soldiers in a northeastern Georgia tavern had been too much for Griff. He shot one of the men and menaced the other two. As a result, they had to flee ahead of vindictive Yankee justice that decreed no white Southerner had the right to protect his property, family, or his own life.

In their flight, something had snapped. In a small glade

on the side of a narrow country lane, Griffin Stark broke out of his self-inflicted shell of defeat and grief. Joyously he had come to her, taken her body and soul and released his pent-up juices in a glorious union beyond anything she had ever imagined. Oh, how good it had been.

Studiously they avoided physical contact for a long while after returning to Oaklawn. In Maryland, unknown forces had been set afoot that threatened their lives.

Marauders came to the plantation in the middle of the night. They appeared like any band of roving brigands, though in reflection her brother and Griff had agreed that the raiders seemed inordinately concerned with killing the three young persons. Even in their hasty retreat, the night prowlers had failed to take along any loot. Gradually, the incident lost its importance. When Griff announced that he would leave, alone, to take up the trail of his brother-in-law, Evan Tucker, and his son, Jennifer thought her heart would break.

The night before his departure, she came to his room and they made tender, poignant love. She still remembered vividly the wonderful feel of his maleness deep within her, the tender chaffing, stimulating slides down, down into a melding of their souls that was then forged on the anvil of ecstatic passion. They pledged their mutual love without reservation. Only the quest for Jeremy Stark lay between them and a wonderful life together. Griff would rebuild Riversend, they planned in the early hours of that delicious night. As her hands skillfully brought his body into readiness for new excursions into delirious love, they dreamed together of that restoration. Then he had gone.

After months with no word, Jennifer set out on her own. Hard-headedness, her brother had accused her of. Well, truth to tell, that fit her exactly. She had followed Griff's trail to St. Louis, then on to St. Joseph, Missouri. There she learned he had departed the previous spring for the high plains of Montana. She bided time that winter in St. Jo, teaching school. With the thaw on the Missouri, she set out in company with Ansel Thorson, a friend of Griff's. At Fort Kearny, she turned northwest to the small outpost where her brother commanded a company of cavalry. And there, at last, she was reunited with Griff.

Oh, how tenderly, yet eagerly, they had made love on the first night after Griff returned from a patrol. He scouted for the army now and the clean air, brazen sun, and hearty diet of the frontier had made him even more lusty than she had remembered. As she recalled it, her body ached for him more with each minute. They had been destined for each other, neither could deny it. Yet, the constant drive to find his son still came between them. When, oh when, would she hold her darling in her arms once again?

CHAPTER TWELVE

Without conscious control, Griffin Stark's hand dropped to the heavy military holster he wore, its flap cut off. The big Starr revolver came free in an instant. Hammer eared back by the web of his left thumb, the weapon came into line and fired before Temple Ames realized his friend had drawn.

"What the hell?"

"Rattlesnake," Griff said simply.

Thirst had long since driven them to one word communications, or conveying meaning by small, slow gestures. Three days had ground by since Paco and Hernando had abandoned them during the sand storm. Progress afoot had been far less than astride. Each day the relentless sun sapped them of more strength. Always, looming on the far horizon, they saw visions of trees, wavering buildings and, tauntingly, cool, rippling water. Each sunset had seen them no nearer those tempting mirages. Griff found himself squinting to peer closely at the snake to make certain that it, too, was not the product of his strangely altered state of reality.

"Yeah," he panted out. "Snake. Real, too." Griff kicked at it half-heartedly where its headless body writhed as though still endowed with life.

"Save it. We can eat it. Get the moisture," Temple advised.

Griff had limited them to one swallow of their precious little water each morning, at midday, and at night. Boots got two handsful in the crown of Griff's hat at daybreak and sundown. Less than half a canteenfull remained. Griff turned his head slowly and looked at his companion.

"You mean, raw? Blood and all?"

"Sure. Iffin you want to survive that is. Got to take in all the liquid we can. This chile only been on one desert. The one by the big Salt Lake. Like the anvil of Hell out there. This ain't much better."

"Save your voice. Need the spit," Griff reminded him.

In silence they staggered on. Temple had slung the rattler over Boots's saddle. The sturdy Arabian-cross tossed his head and rolled dubious eyes. The scent of the snake and its blood unnerved him.

"See 'em?" Griff suddenly cried out. "Up ahead. Turkeys. We'll feast tonight."

"Them's vultures," Temple told him, disappointed.

By nightfall, Griff estimated that they had progressed some eighteen miles from the point they left that morning. Five miles less than the day before. Strangely enough, they had encountered no one along the desolate road. At this rate of decline, Griff figured they would run out of food and water and leave their bones to bleach along the roadside a good seventy miles short of Chihuahua. Exhaustion and dehydration numbed them. Clear reasoning power and a sense of relationship between real objects and the unending torment of their journey had abandoned them the day before. Everything had become two dimensional: the sun above, the sand below. The night's cool air found them too numbed to care.

Griff and Temple lay for an hour staring at the twinkling yellow lights. Neither of them stirred after they had seen to Boots, who munched desultorily on pungent sage and mesquite leaves. They had taken their drink of water and sank into a comatose state resembling a stupor.

"Damn, them stars is close to the ground out here," Temple observed after some time.

"Unnnh. Sure are. Right down to the horizon," Griff offered with his last flagging energy.

"Never seen that before."

"Me neither. Can fool you. Something looks like a

116

star . . . only to turn out to be a lamplight in . . . in some farmer's barn!" Griff ended with a shout. "Mark it," he demanded of Temple. "Mark the direction to those funny stars of yours with some rocks, so we can take a sight on 'em in the morning. We're going to where they are."

"Ya mean, leave the road?"

"Right. Oh, why didn't I think before. These big ranches, lots of land. The upper class would seek seclusion, back from the road, not along the property line. Of course. We did it in Georgia. Why not here? Temple, I think we're gonna find help."

Yellow-green puss squirted from the angry red welts along Jeremy's ribs when Bear Heart opened them with the elk bone needle. Despite the boy's determination not to, he cried out at the pain. The oozing matter had a fetid odor that Bear Heart did not like.

It could only mean that the herbs were not working properly. Snow Rabbit's condition had forced them to remain camped for two days in a willow thicket along a slender silver ribbon of water that trickled over the desert sand. Here in the far southern part of Arizona, even time had become hostile. Bear Heart looked across the prostrate form of the child at his friend of thirty summers, Joshua Lame Deer.

"It grows worse," he stated simply. "I must open the wound again."

"What will you pack it with?" Joshua inquired.

"All of the medicine herbs I have left. They grow weak from age and I really need willow bark and black moss."

Joshua waved a hand around them. "There is plenty of the first. We should be in our mountains instead of this spirit-ridden desert. Then the boy would not die."

"*He will not die!*" Bear Heart declared vehemently. "I will not let him." An unaccustomed moisture filled his eyes and blurred his vision. He turned back to Jeremy.

"Snow Rabbit. You must bite this stick. Clamp down hard. I have to use my knife to open your wound and take out the old medicine, put in new."

"I fought bravely, didn't I?"

"Yes, my son. Now be brave again. Bite down . . . that's it."

Bear Heart drew his hunting knife and tested its edge, then laid the cool steel against Jeremy's feverish body. With one swift, sure stroke, he opened the length of the crimson weal. Blood, pus, and sodden lumps of the medicinal powders rolled out. Healing had hardly begun, he noticed. He could still see the rib bones. Bear Heart cleansed the slash with a damp rag and fished in his pouch for more of the dwindling supply of healing compound. Satisfied, he reached for the bone needle and some dried strips of gut.

Try as he might to stand up to the doctoring, Jeremy Stark uttered a long whine of agony and lost consciousness before the first suture had been tied in place.

His task completed, Bear Heart rose and walked to the stream to wash his hands. He wanted to weep. He wanted to cry out to the Great Spirit and to all the spirits of the earth and sky, wind and water. He needed to release the great hurt that rose to choke him. Why, he wanted to demand, did this handsome, brave little boy lay so still on the ground, slowly dying from the poison in his wound? Why did the Great Spirit need the services of one so young? Why, a mocking part of himself asked, had he let this boy become so important to him? A chill night wind rose, as though in answer, and sent shivers through Bear Heart's body. A foraging owl hooted. These things were omens, this he knew. But, did it mean the child would live or die?

At the rancho, *Santa Cicilia*, Griff and Temple found relief for their thirst, hunger, and fatigue. They rested and recovered from their ordeal on the desert for two days, then started off for Chihuahua. Temple obtained another horse, a handsome animal with Andalusian bloodlines. He and Griff offered to pay for its use, but their host refused.

"Only leave it at the Montez stables, *Señores*. It is my pleasure to assist you," Don Alonzo Cordobes informed them. "I have always been an admirer of your Confederacy, *Señor* Stark. It was with regret that I saw its cause dim and fade. Let this be a service from one gentleman to another, eh?"

When they left the rancho, they also had two burros well stocked with supplies in tow. The rest of the journey went with ease. The nearer to *Ciudad Chihuahua* they came, the more populous the countryside. Griff and Temple spent the nights as guests of a number of Don Alonzo's friends and arrived a mile from the city in good health and high spirits.

Bright rays from the sun made the solid buildings of Chihuahua waver in the air like mirages. The image recalled to Griff their trying days of little water and blistering heat on the grueling trek to *Rancho Santa Cicilia*. He reined in and looked over at Temple.

"From here on, we ride the train."

"At least part of the way. This chile don't never want to see a desert again. Ain't no hospitality in one."

"Let's ride on in. We can get rid of the burros and your fancy horse and make arrangements to board Boots until we come back."

"Back here? Through this gawdforsaken desert again?"

"How else do we get back to our country?"

At the livery barn, Mario Montez, the proprietor, greeted the Andalusian stallion affectionately and readily agreed to make provisions for the burros and Griff's horse. The rates he asked seemed inordinately low to Griff. He accepted, though, and left the stable in company with Temple to locate a hotel, then the railroad office.

By five that afternoon, everything had been attended to. The train would leave the next evening at seven. With time on their hands, Griff and Temple sought out a place to eat.

Whole chickens, roasting over smoldering hardwood on a rotisserie spit attracted their attention. The savory birds came with the ubiquitous bowl of beans and fiery salsa and mounds of tortillas. Their stomachs satisfied, Griff and Temple sought other forms of sustenance.

At the second cantina they visited, Griff halted abruptly a foot inside the plastered adobe block arch that formed the main entrance. He put a hand on Temple's shoulder and nodded toward the long, gleaming mahogany bar.

"Over there, at the end of the bar. There's our guides,

119

living it up on what they must have gotten from selling our gear and the burros."

"Oughtta just gun down those polecat bastards," Temple growled, one hand going unconsciously to his still tender scalp.

"Too quick for them. I think we can get some sort of reckoning. Follow my lead."

With swift, sure strides, Griff and Temple marched to the bar. Their sudden appearance prevented the two thieves from reacting in time.

"Well, Paco, Hernando, how nice to see you here," Griff declared through a wild grin. Then, before either man could respond, Griff sent a hard left crashing into Paco's chin.

The little Mexican reeled backward and tripped over the edge of a table, scattering its contents and bringing angry shouts from the occupants.

Before he could right himself, Temple Ames drove a hard fist into Hernando Castro's fat gut. He followed with an open-handed slam to the bent-over thief's forehead that sent him flying.

Hernando smashed into his companion and their weight came full on the tabletop. The legs gave way and the flimsy piece of furniture collapsed to the floor. Sawdust billowed up as the writhing men surged to their feet. Hernando closed in on Griff, a bit hesitant to test the surprises Temple might still have in store.

Griff saw the big man's fists coming in a blur and tucked in his chin, rolling his right shoulder up so that he slipped the blows without damage. He danced back a step and planted two fast rights on Hernando's cheekbone.

The would-be murderer's head snapped backward with each impact of the rock-hard knuckles. Griff felt a darting pain jangle up his arm and hoped he had not collapsed one. He stepped in to finish his opponent, then pivoted sharply. He took a pointed boot toe, that had been intended for his groin, on the outside of his thigh. Instantly he swung his left arm in a backhand blow that pulped Hernando's nose.

Hernando blinked, eyes involuntarily watering at the pain in his beak. He wanted very much to crush this *gringo*

120

in his powerful arms. Driven by this thought, he closed incautiously. Instantly, stinging punches tore at his face.

"Cabrón! Hijo de la chingada!" he roared in growing fury.

"You left us on the desert to die, you bastard," Griff grunted while he continued to punish Hernando's ugly features.

To his right, Griff caught sight of Temple. The former mountain man's arms churned in and out as he worked on Paco's midriff. The skinny Mexican sagged at the knees and slowly drooped to the floor. Then Griff had to concentrate fully on Hernando as the big man leaped at him, arms wide to grab and squeeze.

Griff stepped in and sent a hard, fast kick straight to Hernando's crotch. It missed its main target, though the pain that shot through the fat Mexican's body sent his breath out in a wheeze. Griff stepped to his left and snapped a solid blow to the side of Hernando's head, above his right ear. Still clutching his savaged groin, Hernando slumped to the sawdust. Griff looked around at the closed, angry faces gathered about them.

"They had it coming," is all he offered in explanation. He saw that Temple had finished on Paco and gestured toward the bar with a sideward nod.

"See what ya mean about that reckoning," Temple panted out. "Lot more satisfaction this way."

"Beer, bartender," Griff ordered. "Ah . . . *cerveza, por favor.*"

The tall *tubos* arrived promptly and the two men slaked their thirst on the cool brew. Suddenly, from behind them, a voice called out urgently.

"Qiudado!"

A glance in the backbar mirror showed Griff that Paco and Hernando had come to their feet. Each held a knife low and stumbled across the floor on uncertain feet. He had no doubt as to their intent.

The Starr revolver cleared Griff's waistband before he had turned completely around. He squeezed off a shot the moment the barrel came into line.

Hernando buckled in the middle and his legs drove him

121

forward. His big skull crunched into the facing of the bar and he fell with his face in a yellow, foam-fringed puddle in the tile trough that ran the length of the fixture to provide relief for the patrons' bladders. Only a split second after his own shot, Temple's Colt cracked.

Little Paco spun around, mouth working like a fish. He took one tottering step and sat abruptly. Griff heard Temple's disgusted growl.

"Damn. Missed his heart. That shoulder'll mend."

The bartender, a beer barrel of a man with a jolly, round face, hurried toward them. His wide-set eyes had gone round and his small mustache moved in an agitated wriggle as he spoke.

"*Señores*, you have acted in your own defense. Everyone here can swear to that. Only, the *policia* do not take kindly to *gringos*. You haven't any wish to visit their jail, no?"

"Definitely not," Griff told him. A quick look around showed that most customers agreed with the bartender. The cowardly attack from behind had changed their minds about who might be in the wrong.

"I have a place where you can stay. I will tell the police that two men, who look very unlike you two, did this killing." He pointed over the bar to the unmoving form of Hernando. "Only you must hurry. The police will be here in a minute."

"Why are you doing this?"

"These two have been in my establishment over several days. They talk about the *gringos* they lead into the desert to die. When you appear, I know that justice will be given these men." He spread his arms to include his clientele. "We are not like this, *Señor*. There are some bad men in any country. Is that not so? I believe in things being put right, in—how you say?—justice."

"Thank you, ah—"

"I am called Jose Garcia."

"Thank you, *Señor* Garcia. Where is this place?" Griff asked.

Garcia shrugged. "It is not much. A cellar room where I put my beer barrels. It is damp and smelly, but you can be safe there."

CHAPTER THIRTEEN

In the hours before sunrise, most people fall into their deepest sleep of the night. The residents of the small village of Silao were no exception to this. Duty caused only a few men to shun the oblivion of slumber. One of them was Capt. Ramon Gomez. Barricaded in the small church on the plaza, he and his men waited and wondered, even in their dreams, of what the next day would bring.

It was not his fault, Gomez thought with wounded spirit. Why, he had many friends in Silao. Even the *alcalde*. Yes, he and the mayor had been on the best of terms. Why was it that no one understood? Particularly a man in so important an office as Don Federico Guzman. Why did the mayor seem not to accept that he, *Capitán* Gomez, was merely following orders?

It wasn't he who signed the warrant for the execution of Moreno and Contrerez. They were notorious Juaristas. Everyone knew that. Gomez shrugged elaborately in the privacy of the vestry, which he had converted to his office. A bank of votive candles illuminated the small desk at which he sat. By their flickering light he read again the second urgent message he would dispatch to General Santos in Guanajuato.

He had outlined how heroically his men were holding out against the rabble of Silao, led—embarrassingly enough—by his old friend, Mayor Federico Guzman. He also pointed out that relief was of utmost importance. His men had little food, only holy water to drink and a rapidly dwindling supply of ammunition. In fact, by his painfully honest estimation, his beleaguered garrison could not hold out for more than two days beyond the next dawn. Gomez sighed as he affixed his signature and sanded the paper. Then his anger rose.

Don Federico, his mind raged, why in the name of all the saints have you done this to me?

Capt. Ignacio Rojas studied the faces of his officers in the pale first light of dawn. They looked fit and ready. The anticipation of battle shone from their eyes. They also grinned a lot, a sure indication that the ever-present fear a man felt when going into combat also accompanied them. Below, in the pocket of the valley, lay the sleeping town of Silao.

"We will attack in force across the bean fields on the south. Lieutenant O'Bannion, your platoon will be the reserve. Keep mobile and be ready to commit your men wherever heavy resistance is encountered. Our scouts indicated that the traitors control most of the town. They are more concerned with our troops in the church than with any possibility of an attack from without. We must take the greatest advantage from this.

"Instruct your men. I want no one to fire a shot until the enemy is actually encountered. Get in as close to the buildings as you can. If we properly use the element of surprise, we should be able to take the village without losing a man. That is all. Take your positions and prepare to move out."

Filipe O'Bannion held back. Rojas had expected this and remained silent until the other troop leaders had walked out of hearing range. He put a hand on the lieutenant's shoulder.

"You are disappointed, Filipe?"

"Yes, I am, Ignacio," the stocky, black-haired son of a Mexican mother and Irish immigrant father admitted. His green eyes did not stay fixed on the obsidian ones of his commander.

"I gather your concern is over more than not having the honor of leading the assault?"

"I . . . yes, Ignacio, it is. Not more than three years ago, we fought alongside the men we are attacking. We strived together to expel the Austrian, Maxmillian, and his French allies. They are our brothers. . . ." O'Bannion finished lamely.

"They are *Juaristas*!" Rojas snarled, making the word sound like an obscenity.

"So were we. This attack on the people of Silao takes us over the line once and for all. It puts us in open revolt against the government in Mexico City. There will be no turning back. And, no forgiveness from Benito Juarez."

"And that concerns you? Why? When we win, we will be the government. Juarez is a philosopher, a soft-hearted man who has no stomach for what must be done to keep the peasants in line and run a country properly. There is a powerful, warlike nation on our border to the north. Once the rulers of *Los Estados Unidos* realize how ineffectual Juarez is, their filthy rag of red and white stripes will be flying over our capitol again. Is that what you want?"

"Uh, no, Ignacio. It's . . ." Filipe O'Bannion suddenly found himself without words for further argument. He stiffened into a rigid position of attention and saluted gravely. "I will do my duty."

"I know you will, lieutenant. Now join your troops. Our conversation will, ah, remain confidential."

As the young officer departed, Rojas made a mental note to remember well the lieutenant's disaffection. It might prove useful to him in the future.

To the consternation of Mayor Federico Guzman, uniformed troops suddenly filled the narrow alleyways that constituted streets in the outer portion of the residential district. Were they soldiers loyal to Juarez? He had sent dispatches explaining the situation in Silao and all of Guanajuato. Perhaps the school teacher had sent him much needed reinforcements. Federico Guzman loved Benito Juarez, a soft-spoken man with vision and the courage to bring it into reality. When Santos had seized power in the city of Guanajuato, Guzman fumed. When the rebel general began to extend his influence over the entire state, he had called together men he knew to be loyal to the Juarez government.

United, they had planned to offer some form of resistance. To begin with, they had sent messages secretly to Mexico City. They also gathered stores of weapons and ammunition. When the time came, they would strike. Had it not been for an informer, their scheme might have succeeded.

Andreas Contrerez and Manuel Moreno had been arrested, savagely beaten in an attempt to make them talk, then stood against the wall of the church and shot. Warning reached the mayor of Silao in time and his small army of volunteers followed him in a preemptive attack against the local garrison. They had met with immediate success and now had Captain Gomez and his remaining troops barricaded in the church. Why had Ramon been so willing to follow the lead of a corrupt *puerco* like Emilio Santos?

It bothered Guzman. They had been friends, fought together against the French. Shared liquor and women during the heady days of the liberation. Then, to have so old a friend turn on him. The mayor sighed. He turned his attention to the troops advancing along the narrow street.

If these newcomers had been sent by General Castillo in Aguascalientes, or General Diaz in Mexico City, then his worries would be over. Suddenly the shooting started.

Three of the mayor's loyal soldiers fell in the first fusillade unleashed by the attacking troops of General Santos. Quickly, others in the open dashed for cover and began to return fire.

Bullets smacked solidly into the thick adobe wall of the building which the mayor had been using as headquarters. Wood splinters flew from the door and glass tinkled somewhere in the sturdy house as stray slugs found fragile targets. Guzman ducked low and sidled across the room to his second in command, a tough, muscular *herrero*.

"Where did they come from?" Ricardo Baltran demanded.

"General Santos, of course," the mayor told him. "We will have to pull back. There is still a chance to make our escape to the west. Then we can join up with any force sent to put down Santos's rebellion."

Heavy .45-70 slugs smacked into a wooden armorie near the mayor's head. The blacksmith swallowed, his face pale under his usual dark complexion. "I'd rather be at my forge," he said in an attempt to be calm.

"And I at my *abarotes*, my friend," Guzman told him. Sadness colored his voice as he went on. "You have all fought bravely. I only pray that we will survive to fight again."

Baltran patted the mayor on one shoulder. "For a grocer, you make a good general, Don Federico."

A loud pounding came at the door, which yielded under the effort. Two soldiers rushed inside. Mayor Guzman shot one through the breast, a thin spray of blood spattering the wall behind the man. Beside him Ricardo Baltran fired point-blank into the face of the second attacker.

"Out the back way," Guzman advised.

Armed men ran through the few streets of Silao. Some wore uniforms, many did not. Occasionally they stopped to exchange shots. More fell among the civilian defenders of Silao than in the ranks of the trained soldiers. The wounded screamed and died, many horribly as bayonettes were driven into their stomachs and chests. A rattle of musketry sounded to the west, where the mayor and some of his followers attempted to effect an escape from the carnage.

Few survived to win.

Heavy fire came from the direction of the church. Yelling at the top of his lungs, Captain Gomez led his men in a charge across the plaza. His unexpected sally scattered the demoralized defenders. Then, swiftly as it had begun, the fighting ended.

Half a dozen men had been rounded up and, at the direction of Colonel Cardoza, dragged to the plaza. Among them was the village priest. His hands, face, and brown Franciscan robe were smeared with blood from tending the wounded. In the silence that followed the short, furious battle, Cardoza walked up to him and struck the cleric a vicious backhand blow that split his lips.

"So, priest, you would join the enemies of Mexico, eh?"

"*You, Señor Ladrón*, and the monster you serve, are the enemies of Mexico, *coronel.*"

"Ha! We'll see how brave your words are when we stand you in front of a firing squad."

"I am a man of the Church. A noncombatant."

Cardoza's eyes narrowed. "Do you plead for your life?"

"No. I only warn you of the imminent danger to your immortal soul. Do what you will. God will see that you are punished."

"*God* doesn't really care, *padre*. Take him off with the others," the colonel ordered Captain Rojas. He turned to Arthur Treadwell. "How did you like our little action, *Señor* Treadwell?"

"I was impressed. Quite efficient. The consortium was right to put its faith in General Santos. If you don't mind, I think I will take a little stroll about the village."

"Wait a moment," Cardoza suggested in a tone of command. "You should find this interesting."

Three more men had been found in the battered buildings of Silao. They had been dragged over to where guards surrounded the other prisoners. After a short consultation with Captain Rojas, the soldiers drove their charges toward the sidewall of the church with punches and vicious buttstrokes from their rifles.

There they lined up the defeated resisters, the priest in the center. A sharp bark from a sergeant brought two dozen men, in two files, to attention.

"Forward march," the NCO commanded.

128

When the detail reached the desired position, the sergeant ordered them to halt. "Left FACE. Second rank, one step to the right. March. First rank, kneel."

"No!" a sobbing woman on the edge of the plaza wailed. "Oh, no. For the love of God, don't do this!"

Captain Rojas and several of the men laughed nastily. At a nod from the sergeant, Rojas stepped forward. He drew the slim-bladed sword from its scabbard at his side.

"Listo! . . . A punto! . . . Fuego!"

Twenty-four rifles cracked as one. The figures against the wall jerked backward and fell, writhing to the ground, blood flowing from their backs, smearing the church wall and the pockmarks of the bullets.

The woman screamed and several others took up their own noisy lamentations. Arthur Treadwell licked his lips and swallowed around a lump in his throat.

"Most, ah, entertaining, captain. I, ah, think I'll take that walk now."

"Take a gun along," Cardoza advised. "It could still be dangerous."

Arthur nodded absently and wandered away. With the execution over, the looting began.

Mounds of goods began to appear from the homes and shops of Silao. First small groups, then individual soldiers started to select women and young girls from the rounded up citizens at the plaza. They were taken away among the empty buildings and in a few minutes the screams began. The troops of General Santos's army seemed to enjoy the rape with equal fervor as the prospect of compiling loot.

Disgusted by this show of man's inherent evil, Lieutenant O'Bannion turned from the orgy of destruction and stalked off toward the edge of town. He had been sickened and angered at the wanton butchery of the priest. Was he not of the Church? Why had he stood by silently and allowed it to happen? O'Bannion continued to chide himself until he had gone far enough that the cries of the abused women and girls faded to little more than the mewing of distant kittens. His heart ached.

Why had he thrown his lot in with Santos? The

rebellion had been dubbed a "holy cause," for the "salvation" of México. His wild Irish side had responded to the siren song of adventure and the eventual adulation of a grateful people. Now it had all begun to sour. When the Spanish had executed a priest, O'Bannion recalled from his Mexican history that, rather than quell the rebellion, it had fanned the flames that eventually resulted in Mexico's independence from the fatherland. Would what they did in Silao today also backfire on the perpetrators?

Sunk in his black thoughts, he turned back to the town. Perhaps he could somehow see to the protection of some of the women and children.

He had enjoyed an excellent point of observation during the short battle, Arthur thought as he walked through the quiet backways of the town. At the peak of the fighting he found himself suddenly aroused. His loins ached and his maimed organ throbbed with an intense flush of passion. Now he needed to find some outlet. He had left his favorite tools behind, yet he would be able to devise a way.

"*Señor* Treadwell?" Captain Rojas suddenly appeared at Arthur's side. "Uh, may I call you Arturo?"

"Certainly, captain. What is it?"

"I, uh, I understand from Corporal Cadiz that we, ah, share certain interests. Oh, I assure you," he hastened to explain, "the corporal was entirely discreet. I have found him, ah, useful in the past myself. His own proclivities recommend him to be quiet about what he does."

"Except to you?"

"Precisely." Rojas brightened. "Well, then. I have arranged to put aside certain, ah, desirable creatures for my own indulgence. Would you care to join me?"

Arthur licked suddenly dry lips. "Uh, as a matter of fact, I was setting out to seek something of the sort myself. The, ah, spoils of war, right?"

"Exactly. Come. I think it should be to your liking."

They were young and terribly frightened. A boy of ten or so and a girl a bit younger waited in a small house on the edge of Silao. They had been stripped of all their clothes and stood trembling under the watchful eye of Corporal Cadiz. The soldier's eyes glowed and he stared hungrily at the tearful lad. When Arthur Treadwell and Captain Rojas entered, the noncom snapped to attention.

"I hope you will find everything to your specification, *capitán*."

Rojas examined the merchandise. He smacked his lips in appreciation and rubbed his palms together. "Marvelous. Why, they're actually good-looking, for peasants. Watch the door, Cadiz. From, ah, outside. When we've done, you can have your turn."

A grin of anticipation spread on the youthful corporal's dark face. "Thank you, captain." He executed an awkward about-face and left the room.

"Now, my dear Arturo, take your pick. Or you might enjoy both, as I shall surely undertake to do."

Unsteadily, Arthur stepped forward and stroked the cringing flesh of the naked girl. He swallowed with difficulty. "Ah, she's, ah, just right for me. At least for the first go around, eh?"

His heart pounding, Arthur wondered for the first time in many long months how it would be with the boy. Perhaps with the girl looking on? Eh? That would be something, wouldn't it?

Rojas opened his fly and stepped close to the small, crying lad. He soon gave Arthur a graphic demonstration of what could be accomplished.

CHAPTER FOURTEEN

A magenta and orange glow lingered over the distant Sierra Madres, a thin band of pale blue separating it from the deep black of night. The rickety coaches rattled along the iron rails of the narrow-gauge railway as the train ascended off the desert floor. Chihuahua lay far behind as the grade leveled out onto the high plain that stretched in the direction of Torreón and distant Aguascalientes. Griffin Stark and Temple Ames enjoyed the relative comfort of first class accommodations. Well-caulked windows freed them from the soot and smoke that assailed passengers in the second and third class cars. After several long minutes, Griff looked away from his appreciation of the spectacular sunset.

"I wonder when that taco vendor will be through here again. I could use some supper."

"And a cold beer," Temple added.

"Day after tomorrow we should be there."

"This chile hopes the stage ride from Aguascalientes to Guanajuato is smoother than this rattle-trap."

Griff chuckled at his friend's discomfort. "Don't count on it. Ah, there comes the beer man. We can have one while we wait to eat."

A surprise lay waiting for the passengers. When the train reached Jimenez, the conductor announced a stop of one hour. This was necessary for the arrival of an additional locomotive for the long pull up to Torreón.

133

Griff and Temple left the station, in search of a restaurant.

"Hot food," Temple enthused. "This chile's belly don't remember the taste."

"You ate well in Chihuahua," Griff observed in amusement.

"Shore. Only that was more'n eight hours ago."

They settled for a place that advertised *carnitas*, chunks of pork, cooked in oil over an open wood fire and served bite sized with a tray of vegetable condiments, beans, and corn tortillas. After the meal they returned to the depot. In their coach, they settled back in the cushions and watched the stars fill the high vault of the mountain sky. Griff felt real peace and contentment for the first time in a while.

"Breathwaite will be well protected, you know."

Temple's words ended Griff's moment of repose. "What else? I didn't figure to walk up and tell him he was under arrest."

"Well then?"

A grim line formed from Griff's generous lips. "I considered something at a bit longer range. Say, a rifle shot from two or three hundred yards."

Temple considered that for a while. "Don't calculate as bein' all that sportin' for the feller."

A violent lurch, followed by lesser tremors, signaled the train's departure. Griff replied without hesitation.

"Didn't expect it to. The Yankees used the same method on some of our officers during the war. From as far away as a mile, too. It involves the least risk. The only problem is that then we will probably never know anything more about the consortium or why it is they want me dead."

"Does put a crimp in things."

Two porters entered and began to light the oil lamps that hung from the ceiling on short, brass rods. In their yellow glow, Griff studied the backs of his square, blunt hands and thought over what he had learned the year before. Breathwaite had made it clear enough that he had set Griff up at the Wilderness. Also that he had been trying since to kill the ex-Confederate.

"Breathwaite tried to have me killed at the Wilderness.

He told me so. Only it didn't take. But he didn't say why.''

"Could be he was already workin' for the consortium and didn't want you findin' it out.''

"I'm sure he was. It wouldn't have made any difference, though. I didn't know what questions, or whom to ask. He did it on someone's orders. There's no doubt of that. Who, though, and why?''

Temple shrugged. "Wel-l, you've got lots of time to think on it.'' Temple rose. "I gotta go make some water.''

Alone with his thoughts, Griff ran back over everything he could recall connected to Breathwaite and the war years. As he did, the train reached full momentum, only to begin to slow some ten minutes later as the locomotives labored into the steep upgrade. Within minutes the speed reduced to a walk. As the creaking conveyance rounded a big bend, Griff saw from the corner of his eye a bright orange blossom.

A fraction of a second later, the window beside the seat in front of him exploded inward under the impact of a slug. Instantly, more shots blasted out of the night and bullets slapped into the wooden sides of the cars.

"A holdup,'' Griff correctly diagnosed. He dived below the sill and brought his Starr revolver from under his coat.

Diego Bargas commanded twenty-three men. Over the years, due to his cunning and the gang's ferocity, they became known as the most powerful bandits in the central part of Mexico. They raided stage coaches, shipments of ingots from the mines, and an occasional village. The latter was done primarily to provide sexual release for his followers. The small collections of mud huts and palm-thatch *palapas* offered little to enrich them. Since its completion two years earlier, Bargas had graduated to robbing trains.

"Why not?'' he would say to those who questioned his actions. "I am only robbing from the rich and giving to the poor.'' And he quickly pointed out that he and his men had been extremely poor until opportunity, in the form of the railroad, came his way.

On this particular dark, moonless night, he had chosen to relieve the passengers and freight cars of whatever of value might be at hand. He sent six men forward to deal with the engineers of the two locomotives and the usual guard of three *Federales*, while the remainder of his men slid their mounts down the crumbly slope to the tracks to board and make their collections. Diego had made only one slight miscalculation this time.

Among the passengers this particular night rode a company of the Mexican army. Enroute to join General Diaz at León for a punitive expedition against the traitor, Emilio Santos, they came fully armed and gamecock-ready for a fight. Suddenly the doors of two cars flung open and, before Diego Bargas's astonished eyes, brown-uniformed men began to pour out, rifles in their hands.

"Ataque! Ataque!" a young army captain shouted to his soldiers as they spilled from the two cars assigned them. *"Matalos!"*

Rifle fire from the surprised bandits became rapid and hastily aimed. Few rounds hit the troops as they spread out along the stalled train. Diego took a shot at the officer and missed. Subalterns appeared and took command of their men. The government forces fired in a smooth, disciplined rhythm.

From a broken window above the captain's head he heard supporting fire. He risked a glance up and saw a blond-haired *gringo* taking careful aim and shooting a strange-looking revolver. A grim smile of satisfaction split the officer's sharp features.

"Bueno, Señor. They are *bandidos.* Give us cover while we advance. We must kill them all."

"Seguro, capitán," a vaquero kneeling at the same window replied for the *Norteño.*

"Dang bandits!" Temple swore as he came back into the car. "Caught this chile with his pants down. I mean *down."*

136

"Kee, low, they're shooting into the cars," Griff shouted over the blazing of several more weapons, produced by the passengers.

"Then let's get them damned lights out."

Ames hurriedly smashed glass and blew out the wicks. As he rushed down the aisle, the railroad car dimmed into darkness. When the task had been completed, Temple hunkered down next to Griff.

"Now what?"

"There's enough people in here to keep the bandits ducking. We're going outside."

"This ain't our fight," Ames protested.

"The hell it isn't. Those bullets don't make any distinction between Mexican and Anglo targets. Let's get moving."

Riderless horses neighed and milled about amid the flashes of exploding rifles and handguns. Men screamed in agony while others died silently. As Griff's eyes adjusted to the dark, he saw the soldiers moving slowly uphill under control of their officers. As they walked, they worked the actions of their rifles and kept up a steady fire that slashed into the outlaws, making more gaps in their dwindling number. Suddenly one man, wearing a huge black, silver-trimmed sombrero, broke away from the cornered bandits and charged at an angle downhill along the length of the stalled train.

Griff turned that way and let go a round from his Starr. The horse shrieked and reared, throwing its rider. Quickly the ex-Confederate ran toward the downed man.

Bullets moaned through the night, some close enough to cause Griff to crouch lower. When he reached the fat, groaning man, he dropped to one knee.

"My leg is broken," Diego Bargas gasped in Spanish.

"Lay still," Griff advised, although not positive of what had been said.

Bandoliers of cartridges crossed over the protruding belly of the bandit leader. Griff located the man's revolver and chucked it out of the way, then slid the rifle from the saddle scabbard.

As the *gringo* worked, Diego Bargas cautiously inched one hand toward his side. He managed to maneuver it behind his back unseen by Griff. Slowly he closed his fingers around the hilt of a long, wide-bladed knife. As Diego had hoped, the strange *gringo* came to his side again.

Griff knelt down, reaching with his right hand to where Bargas's leg lay at an odd angle to his body. Blood soaked the black trousers the bandit wore, and through a tear in the material, Griff could see the splintered, yellow-white end of a bone. He bent forward.

Diego Bargas struck in that instant. He pulled his arm from beneath him and swung it in a vicious arc. The tip of the razor-honed blade rushed toward the left side of Griff's ribcage.

Griff saw the movement and his left hand reacted with combat-seasoned reflexes. The Starr came free, his arm now blocking the deadly steel from his body. Pain flared along the meaty portion of Griff's left forearm a moment before the hammer ratcheted back on the Starr.

The earth lit to day brightness in the muzzle bloom of the .44 calibre Confederate revolver. In its momentary brightness, Griff saw the bandit's head snap backward and a hole appear in his throat.

"Fool."

Above him the shooting continued. Griff rose and started that way.

"It will not be necessary, *Señor*," the young officer said in passable English from behind Griff. "My men are only taking care of the wounded bandits. Let me thank you for your invaluable assistance. My name is Capt. Luis Manuel Hertado, Third Lancers, army of Mexico."

"My pleasure, captain. I am Griffin Stark of Georgia."

"You are a fortunate man, *Señor* Stark. Oh, not to have survived. I mean to have been the one to kill that *cabrón* there. He was Diego Bargas, the most feared *bandido* in this part of Mexico. There is a substantial reward offered by the governor of the state and the *presidente* of Mexico."

"I never say no to money," Griff replied, wondering at

the change the years had wrought since that time when he never had to carry money with him or wonder how bills would be paid.

"Tell me, how is it that you are on this train?" Hertado inquired. "We get few visitors this far into Mexico."

"I'm here on, ah, business."

Captain Hertado eyed the dead bandit speculatively. He had seen the speedy draw employed by the *Norteño* to evade death at Bargas's hands. It gave rise to his next question.

"The sort of, ah, business you employed to finish Diego Bargas?"

"Hummm. Now that you, er, mention it, something like that." Griff winced as he moved his left arm. He was surprised to see blood dripping from his fingertips.

"You have been wounded, *Señor.* We have a man to care for these scrapes. Come with me, please."

The Mexican army medico proved to be swift and efficient. He cleaned the slash on Griff's forearm, sprinkled a bit of sulpher and salt into the open lips and wrapped a bandage around the injured appendage.

"There. You will survive, I am sure. Next," the portly, graying man called to his orderly.

Outside the passenger car again, Captain Hertado came to Griff. "I do not wish to pry, *Señor* Stark. But would you mind naming the person you have come here to kill?"

"I didn't say I intended to kill anyone," Griff returned hotly.

"Come, come. That is only a matter of form, no? Who is it, shall we say, that you come to transact your business with?"

"A man named Chester Breathwaite." Quickly Griff related the facts regarding Breathwaite and the consortium. As he did, Captain Hertado scowled darker and darker.

"And this *Norteño*, Breathwaite, is with the traitor, General Santos?"

"According to the information I received, yes."

"It will be difficult for you to enter Guanajuato."

139

"I doubt that. Breathwaite has no idea I am coming."

"Hummm. In a situation like this, rebels are always in the need of recruits. Cannon fodder for their engagements with the government in power at the time. It would not be unusual to suspect that Santos is buying men and arms. We could easily enter the city as prospects to join his war of liberation, no?"

"We?"

"Sí. My troops and I, an entire company of the Third Lancers, are on our way to León to join Gen. Porferio Diaz. He has been placed in charge of the punitive expedition against General Santos. My specialty has always been in scouting and intelligence gathering. Naturally, if one so professional as yourself were to join me, I would be certain of obtaining information on the traitor and what he is doing in Guanajuato."

Griff gave the Mexican officer a brief, nasty smile. "In other words, provide you with protective coloration, eh, captain?"

"You understand only so well, *Señor* Stark. Tell me, did you serve in the recent conflict in your country?"

"Yes, sir. I had the honor of serving with Jeb Stuart's cavalry, Army of Northern Virginia."

"Well, then, what I proposed will not be so much to ask, will it? Come, let us share a bottle of brandy on the train and we can talk of it. I will take you to see the general personally and see about affecting your temporary enlistment in the Army of Mexico."

"I have a friend along."

"The one who swears like a sailor and shoots better than any three men? He has come to the attention of some of my men. Now that the fighting is over, he and they are swapping lies about previous encounters. He, too, will be most welcome. General Diaz will be so happy to see you."

CHAPTER FIFTEEN

A tall, smiling man with long, curly blond locks faded in and out of the mists that clouded everything. In his left hand he held a revolver that spit fire into the darkness.

"Father!" Jeremy Stark, wracked with the delirium of his fever, cried out in Cheyenne.

Bear Heart rose from his sleeping robe, a sharp scowl of concern cleaving his tall brow. He had left the boy's side only when near exhaustion compelled him to try to get a few moments of sleep.

Suddenly, small dark figures swarmed around the blond man.

"Father, look out!" Jeremy moaned, this time in English.

The dark men came closer and their big, black hats could be clearly seen in the night. Drooping black mustaches framed their screaming mouths and they began to fire their weapons.

"Oooh, Father, Father," Jeremy wailed in Cheyenne. "Watch out for the black hats!"

"He grows worse," Bear Heart confided to Joshua Lame Deer, who had also awakened. "The poison eats at his body."

Bear Heart pulled back the covers to reveal Jeremy's wasted body. Pale under his usual deep tan, except for where the infected wound made an angry red line, his skin had become tightly stretched over his ribs. For two days

141

now he had been unable to eat and his body had rapidly consumed its own sustenance. His eyes had sunken into the sockets, surrounded by dark circles and his cheeks had grown hollow. Bear Heart extended a hand.

Jeremy's high, smooth forehead felt hot to the touch and slimed with the oily sweat of fever. His continued illness had forced a change in the Nez Percé's plans. They had turned northward and now camped among sheltering rocks on a hillside in what they considered hostile territory. If only, Bear Heart thought, we could get some buffalo meat. Make a broth to strengthen Snow Rabbit. Beaver Tail roused from his sleep on the opposite side of his small friend. His boy's face quickly became lined with worry.

"He needs a drawing compress," Joshua suggested.

"True enough," Bear Heart agreed. "But we have none."

"There is a village near here," Beaver Tail suggested.

"Yes. Pima," Bear Heart replied with a contemptuous curl to his lips.

"We must take him there," Beaver Tail persisted. "They will have a medicine man who can provide the herbs that Snow Rabbit needs."

"The Pima are enemies of the Nez Percé," Joshua told the boy. "They would delight in killing us all."

"Snow Rabbit and I are Cheyenne. They would not hurt us."

"You are wrong, Beaver Tail. Like the Apaches, the Pima are suspicious of all strangers and so will fight them before making friends." Tears suddenly flooded Bear Heart's eyes. "My son is dying and I can do nothing for him."

"We *have* to take the chance!" the Cheyenne youngster demanded. "Can't you see? Snow Rabbit is my brother—in the Cheyenne way—and I have to help him. Please, Bear Heart. If I go first, they will not harm me, I am only a boy. If I carry a peace belt, I can talk for us and get a truce. Let me try. *Please* let me try."

"It is not possible," Bear Heart growled bitterly. "Go to

142

sleep now. I will sit with him until his spirit leaves his body."

Beaver Tail lay down and covered his head with a buffalo sleeping robe. His small body shook with silent sobs and he hid his scalding tears from the others. Gradually his torment eased and his heart no longer weighed heavily with grief. A cold, hard determination replaced his sense of defeat.

He would not let Snow Rabbit die!

It would not be easy, Beaver Tail calculated. He would have to be careful. Wait for the right time. In addition to their own mounts, they had two hands and two left of horses for trade. Could he put any of those to use to help Snow Rabbit? His friend would have to be tied on his pony. First, Beaver Tail thought, he would have to get Snow Rabbit out of camp and to his pony. Sleep threatened to send him drifting from his purpose.

Beaver Tail viciously pinched himself at a tender spot on the inside of one thigh. The pain would keep him alert. He heard no more voices. Slowly he eased the robe down until he could peep out at the figure of Bear Heart, silhouetted by the camp fire.

Bear Heart's head bobbed ever downward toward his chest. As Beaver Tail watched, the Nez Percé's fatigue betrayed him once again and he slumped forward slightly, propped on his elbows. In a few more minutes, he became wrapped into a sound slumber. Slowly, Beaver Tail slid from under his sleeping robe.

He tugged on his breechcloth and hesitated. No sound of alarm came from the two Nez Percé. He could, he decided, move even quieter barefoot, so he carried his moccasins with him as he made his first trip.

Beaver Tail quickly located his pony and Snow Rabbit's. One by one he led them some distance from the camp. There he left them hobbled and returned to the fireside. Quietly he gathered up his few belongings and an armload of his friend's. These he took to the waiting Appaloosas. His next stop was at the small herd of grazing trade stock.

With studied effort, he selected the four best horses and cut them out from the rest. A young, flighty mare wickered softly and Beaver Tail froze, fearful that one or another of the Nez Percé would be aroused. He moved on, leading the chosen ponies. These he left with their own animals, rawhide hobbles slipped on opposing front and rear hoofs. Once more he went to the circle of sleeping forms.

"Oh, please don't cry out, Snow Rabbit," he whispered softly.

In a pile of camp supplies, he located the braided horsehair halters and chose four. Also a long lariat of cured and oiled elk hide. Then he paused, fearful of how to go about the rest of his plan.

Snow Rabbit had lost weight. That was good. He would have a hard time carrying his friend anyway. And right then he had his hands full. It meant one more trip to where he had taken the horses. One more chance at discovery. Beaver Tail bit his lower lip and sucked air deep into his lungs. Then he started his hazardous trip once more.

Excitement and relief tingled through the Cheyenne boy when he made the short journey once again without discovery. Now came the hard part. He crossed to where Snow Rabbit lay and knelt. He tried to lift his friend, buffalo robes and all.

Although sickness had made him frail as a bird, Snow Rabbit's weight proved almost too much for him. He would, he decided, have to leave the robes behind. He could cover his friend with his own. Working slowly, so as not to make any noise, Beaver Tail pulled off the robe and lifted the naked form of his friend into his arms, in sort of a clumsy embrace. Before he stood, he hefted the unconscious boy so that Snow Rabbit's head, shoulders, and arms dangled over his own back. With all the strength he had, Beaver Tail rose unsteadily and swayed a moment before regaining his balance. When he took his first tentative step, he nearly grunted with the effort.

Sharp grains of sand bit between Beaver Tail's toes as he cautiously raised one foot, then the next in silent steps that took him away from the fireside. Inch by inch, then yard

144

by yard, the distance grew. Practice improved his stride until he nearly walked at a normal pace.

Then sudden pain lanced up his leg when one big toe stubbed against a barrel cactus and drove a long, sharp spine deep into the flesh. Only his Cheyenne upbringing prevented Beaver Tail from yelping aloud at the numbing agony that pressed hotly on his ankle. He staggered and, for a long minute, had to let Snow Rabbit down. His fingers found the offending barb and he bit nearly through his lower lip to stifle any outcry as he yanked it out.

His blood tasted salt-sweet and metallic in his mouth. Acting from remembered advice, he squeezed the wound until a thin flow of crimson trickled out. His leg throbbed clear up above his knee. Tears formed and he blinked them back. No time to give in to the hurt. With greater effort than the first, he hefted his friend over one shoulder and continued on, limping markedly on his right foot. A moment later he found the horses.

How to get Snow Rabbit onto his pony? Beaver Tail pondered the question for only a moment. The obvious logic of his answer came naturally to a child almost born on a horse. He heaved and pushed until his friend lay athwart the Appaloosa's middle. Then he mounted behind Snow Rabbit and started to tug and pull to get the other boy into a reclining position along the animal's neck.

"Help, Snow Rabbit," he pleaded in a whisper as his strength waned. "Wake up and help me." He tugged harder and the youngster in his arms groaned. "Please help, Jer-a-my," Beaver Tail urged again, using the strange name the boy had called himself when he first came to the Cheyenne camp.

The word seemed to rouse Jeremy Stark and he clutched the horse's mane with his fingers. It let Beaver Tail shift his position and slide from the pony's back as he swung his friend's left leg over. Now he had to tie him in place.

His task took only a minute. When he finished, Beaver Tail looked up into the open eyes of Jeremy Stark. Both boys blinked. A croak came from deep in Jeremy's chest, the words in Cheyenne.

"You . . . you are my . . . friend . . . B-B-Bea . . ." Then he lapsed back into his coma.

"It is done, as it should have been," Bear Heart told Joshua the next dawn when both awoke to find the boys gone.

"They have gone to the Pimas?"

"Yes. Beaver Tail was right. Being small boys and Cheyenne, the Pimas might not hurt them. We could not do it and I hadn't heart to prevent them from trying when I heard scuffling around the camp in the night. With one eye I watched a brave boy become a man in order to save a friend. My heart is big for them both."

"It will be a lonely trip home, brother."

"Yes. I know that only too well. Let us pack and gather the horses. Some Pima medicine is going to be puffed up with his gift of four of our best."

Joshua Lame Deer snorted derisively.

The sun rode an hour high in the eastern sky when Beaver Tail led the string of horses and the one with Jeremy's supine body down out of a small copse of spindly pine. His right big toe had swollen and he had removed his moccasins to ease the pressure. Red lines ran up his coppery skin from ankle to knobby knee. He looked around, then selected the proper trail. He followed a narrow path that led to the edge of the Pima village.

"Hello," he called in Cheyenne. "We come as friends." Quickly he made the plains' signs for his words, though he saw not a person around.

Silence answered him.

"Hello," Beaver Tail shouted louder. "I have horses to give for the life of my friend."

"Hello, yourself," a boy about his own age returned in a strange tongue. He climbed, dripping and naked, from a sink hole of chill mountain water. "I am Feather Hat.

146

Who are you and why do you come to our village?"

Beaver Tail frowned in concentration. He made nothing of the language, though he knew the boy gave his name when he had pointed at his chest. "I am Beaver Tail of the Cheyenne," he replied. "My friend and I have stolen horses from the Nez Percé and he has been hurt. We need a medicine man."

An equal lack of comprehension made communication difficult for both sides. Feather Hat studied the two youngsters, one sitting proudly erect, the other slumped and tied to his mount. "He is sick," he stated the obvious.

"Yes, sick, sick," Beaver Tail tried, using the unfamiliar words in hopes it meant what he had previously explained.

"Come," Feather Hat commanded. He slid into his high moccasins and pulled a deerskin shirtlike garment over his wet, glistening body. It turned dark in places as it absorbed the water. The hem struck him at mid-thigh, leaving a wide expanse of bare legs between it and his high-topped moccasins. He shrugged as he gave the newcomers another appraising glance. Then, he started off toward the center of the village.

Feather Hat had recognized the words *Nez Percé*. These boys did not dress like the hated men of the north who refused to trade with the Pima for their ponies. That meant they must be slaves who had escaped from a band. They had the spotted horses, though. Maybe they had stolen them, fought with the Nez Percé and gotten away. If so, they must be friends of the Pima. Feather Hat's chest swelled with the importance of the news he brought. He would see these strange boys got the help they needed.

CHAPTER SIXTEEN

Three freight wagons and an army ambulance had been drawn up on the small parade ground at the temporary, sod-block military post commanded by Damien Carmichael. The handsome young officer stood beside his sister on the small stoop in front of the building that housed his office and living quarters.

"It's the best thing, Jen. I'm glad you finally realized that. There's no telling when or if Griff will locate Jeremy. Or when he will grow tired of searching. At least, in St. Joseph you will have the comforts of civilization to make the time pass by easier."

"Brrrr. Only the very minimum of social whirl, I assure you, dear brother." Long lashes closed their shutters over Jennifer's green eyes. She had chosen a blue velvet traveling dress with puff sleeves and lace bodice for her departure. Her tiny feet were encased in black, high button shoes, and a small hat of material matching her skirt was perched on her head. She had done her long, black hair in sausage-roll curls for the journey to the Missouri and a mail packet side-wheeler to St. Jo.

"All the same, it beats being out here." Damien's thoughts turned to his friend. "Griff's last letter came from Chihuahua. What strange names these towns in Mexico have," he added in an aside. "He ought to be nearly to Guanajuato by now. If only there had been some way to warn him of the situation."

Jennifer Carmichael put a small, soft hand on her brother's arm, fingers pressing into the blue wool of his uniform. "Griff will be all right, I just know it, Damien."

"I certainly hope so. Breathwaite is a dangerous man. He's cunning and slippery. Every time we have come close to capturing him, he's managed to get away. And he's hurt or killed someone each time."

"Like poor Ansel. At least he is mended now and working his wheelwright shop in St. Jo. I'll be happy to see him again."

"Uh, well. We can't keep those teamsters waiting any longer. I'll miss you, Jen."

"And I'll be lonesome without you, Damien."

"I'll write you."

Jennifer smiled engagingly. "And I'll probably get all of them on the first packet after the spring thaw," she replied lightly.

"No doubt. Take care of yourself."

"Good-bye, Damien."

"Good-bye, Jen."

Jennifer walked with stately grace to the ambulance and accepted a hand up from Sergeant Mallory.

"We'll all be missin' yer smilin' face, Miss Jennifer. The men will be a long time fargettin' ye."

"Why, thank you, sergeant. What about yourself?" Jen asked coquettishly.

Sean Mallory blushed. "Well now, an' ye see, ah . . ."

"Why, sergeant, I do believe I've embarrassed you. Tanow. When you come to St. Joseph, please stop by for tea."

"Thank ye, Miss. Sure an' that's what I'll do."

"Heyupp!" a teamster called to his animals.

The six-span of mules leaned into their harness and one of the supply wagons strained forward. When its wheels began to roll smoothly the second freighter started his team. The corporal on the driver's box of the ambulance flicked the reins lightly and clucked to his four-up of spritely bays. The lighter load sprang forward and took position at the head of the small column. Preceding it were an officer and three soldiers of a twelve man patrol

150

detailed to escort the wagons to Ft. Kearny. Jennifer turned back and waved until the small fortification's earthen walls obscured her vision of the headquarters.

Poor Damien, Jennifer thought impishly. He'll get over it, of course. By the time he hears that I never arrived in St. Jo, it will be too late to stop me. No, I'm not going to spend this winter, or any of the winters to come teaching school in Missouri while I wait for Griff to come back. On the contrary.

The next stop will be Chihuahua, Mexico and a start on finding Griffin Stark.

Gen. Porfirio Diaz listened politely to the Lancer captain while Luis Hertado explained the bandit attack on the train. He concluded by summing up Griffin Stark's fight with the outlaws and the killing of Diego Bargas. In the silence that followed, Diaz studied the tall, stocky *Norteño*.

The general liked what he saw. This *señor* Stark had an air about him of confidence and competence. A former military man, of that Diaz was certain. Perhaps he could be prevailed upon to assist in some means? The idea played about in the general's head as he responded to the information given.

"You did well in killing that one, *Señor*," the general began. "He was a very bad man. But tell me, why is it you come this far into Mexico?"

Outside the small room in the walled-in house General Diaz had chosen as his León headquarters, birds chittered in the vines and fluttered about the orange and lime trees. The restful splashing of a fountain could be clearly heard. Griff let the peaceful sounds ease him while he considered his answer.

Porferio Diaz was a short, rotund man with sharp features, despite his portliness. He had straight, thinning black hair which he wore long and combed to the left over his receding hairline. His small mouth seemed to register disapproval of the world in which he had been condemned

151

to live and his blunt fingers were never still. A tough man to attempt to deceive, Griff realized. He forced a smile he didn't feel and launched into a slightly edited version of the truth.

"My associate, Mr. Ames, and I are looking for a fugitive from the United States. He is believed to be in Guanajuato."

"You are officers of the law, then?"

"No. We are scouts for the United States Army," Griff stretched the truth. "The man is wanted by the army in connection with stirring up certain dissident Indians into attacks on settlers living in Montana Territory."

"I . . . see." Diaz withdrew into contemplation for a moment. "Hummm. Of course we must feel a certain, ah, gratitude to the United States. It was the threat of your General Sheridan's army on the Rio Bravo that convinced the French to withdraw support of Maxmillion. Otherwise, we might not yet have our freedom. Well then, who is this man and what is he doing in Guanajuato?"

Reassured now, Griff explained in greater detail. General Diaz took particular interest in the possible connection between rebellious General Santos and the Federated Rail Consortium. When Griff paused, he asked a question.

"Why would this organization of international bankers and industrialists be interested in Santos's revolt at all?"

"Mexico is a rich country, General Diaz," Griff explained. "Gold, silver, copper, and other minerals abound. Your people and cities are isolated for lack of good roads and rail facilities. Buildling railroads makes a lot of money for a few people. The consortium had a scheme to develop and ultimately control a large portion of the American West through manipulation of right of ways granted for railroad construction. We, er, the army managed to thwart that plan. Since Breathwaite and his masters are already geared toward railroad development, it would seem natural that they would sponsor such a program in Mexico. At least in a Mexico whose government is beholden to them for being in power. I have been giving this some thought on the way down here and I can see other possibilities."

"Such as?"

"Control of imports. Mexico needs industry to advance. Also your banks and monitary systems. From what little we know of the consortium, its members comprise some of the largest banking firms in Europe and the United States."

"In other words, more direct foreign intervention into the workings of our government."

"Exactly, general."

"Since you work for your army, *Señor* Stark, would that preclude you from doing a service for Mexico?"

Griff and Temple exchanged a thoughtful glance. Ames nodded imperceptibly. "Uh, no, general. What is it you had in mind?"

General Diaz considered this a moment before answering. "You seem determined to go to Guanajuato to apprehend your fugitive, regardless of the, ah, military and political situation. In light of that, you may as well do double duty. You could provide invaluable assistance to *Presidente* Juarez and myself by collecting information on the traitor, Santos. Captain Hertado has informed me that you once served with the intelligence corps of the American army."

"Yes, sir. That was back before the War for Southern Independence, though."

"All the same, I assume you could easily make estimates of troop strength and deployment, morale, supply problems, and such like. Also determine the attitudes of the civilian population."

"Yes, general."

"Fine. That is decided. You and *Señor* Ames will be enlisted into the ranks of the officer corps of the Army of Mexico. You shall both have equal rank to Captain Hertado and work with him in obtaining this data. You are excused now. Go rest yourselves from your journey.

Tomorrow morning you can begin preparations for your mission."

●

Four days later, Griffin Stark, Temple Ames, and Luis Hertado, all in casual, civilian clothing, rode into Guanajuato. All about them they saw the signs of privation. The people looked hungry and they went about with a furtive air as though they feared someone might be spying on them. The three newcomers soon discovered that the local residents had good cause to suspect such a situation when they arrived at a small inn near the center of the city.

"Ah, yes, the three men who rode into town this morning," the desk clerk remarked when Griff and his companions inquired about rooms. The man had a brisk, military air about him that belied his supposed civilian occupation.

"What has brought you to Guanajuato?"

Hertado answered for them all. "We wish to enlist in the army of General Santos for the liberation of Mexico."

"That is refreshing," the square-jawed young man replied. "I am sure you will be well received at the barracks. I have but two rooms left. Though you shouldn't need them for long, considering your intentions."

"At least five days or so," Hertado told him.

An eyebrow raised inquisitively on the soldier-clerk. "Oh? Why is that? If you are here to enlist in the army—"

Hertado gave him a deprecatory smile. "I saw the *noticias* about the festival. I am an *aficianado practico* and, if the *cartel* is not filled, I would like to fight. After that, we can join General Santos's army."

"*Verdad?*" the clerk asked in a tone of sudden respect. "I can assure you that if you were in the army first, you would not be permitted to *torear, Matador*. I am pleased to make your acquaintance. I am called Filipe O'Bannion."

"I am called Luis Manuel Hertado. *Con mucho gusto, Teniente.*"

A look of surprise flashed across O'Bannion's face.

154

"You, ah, are mistaken, *Matador*. I—"

"Oh, come now, Filipe," Hertado interrupted. "You *are* an officer in General Santos's army, *verdad?* It is obvious. Your military bearing speaks well for your abilities and your training."

O'Bannion's frown changed to a smile as he accepted this as a compliment. "So, then a peacock cannot hide its plumage, eh? Yes, I'm indeed in the army. Many things have changed in Guanajuato. Among them is a need to observe strangers. So, such jobs as this have been taken over by junior officers. I will be happy to watch you fight and will put in a good word for you and your companions with the general. Now, let me show you to your rooms."

"What is this about fighting, Luis?" Griff asked a few minutes later when the three met in the tiled patio of the inn.

"Oh, *that*. The *corrida de toros*. It is the—how you say?—bull fights. I am, ah, an amateur *matador*, a, ah, killer of bulls."

"You mean you kill them for sport?"

"No, no, Griff. It is a ritual, a classic drama, a, ah, ballet if you wish. But never, no, *not ever* a sport." Launched into his favorite subject, Luis called for tequila, limes, and *Sangrita de la Viuda*, a reddish, spicy concoction made of orange juice, chili peppers, and other spices. Then he continued.

"There is nothing 'sporting' about *la fiesta Brava*. As surely as the sun rises on the morning of the *corrida*, one or the other, or both, who enter the ring will die." His gaze rested above the seated Americans, far away in some distant place where crowds shouted their approval, bulls bellowed and the clarion call of the trumpet announced the orderly procession of the *lidia*. His features first softened, then firmed and played through a gamit of emotions as he described the ancient spectacle.

"Everything is done to a strict formality. The costume worn by the matador is determined by tradition. A custom so rigid that it often takes a hundred years to affect a single, minor change in design or decoration. The suit of tight pants, bolero jacket, and small, black slippers is called a *traje de luce*, a suit of lights. There is much gold or silver embroidery, sequins of gold leaf or silver. At one time, bits of mirror, a very rare commodity in those days, were incorporated to show the wealth and magnificence of the matador. On his head, the matador wears a *montera*. A small, black-embroidered hat with puffy points on each side. This he doffs when he entered the arena for the first time to ask permission to run the bulls.

"That is called the *paseo*," Luis went on, enraptured with his own acount of the festival of death. "In the lead is the *aguacil*, or official of the *corrida*. From the judge he receives permission to put on the fight and also a symbolic key to unlock the *torril* gate. That is the portal out of which the bulls come. After making a circle of the arena, the matadores make ready to perform their passionate tryst with death. The *clarin* is sounded by a trumpeter and the *torril* gate is opened.

"Out rushes the first bull! Ah! It is magnificent." Luis paused to sip from his tequila. "I could go on and on, explaining. The simple thing will be for you two to come to the festival and watch me fight."

"What? When is this?" Griff inquired with surprise.

"Two days from now. Did you not see the notices?"

"If I did, they didn't make any sense to me."

"It will soon, my friend."

"Will you be attending the festival tomorrow, Excellency?" an aide inquired of General Santos the next morning.

"Yes. It will be good for the people to see me enjoying the same things that they do. I have scheduled the execution of the two Juaristas for three days from now. Right before the final *corrida* of this fair. It will give people something to think about."

"For certain it will, Excellency." On a new tack, the aide presented some papers. "I have a report from our officers who have been out in the city, general. *En particular*, you

156

should look at the one from Lieutenant O'Bannion. It appears that already volunteers are arriving from other parts of the country. Even two *gringos*. They came in company with a very military-looking man who claims to be an *aficianado practico*."

The idea amused General Santos. "Is he?"

"I would say so. He has signed up to participate in the *festival*."

"So. And after that he wants to join my cause? Well, we shall make him and his friends welcome." Santos rifled through the reports until he came to the proper one. "Ah. They are staying at the Posada de la Paz. We will send a summons for their appearance, say, when the *faria* ends."

"Yes, Excellency."

On the streets of Guanajuato, while General Santos laid plans for their future, Griff, Temple, and Luis walked among the people. They heard plenty of complaints about the lack of vegetables, chickens, and other items in the market place, high taxes, and the number of young men being conscripted to fight against Don Benito. It became evident that the emnity between General Santos and the government of Benito Juarez was not shared by most citizens of the city or state. As the soldiers took over more and more houses for quartering troops, the residents thronged in the narrow passageways ambitiously called streets.

A condition resembling the worse squalor of such cities as London and Paris resulted. Unpleasant odors rose from open sewers and the crying of babies followed the trio everywhere. As they worked their way through the throng, counting and making note of the number of soldiers and the units they represented, it became clear to Griff that Luis had a specific goal. When they reached it, Griff put out a hand to halt their Mexican friend.

"Wait a minute, Luis. What do you propose to obtain in a house of ill-repute?"

A carefree smile lighted Luis's face. "Outside of the obvious, *amigo*, I expect to get a great deal of information. Also meet our local contact, a young lady, by the way, of

157

considerable social standing."

"In a bawdy house?"

"Only temporarily, I assure you, Griff. She has been forced into this pass by extortionate means. Representatives of General Santos saw to it that certain members of her family . . . ah, but I shall let the lady tell her own story. Come, let's go in."

CHAPTER SEVENTEEN

She turned out to be one of the loveliest women Griffin
Stark had ever seen. Her name, he learned, was Consuelo
Alvarez. Unbidden, he addressed her with the smooth
grace of a Southern gentleman. She responded with all the
breeding of the ancient strain of *hidalgos*, those "gentlemen and gentlewomen adventurers" who had represented
Mexico's upper class since the time of the Conquistadors.
In keeping with the house regulations, he paid for his visit
and accompanied her to a room at the back of the
establishment.

"You are from General Diaz?" she asked in a whisper
after closing and securing the door. To Griff's pleasure
and surprise, she spoke excellent English.

"Yes. So are the others who came in with me. Why are
you making contact with me, instead of Captain Hertado?"

"It is less an obvious thing if each time a different one of
you is my 'customer.' I have much to tell you. First," she
began as she started to remove her clothing. "It is better if
we appear to be engaged in the expected things. In the
event someone visits the peep holes built into each room,
you see." Her dark eyes, slightly almond in shape, glowed
with inner fire. She had dainty hands and feet, an
aristocratic profile, and lips that pouted slightly in a bold
invitation to be kissed.

"I, ah, yes."

159

"Then you should call me Consuelo and I will call you Griffin."

"Make it Griff."

"Ah, Griff, it is musical, no?"

As her stirring figure emerged from the gaudy clothing of a prostitute, Griff felt a tingling in his loins. Growing warmth radiated through his body and his breath became roughened. He licked the tip of his tongue across dry lips and swallowed with effort as he felt his own response. With eager expectation, his manhood swelled to its fullness as the girl removed her undergarments with a sensuous wriggle that would have excited a marble statue.

Consuelo gave him a tender smile that sent the blood throbbing in his erect phallus. Swiftly he shed his coat, shirt, and trousers. She looked at him not with the eyes of a bawd, but with those of a young girl in the presence of her first love. Her gaze became locked on the protrusion of his ready weapon. Slowly at first, then with a gush unlike any she had experienced since being forced into this place, Consuelo felt herself moisten and the contractions began that would open the leafy portals that guarded her inner being.

"I . . ." she stammered. "This is not effecting me like the others."

"Your other contacts?" Griff prompted.

"No. The men who come to . . . to *use* me," Consuelo gulped out. She lowered her eyes and her face and neck colored with shame.

Moved to sympathy, Griff took a step forward and put his hands on her shoulders. She trembled at his touch. Her physical presence sent a powerful ache through Griff's body. She wore only a thin shift. The rosy circles of her areolas and tiny bud nipples could be seen through it. Before he thought the action through, he took her in his arms.

Their lips met, cool and impersonal at first. Then their mutual ardor grew with the lengthening contact. Consuelo writhed in his embrace and her tongue probed at his lips and teeth, parting them. In a surge she entered his mouth. Griff pressed his turgid maleness against her slender body and felt a lunging response that only encouraged his determination. In the next moment, as though reading his pounding thoughts, her hands went to his waist, undid the drawstring of his underdrawers and released them.

As the kiss ended, Griff slipped her out of the shift and lay it aside. "Contact with a local agent should always be so pleasant," he murmured.

"Oh, Griff, Griff. You do wonderful things to me."

Her one hand encircled his pulsing organ and directed it to the fount from which flowed her heady perfume. "Later. We will talk of important matters later."

"Yes. Much, much later," Griff agreed as he lifted her from her feet and carried Consuelo to the bed. All thoughts of their mission and of the danger of playing in Emilio Santos's backyard fled his mind as he knelt between her lovely legs.

Slowly he lowered his body and his manhood found its eagerly sought haven. With gentle, deliberate strokes he entered her. Consuelo cried out in overwhelming desire and they lost all track of time and the world.

Later, when each had recovered their equilibrium, Consuelo turned to Griff and began to relate her information. All the while her eyes haunted him, as did the glorious memory of her wild abandon and the silken texture of her magnificent tawny hide. She had a lot to tell.

At last the string of anecdotes, complaints from officer customers, and minor observations ended. Griff made ready to rise.

"Oh, not now, *querido*. Stay with me for a while. For the first time in my life I have found happiness with a man. For the first time since I came to his horrid place, I want more and more of the joy you have brought me."

"How is that you are here, Consuelo?"

"Ah, Griff, that is a story for another time. A sad tale that would only put bitterness on our tongues to spoil the sweetness we have tasted together. Come to me, my love. Let's share that rich, wonderful moment again and again."

Griff found his lusty organ rising to the occasion and moved closer. Perhaps, he thought, he might as well stay all night.

Astonished, Griff sat in the stands of Guanajuato's Plaza de Toros Santa Fe the next afternoon, lost in the amazing exhibition of raw courage and indomitable skill displayed by Luis Hertado as he faced the deadly horns of a truly monstrous black menace. The bulls were big ones, though Griff had only a neophyte's understanding of this. To him they all looked gigantic and ferocious. Especially when considered in the light of having to stand alone on the sand and face one. For his benefit, and that of Temple Ames, Luis had explained the different movements and terms. Now Griff watched in utter fascination as Luis wove a pattern of splendid grace and defiance of death in the arena before him.

Lance after lance, the figures executed with the large magenta-and-yellow cape that Luis called a *capote*, and pass after pass with the small, red pendulum cape Griff knew as the *muleta*, Luis worked closer and at shorter range than any of the other amateur *toreros*. At one point, prior to dispatching his animal, Luis brought Griff to his feet, shouting and clapping his hands in approval. The bull charged straight across Luis's exposed body, following the *muleta* in his left hand, only to have its front hoofs jerked high off the ground, neck thrusting upward, horns dangerously close to the matador's armpit, in a spectacular *passa por alta.* So rapt had Griff's attention become that he failed to take notice of the others in attendance.

"Over there to your right, Excellency," Chester Breathwaite remarked behind his hand to General Santos. "That man in the first row."

"You know him?"

"Only too well. That is Griffin Stark. The one I told you about. There is only one thing that would bring him here. He is after me."

"Then we will simply send soldiers down to arrest him."

"No, Excellency. Let us be more clever than that. It is certain he is not here alone. Set men to watch him after the fight. He will lead us to his confederates. Then we shall have them all."

"Hummm. An excellent idea, *Coronel*. It shall be as you say."

"We are being followed," Temple Ames informed Griff as the two of them and Luis Hertado left the rolicking barbecue that had been staged following the festival.

"I think I see them. Could that be standard practice?" he asked Luis. "After what Consuelo told me last night, it wouldn't be much of a surprise."

Luis considered it. "No. I am afraid we have been found out in some manner. Come on, we can take the underground roadway, slip away somewhere and lose them."

Ten minutes later, footsteps echoed along with voices as the trio made their way through the subterranean passageway that ran the two mile length of the town. "This was built as a drainage system," Luis explained, his words oddly hollow in the long, dimly lit tunnel. "Children use it to play in, and of course the *ladrónes* employ the roadway as a means of escape after their crimes. There are offshoots that will take us nearly anywhere in town."

"Where are we headed now?" Griff inquired.

"The only place we have a friend," Luis responded cryptically.

"Unless this chile is hearin' things," Temple remarked, "we've got company. About six of 'em right behind us and comin' on fast."

Griff glanced back. Three men, armed with clubs, and three more with knives hurried forward at a trot, closing the distance rapidly. This had gone beyond surveillance, he acknowledged. This was an attempt to capture them. At all costs they had to avoid that. An expert himself in interrogation, Griff knew only so well that any man could

163

be made to talk. With the right methods, even torture would not be needed. At this point, they had only one choice. He stopped abruptly, his companions doing the same.

Instantly, Griff turned around. The men following them had closed to some ten feet. Two of them, he saw, wore the uniforms of Santos's army. All doubt as to the purpose of the attack ended. The ex-Confederate reached under his coat and came out with his Starr revolver in his left hand. As it swung level, the hammer clicked into the last sear notch. In front of him, six men showed wide, round eyes. A light pressure on the trigger sent the hammer forward.

An agonizing roar that punished ears and pulsated down the passageway came from the .44 revolver in Griff's hand. One of the pursuers threw up his arms and slammed back into the man behind him. His club struck the stone flags of the drainage tunnel with a ringing clatter, dimly heard due to the explosion. Already Griff had cocked the Starr and settled on a second target.

His next shot seemed not so loud, though the stench of black powder smoke in the confined space made everyone cough. A fat soldier spun to one side and dropped to his knees, hands clutching the bubbling wound in his chest. Immediately, Griff sought a third point of aim.

At his side, Temple Ames flicked his arm forward and a twinkle of bare steel could be seen a fraction of a second until it buried deep in another soldier's gut. His mouth worked like a beached fish and his knees went limp. He fell face-first to the cobbles. Again, Griff's Starr bellowed.

Two of the arrest squad had given up and tried a hasty retreat. One of these suddenly catapulted forward, as a black hole appeared in the back of his skull and the right side of his jaw exploded outward in a shower of blood and bone fragments. The .44 slug passed through air and struck the stone side of the passageway. It moaned off in the direction from which they all had come.

"Over there," Luis cried as he clamped a strong hand around the throat of the nearest soldier.

The gagging man clawed frantically at Luis's skin and writhed uselessly as his strength rapidly ebbed. Griff braced his gunhand and took steady aim on the last, fleeing, attacker. The Starr bucked in his grasp and a yellow-orange flame leaped from its muzzle.

With a grunt of pain, the surviving soldier pitched forward and sprawled on the stone floor, skidding three feet from the momentum of his flight. In the silence that followed, his boot toes drummed a final death song for several long seconds.

"Quickly," Luis advised. "We must reach Consuelo. She can help us get out of the city."

"They have escaped, general," a nervous aide informed Santos some twenty minutes later.

"How is that possible?"

"They turned on the men sent to follow and killed them all. The sounds of fighting were heard by others waiting outside the drainage canal to take custody of the whole group. Lieutenant Balances sent more soldiers to investigate. They found the corpses."

"Any indication of where they have gone?"

"None, I regret to say, Excellency."

"Organize a manhunt. Search every warren in this city. Turn out every hotel, cantina, house, and store. I want those men!"

"Immediately, Excellency."

"Don't worry," General Santos said as he turned to Chester Breathwaite. "They came here for you, so they won't go far. By morning we will have them in custody. By afternoon they will have told us everything they know. And, by sunset, that will be standing at *el paridón*."

CHAPTER EIGHTEEN

"There are soldiers in the street," Consuelo told Griff and Temple as she hurried into the room at the bawdy house where they hid with Captain Hertado. "They are searching every building."

"We'll have to leave," Griff decided.

They had only been in the establishment for half an hour. It had taken ten minutes at a trotting pace to reach the exit from the underground sewer system nearest the bordello. That meant, Griff calculated, that Santos had reacted with exceptional speed.

"Where can we go?" Luis Hertado asked, his face betraying a slight nervousness.

"There is a place," Consuelo informed him. "We used it for a while when General Santos first started arresting those loyal to *Presidente* Juarez. It is a played-out silver mine. Abandoned during the time of the Dons. Only, the soldiers are everywhere. How can we go out in the streets?"

"The drainage system," Griff suggested.

"They'll be watching that," Temple observed.

"Then we'll fight our way out. Most of the troops will be conducting the search. That will leave few to guard the exits."

"Hurry, then," Consuelo urged. "We will go out a special way. It is an, ah, arrangement for those who did not wish to be seen coming here."

"A tunnel?" Griff inquired.

"No, a passageway through the walls of other buildings. Come. I will show you."

"You can't stay here," Griff said roughly. "Someone is bound to tell the soldiers about our coming to this place."

Consuelo gave him a radiant smile. "It will take only a minute to pack a few things. I expected to go along."

Five minutes later, the four people entered a dark, cobwebbed passage behind a section of cupboard in the kitchen. A candle, shielded in a punched-out design tin lantern, provided scant illumination. Familiar with the secret entrance, Consuelo led the way.

"I planned to escape this way," she confided. "Once I knew my family was safe . . . or killed."

"How do you mean that?" Griff asked her as they proceeded slowly along the narrow course.

"It is why I am in the *putaria*. My family are Juaristas. My father was in the state assembly until that pig Santos threatened all of the Juaristas with arrest. He is in hiding, with the help of Colonel Cardoza. If I do not serve here, to pleasure those of Cardoza's choosing, he will betray my father and my brothers to Santos." She shrugged, an alluring sight to Griff's hungry eyes. "Now it is too late anyway for them. I have sent word. Perhaps they will have a chance to escape. If they are killed anyway, I have no desire to stay."

"Another reason to take a few more along besides Breathwaite," Griff muttered.

"Oh, no. I want *Coronel* Ramon Cardoza all to myself," Consuelo spat vehemently.

"Where are we?" Luis Hertado inquired.

"Three buildings away from the *putaria*," Consuelo replied. "A little further on, the passage ends in a small alley that connects with *El Callejon de Besar*—The Kissing Alley," she added shyly in English.

Three soldiers occupied the alley where the hidden maze opened to the outside world. When the small, concealed door creaked open, it caught them by surprise. The young, partially trained recruits had been assigned to watch the back walls of houses and apartments along the two parallel streets. The sudden appearance of four armed persons out of a supposedly solid adobe wall momentarily paralyzed their thinking and actions.

Temple Ames used his knife. He threw it in a smooth, controlled rhythm that had the deadly bowie buried to the hilt in one inexperienced trooper's chest before any of them could call an alarm. Griff ran to the nearest soldier, wishing he had not left the magnificent sword he had received from Damien at General Diaz's headquarters.

His fist crunched into the hinge of the rebel infantry-man's jaw, followed by a smashing blow to the back of his victim's head with the barrel of the Starr. To his left, Luis Hertado closed with the last man. Starlight twinkled off the thin blade of a stiletto he held low, driving it up deep into the helpless recruit's belly. Swiftly as it had begun, the grisly encounter ended. The only betraying sound came from three bodies flopping in the dust and refuse of the alley.

"Keep moving," Griff urged.

Consuelo gagged and covered her mouth. She seemed numbed by the experience and Griff had to take her by the elbow.

"Where is the underground entrance from here?"

"Over that way, Griffin," she replied in a weak voice.

At Griff's direction, they exercised more caution in their approach to the subterranean corridor. Four men, with lighted torches, stood watch over the roofed-over shaft that slanted downward at one steep-angled intersection. By the time the fleeing quartet arrived, Luis's chest heaved and he gasped for breath. Accustomed to the low altitude of the Sonoran desert, the seven thousand foot altitude at Guanajuato had a decided effect on him. When he sighted the sentries, Griff signaled for a halt.

"Temple, you and I will backtrack. We'll go around the block and come at them from two different directions. Luis, you and Consuelo walk directly up to the guards. You are, ah, two young lovers out for an evening stroll. Suggest to them that you want to go into the underground for, er, romantic reasons. Argue with them. Keep the four occupied until we get into position to strike from the rear."

"I shall appeal to their romanticism and their, ah, *machismo*. Who knows? They might even let us go by. No one is looking for a woman and a man alone."

"That's what I'm counting on. Now, let's do it."

After a five minute wait to give his allies a start, Luis put his arm around Consuelo's waist and they strolled around the corner and down the block toward the waiting sentries. He engaged her in animated conversation as they neared the soldiers. He stopped abruptly, a few short paces from the guards.

"Ah! What is this?"

"You don't know, *Señor*?" a corporal inquired.

"Uh, no. I have been, as you can well see, ah, otherwise occupied. My *enamoratta* and I wish to view the strange sights of the underground world. Please step aside, *soldado*."

"I'm sorry, *Señor*. But that will not be possible."

"Why not? It is most condusive to, ah, romance down there, is it not? Surely you know this for yourselves. *Por favor, compañeros*. Where is your spirit of amour?"

"Suspended, I regret to say, by this damnable manhunt."

Luis affected surprise, cocked one eyebrow in an aristocratic manner. "Oh? Who is this fellow? What does he look like? What, pray, has he done?"

"It is not one man, but three," the corporal replied. "They are enemies of the state, spies for the Juaristas. The general, himself, has ordered their arrest. They are to be brought to his own office."

"My, my. They sound highly dangerous."

"They have used the underground once before. That is why we are here. Also why you would not want to continue your, ah, stroll through those confines."

"I see. Yes, you might have the right of it, *capitan*."

"I am only a corporal, *Señor*. We have orders to let no one in and capture anyone coming out."

"A prudent idea," Luis agreed. "Well then, we shall—"

"Say," a curious private interrupted. "If it wasn't that you are with the *Señorita*, you could be one of those men. You look very like the description we were given."

"What? Why, that is most droll. But, you should not make jokes like that, soldier."

"It wasn't a joke," the observant soldier countered in an ominous tone. As he studied Luis in the light of the corporal's torch, he labored to convince himself he had been right.

"This has gone too far," Luis protested. His eyes narrowed and he tightened his grip on the stiletto in his left hand, concealed by the folds of Consuelo's skirt. "To make such insolent sport of one's betters is to ask for most unpleasant consequences."

"Such as what?" the young private demanded pugnaciously.

"It can get you killed!" As he spoke, Luis freed his arm and thrust the slim dagger forward, burying it to the hilt in the surprised soldier's chest. The thin blade slid between two ribs and pierced his heart.

The man's mouth worked frantically and he tried to cry out.

At the same instant, Griff and Temple struck the other enlisted men from behind, burying knives in their kidneys, thrashing the blades about for maximum damage and releasing the dying victims. They started forward as Consuelo struck.

Torchlight glinted on the small blade that Consuelo whipped out of her clutchpurse. With unerring accuracy, she buried it in the hollow at the base of the NCO's throat. He gurgled and flailed out wildly.

One fist struck Consuelo's arm and knocked her grip free of the diminutive knife. It remained embedded in his flesh, the esophagus severed, so that large red bubbles formed around the sides of the intruding steel. Before any alarm could be given, the four men lay dead in the street.

"Where did you come up with that?" Griff asked, impressed by her swift and decisive action.

"The *cuchilla*? It is something I have kept, hoping for

the opportunity to use it on that *cabrón*, Cardoza."

"We had better drag the bodies down into the tunnel. It might delay anyone giving the alarm," Griff suggested.

Quickly they completed the task and started off toward the far end of town through the underground system of drainage canals.

When the four fugitives reached the abandoned silver mine, they found ample evidence of its use by the dispossessed, the oppressed, and people fleeing the persecution of Emilio Santos. The dead coals of many cook fires lay heaped inside stone rings that made impromptu stoves for many a family or lonely, hunted man. At the present time, no one else occupied the temporary haven. Gratefully Griff and his companions settled down to take stock of their supplies and assess the situation.

"We are low on ammunition," Griff observed.

"And weapons," Luis added.

"No food," Consuelo contributed mournfully.

"The way this chile figgers it," Temple put in, "we been lucky so far. We wickered them guards easy. Now the hard part begins."

They *had* been lucky. When Griff, Temple, Luis, and Consuelo arrived at the exit closest to the trail that led into the high hills surrounding Guanajuato, they contrived to use a reversal of the ruse that had worked so well before. Griff and Temple eased up the worn stone steps to within a few feet of the entrance. There they drew back into shadow, standing precariously on a narrow ledge that ran the length of the main tunnel. Once in position, Luis and Consuelo went into a different act.

"Stop it!" Consuelo had cried in a tone denoting rejection and fear. "*Señor*, you go too far. Take your hand off there!"

A moment later, the guards above ground heard the sound of a slap and a woman's scream. More experienced than those who fell so easily near the bordello, the corporal in charge sent only two men to investigate.

They no sooner entered the tunnel than Griff and Temple grabbed them from behind and jerked their heads back. Each shoved a knee in the small of a surprised sentry's back. Swift slashes with knives across bared throats ended the lives of the would-be rescuers. They writhed momentarily, a bright crimson spray spurting from the deep gashes in their flesh.

Next Griff led the way while the other three followed up above ground.

Surprise registered a moment before the first guard died with Temple's knife deep in his back. The corporal had been watching the entrance where his men had disappeared. He was first to see them. He started to raise his rifle, only to realize the uselessness of dying for nothing. He lowered the weapon and surrendered.

Only to die for nothing anyway, as Luis slashed his throat with his razor-sharp stiletto. Soundlessly, the foursome disappeared into the night, on the long climb to the mine.

"We'll rest here for an hour," Griff determined.

"Where are we going?" Consuelo asked.

"The only place we can. To General Diaz's headquarters. We travel by night, hold up during the day. How far is it to Léon, Luis?"

"About fifty of your miles. We can requisition transportation, if you wish."

"Good. Where?"

"The first peon with some burros, or a ranchero who has fine horses."

"That cuts down the time. Will they cooperate?"

"It is certain many of them supported Santos out of greed and ambition. Now they will know General Diaz has come here to enforce the will of the government. They are wise enough to realize that continued resistance would be most unfortunate to them." The young Lancer officer smiled icily. "We will be met with open arms. Of that I can assure you."

173

CHAPTER NINETEEN

Gently cooing doves belied the belligerent nature of the business being conducted inside the high, pink-tinted walls of the house in Léon. Two days after their escape from Guanajuato, Griffin Stark, Temple Ames, Luis Hertado, and Consuelo Alvarez arrived in the small mountain town and reported to General Porferio Diaz. After being given time to refresh themselves and change clothes, they returned to discuss what had occurred.

"It is good to see you back safely," General Diaz declared once all had taken seats. "I trust you had some success?" the general added, looking pointedly at Captain Hertado, a brief twinkle of amusement in his troubled eyes.

"Ah, *sí, general*," the lancer captain replied. "I, ah, cut two ears at the festival. Seriously, though, I feel we can honestly report that the level of efficiency among Santos's troops is shamefully low. There are many new recruits, including some *Norteños* who have arrived within the past week. The latter seemed more inclined to seek personal fortune than fight for a cause. The former are peons for the most part, entirely unschooled in warfare."

"I wish I could share your evaluation of all of that traitor's forces," Diaz remarked with a sigh. "Those my commanders have encountered are well armed, disciplined, and capable fighters. There have been several small engagements. Although we have not suffered a defeat, I find us to be at a standstill."

175

"General, may I make a suggestion?" Griff inquired.

"Certainly, ah, *Señor* Stark. Please share anything you have."

"Given what we saw," Griff began, thinking through his evaluation as he spoke, "and what your officers report, it is obvious that Santos has placed his best troops in a defensive perimeter around Guanajuato. The core of his small empire is weak. There is confusion and poor discipline. The place to strike, then, is directly at the city."

"In this terrain, infantry works best, but moves slowly, *Señor*," Diaz replied, his mind busily trying to visualize what the American intended.

"A concentration of mounted men can maneuver much faster. They can strike hard and penetrate defensive screens. Infantry, coming behind, can then mop up the enemy and secure these positions."

Understanding brightened Diaz's face for a moment, then he scowled again. "You are proposing that we employ the lancers. Well and good, *Señor*, but we have only one company."

"Lancers are too lightly armed for what I have in mind. With only revolvers and their lances, they cannot deliver sufficient shock power to break entrenched infantry. What you need is a force of cavalry, like that employed in our recent War Between the States."

A smile broke out on Diaz's austere face. "Now here is a man who gets right to the heart of things. Only, tell me, *Señor* Stark, where shall I get this cavalry?"

Griff hesitated only a moment. "We will have to train them. Oh, they'll never do for fancy parade ground drill, but they will be able to fight mounted and afoot, deliver their firepower directly in among the enemy and rout them."

"You seem so certain. I, ah, wonder. There is little time, you see. *Presidente* Juarez expects results."

"Better he gets the results he wants, rather than something unpleasant," Griff countered. "Even if it takes a week longer."

"*Una semana!*" Diaz exploded. "You say this can be

176

done in one week?''

"Yes, sir." The plan unfolded in Griff's thoughts as he explained. "We can start with Luis's company of lancers. They already know basic horsemanship, the bugle calls, and battlefield maneuvers. Remember, general, we're striving for a capable shock force, not polished cavalry. So then," the former Confederate squadron commander went on. "Each of Luis's men will train two more. That will give us an effective force of a squadron of cavalry. They all know how to use their weapons. The only difference for them will be that they ride to battle instead of march and fire from horseback rather than compact infantry formations. Every man will carry a rifle and twenty rounds of ammunition. Also a sidearm and four loaded cylinders ready to change as needed."

"What about our lances?" Luis inquired in a wounded tone. "My men would mutiny if they were deprived of their greatest symbol of pride. So, I think, would I," he added as an afterthought.

"I know you're not serious, Luis," Griff returned. "Though you have brought up a valid point. Once the training is completed, and your men have become proficient with rifles, they can carry their lances as well. Your company can be employed as flankers, striking to the sides and rear of enemy positions. That way their lances can provide a special advantage. Being ridden down by men with sharp spears is a frightening experience for infantry. Committed at the right time, your company can swiftly demoralize the enemy and send them running from the field."

"I, ah, like your idea, *Señor* Stark," Porferio Diaz said cautiously. "In fact, I think it is splendid. Yes. We'll do that. I believe you told me you were once a squadron commander, *Señor* Stark?"

"Yes, sir."

"Then you are familiar with all the requirements and training problems, is that not so?" At Griff's assurance, he went on. "Well, then, I will overstep my authority a bit here and appoint you as squadron commander of this new

177

force of cavalry. Organize it as you see fit and begin training at the earliest convenience."

Surprised and suddenly filled with a swelling sense of excitement, Griff rose to his feet and saluted. "As you wish, general."

"Excellent, *Mayor* Stark. You see? I also give you the rank sufficient to the task you wish to accomplish. This decision may *me puso en aprietos*—how do you say it?— put me on the spot with *Presidente* Juarez." The short, rotund general spread his hands in a depreciating gesture. "But, by the time he learns of it, perhaps we shall have taken Guanajuato and have Emilio Santos ready for a hanging. In which case we will be praised. Fine, then. Get started immediately, Major Stark."

Griff's companions rose to depart. General Diaz lifted a hand and called out to stop them. "In the meantime, what can we do to keep the pressure on effectively without losing a lot of men?"

"Walp," Temple Ames commenced. "Iffin yer askin' this chile, gen'ral, then what about some small sneak attacks? Injun-style raids against Santos's supplies, his horses. Usin' the method we did to get here, you might even slip some men into town, have 'em kill off some of Santos's officers, blow up powder supplies, that sort o' thing."

"Assassinations and espionage are hardly honorable ways to fight a war, *Señor* Ames," General Diaz admonished.

"*Pardon this chile*', gen'ral," Temple returned dryly. "I thought we was talkin' about winnin', not jest fightin'."

To Luis's surprise, his commander smiled. "A point well made, *Señor* Ames. How would you go about this?"

"Ya got any old Injun fighters among yer troops? Or mountain men used to huntin' for their table? They's the ones to best know how to sneak and peak."

"Hummm. I'll look into it. Another excellent idea, I must say. Carry on. I will be in touch with you on this matter, *Señor* Ames."

* * *

"You were remarkably quiet, Consuelo," Griff observed half an hour later as they sat on a large granite boulder overlooking the small town of Léon.

"I made my report to the general while you men were shaving and making yourselves presentable. He was most interested in the conditions in Guanajuato. I . . . to be honest, Griff, I don't like this life as a spy. I . . . it is hard for me to say it in words that mean anything. It makes me feel dirty."

"Like being where you were?"

Tears formed in her eyes. "That's unkind. For that I feel even worse. It was life in Hell, Griff. Life hardly worth living."

"It's over now. Forget it." He put his arm around her shoulders and drew her closer. Sudden heat radiated from his loins and he caught his breath.

"Griff . . . Griff . . . I can never truly love any man after what has been done to me. I want you to know that."

"But we can have . . . oh, damnit, Consuelo, my own life hasn't been exactly exemplary. Nor have I been entirely honest with you. When this is over. When Breathwaite is captured or killed, I'll be leaving. I must find my son. He is with some Indians . . . somewhere. That is foremost in my mind. We heard rumors that he may have been brought to Mexico. If so, I will search for him. If not, I go back to the last place someone saw him and start from there."

"Your son. How old is he?"

"Ten now. I've not seen him in six years." With an effort beyond his usual, Griff restrained himself from pouring out the entire story. He sighed heavily and embraced Consuelo with a firmer hold.

"Ah, Griff, we are truly outcasts in this world. It is men like General Santos who make things happen. They are evil, *verdad*, but they are the ones who seem always to come out on top."

"In this case, 'top' is going to be at the end of a rope," Griff assured her grimly. "All I can say, suggest, I suppose would be better, is that we find what little happiness we can. Separately or together."

179

"I'd much prefer 'together,' *corozon*." .

Griff looked into her eyes and knew the limits he would go to in order to bring pleasure and consolation to this lovely girl whose features clearly fixed her ancestory as dating back to the fabled Aztecs, as well as to the bloodlines of the Conquistadors. He reached out tentatively and lifted her chin with two blunt fingers. Consuelo gave him a hesitant smile.

"So would I," he whispered as he pulled her close and kissed her fleetingly on the mouth. She sighed as he moved on to lightly touch her closed eyelids, nose, cheeks, and back to the lush, welcoming warmth of her soft, moist lips.

They held their embrace a long while. When he at last spoke, Griff's voice had roughened and he breathed in deep gulps. "Is there . . . anywhere around here?"

"In the out of doors? *Ah, querido, tu tienes mucho amor.* Come, I think we can find just the place."

With the eagerness of a young swain, Griff came to his feet and drew her uptight by one tiny, silken hand. Consuelo led the way to a sheltered place between a cluster of boulders. There she lay her long, woolen rebozo on the ground, spread her scarf and sank to her knees.

It took them only moments to remove their outer clothing. Again they kissed with mounting passion before Griff slipped a hand under her blouse and gently cupped one firm young breast.

"Oh, yes, Griff. More. Please hurry. Fill me with delight."

"No, no, *estupido*!" Sergeant Alvardo "Gordo" Ruiz bellowed at a hapless infantryman whose inept horsemanship had drawn the NCO's wrath. "Hold on with your knees. You need two hands to fire a rifle, no? Now . . . now . . . that's it . . . that's it. Clamp those knees! And the . . . jump! *Idiota*!"

The soldier looked up helplessly from where he sprawled ignominiously on the ground. Slowly his face colored with a flow of embarrassment. Ruiz charged at him, riding quirt flailing the air.

"You are to stay on the horse, eh? Do you know what that means? *Stay . . . on . . . the . . . horse!* A simple thing, no? Then do it, you lump of *mierda.*"

In the third day of the training most of the soldiers had taken to their new duties with a will. Only a few, who turned out to have no better seat on a horse than they had marching ability on a parade ground, remained unreconstructed into cavalrymen. Ruiz turned away from the unfortunate Private Bienavedes and stomped over to where a trooper led his limping mount.

"There's a rock in the frog, you fool. Take your field knife and dig it out. At once!"

"But, *serjento*, it will dull my beautiful *cuchillo.*"

"Right now that horse is more important than your blade . . . or your own miserable life. He gets you to battle, he fights with you and he takes you home again. It is *his* comfort you see to first. If it rains, he keeps dry and you soak. If it is hot, he gets the water first. If supplies are low, *tu caballo* eats while you go hungry. Do you understand, *gorron?*"

"*Sí*, sergeant."

"*Then do it!* You live because your horse lives. Remember that and you might make it through the next battle. Clean that hoof and remount."

"*Sí, serjento.*"

"Hopeless. They are all hopeless," Ruiz growled as he walked up to Griffin Stark and Captain Hertado and executed a smart salute. "*Mayor, capitan*, they will never learn."

"Yes they will, Gordo," Luis told him in a friendly manner. Keep on them. Kick their butts if they don't do right. Use that quirt if you have to."

"We have a night maneuver on the schedule, Sergeant Ruiz," Griff told him. "Try to see to it that not all of our fine new cavalrymen get lost."

Ruiz looked pained. "As you say, *Mayor.*"

*   *   *

"Company on line . . . march!" Captain Cantrerez bellowed.

Sixty men swung their mounts into formation for the attack.

"Trumpeter, sound the charge."

Bell notes floated out from the golden instrument in a corporal's left hand. As one the mounts of Second Company, Provisional Cavalry, of the Mexican army leaped forward into a gallop. Calling themselves *Los Alumbrados*, the Lightnings, they took pride in the precision with which they could perform the basic tactical movements after only a week's practice. Now they gave themselves entirely to the exercise.

Seated in a carriage, General Porferio Diaz watched his new cavalry thunder past him, dust billowing in their wake. From directly ahead, another unit swung onto the flank and charged an imaginary enemy. Then, from the rear came fearsome screams and blood-chilling yells as the lancers struck at the mythical rear of the opposing forces.

"Most impressive, Major Stark," Diaz complimented. "They almost look like they can carry it off. Will they do as well against real men with real bullets?"

"It would be better if we had more time, general. It takes many repetitions to make such actions automatic so that a man does them without thinking, even under fire."

"Would another week help, major?"

"Every day shows some improvement. A week would be a blessing."

"Then you will have it. In the meanwhile, I have been giving thought to *Señor* Ames's idea. I think the time is right for a few of your, ah, 'Injun-style' skirmishes against Santos's supply lines."

CHAPTER TWENTY

Seventeen men, led by Sergeant Ruiz, waited in the dark of a moonless night. Their faces had been blackened with burnt cork. In the dim illumination of a full sky of stars, only the flash of their teeth and the whites of their eyes showed. Griffin Stark and Temple Ames joined them after a short wait.

"Men," Griff told them, with Ruiz translating, "we will walk our horses out of town, then remove the sacking from their hoofs. Our objective is the granary at Irapuato. Two miles from town we'll halt, put on the sacking again and prepare for the attack. When we reach the village, try to avoid any contact with the enemy until we are within striking range of the storage buildings. Make sure you have nothing that reflects light, no loose bit chains or other trappings that will make noise. Our report is that the guards in Irapuato are lazy. They have never had reason to worry and don't bother to stay alert." His voice grew grim as he covered the next item.

"Kill as many as you can. Our purpose is as much to spread terror as it is to destroy supplies. The men charged with setting fires are to act independently from the rest. When we leave here there will be no talking until the first shot is fired. Any questions?"

There were none.

Temple Ames grinned in the darkness. "This chile gets the feelin' these here Mezkins is rarin' for a chancst to play

Injun. They's likely gonna shoot as many of their own as the enemy, though."

"Don't count on that, Temple," Griff contradicted. "They are all crack shots, the best in all of Diaz's army. They've all seen combat. I think you'll be surprised."

Midnight had come and passed and the wheeling constellations above had turned the clock of the universe to three in the morning by the time the small force reached Irapuato. The village, located in a flat bowl below a ridge of hills that separated it from the distant town of Celaya, lay along the course of a wide, swiftly flowing river. Its inhabitants had long since fallen into deep slumber. Even the few soldiers assigned to sentry duty at the granary, stables, and barracks had grown drowsy and inattentive to their assignments. On a low plain to the southwest of town, Griffin Stark called a halt and gathered his tiny command around for final instructions.

"Temple will take six men and circle around to the north. Come in on the warehouses from the city side. It should cause less suspicion and let you get closer before the shooting starts. You six," he indicated the Juarista soldiers to his right, "will come with me. We will go for the barracks. Santos's troops are quartered off the small park near this end of town. Sergeant Ruiz, you and the remaining men will act as reserve for our attack on the troops, also a security screen to cover our backs. Once both of our forces are committed, move in to mop up any stragglers or survivors at the barracks. I'll give you ten minutes to get into position, Temple, then we take the billets."

"Yep. Figgered there wouldn't be time fer any dilly-dallyin' on the way. How you expect us to handle the grain?"

"Stop off in the *mercado* and get some kerosene. Soak the stores with that and set them afire. Any ammunition or weapons you encounter, save aside for General Diaz."

"Right. These fellers is rarin' to go. Reckon we might as

well head off now."

"Keep quiet until you are sure there's no one behind you to interfere. Try not to draw fire from the sentries until after you hear our first shots."

"Yep. Luck."

"Same to you."

Seven figures detached themselves from the huddle of men and walked their mounts quietly into the darkness. Griff turned and nodded to Gordo Ruiz.

"Keep with us until we enter the village. Then hold fast along the first line of houses. When we open up, start closing in."

"*Si, Mayor.* My men are hungry to spill the traitors' blood. We will be most certain of our targets and will have no mercy. It is, ah, tradition, *señor Mayor*, that in an operation in which we are to kill everyone before battle, the trumpeter plays a certain song."

Griff grimaced at this suggestion. All he needed was the Mexican penchant for *machismo* and tradition to destroy their element of surprise with such a serenade. "What is that, Ruiz?"

"It is called, *El Diguello.* It means that no quarter will be given. It is only courteous and manly to give the enemy some idea of what is going to happen to them, no?"

"In this case, I think we will have to forego it."

"*Porque, señor Mayor?*"

"This is a *surprise* attack. We don't want them to know anything until it is too late."

Ruiz sighed. "Very well, we shall keep silent as the mice in church, no?"

"Exactly. Until the shooting starts. Then make all the noise you can. We want them to think they have a whole regiment attacking the town."

Ruiz grinned in the darkness. "So that they fill their trousers in fear, eh? Perhaps then, our trumpeter can play *El Diguello* after the attack begins?"

"If it loosens the bowels and freezes the hearts of the enemy, yes," Griff relented.

"It shall be done then. Go with God, *señor Mayor*."

With practiced ease and total silence, Griffin Stark led his men toward Irapuato. Not even a curious dog roused to challenge them until they had passed the first screen of houses and wended their way along dirt streets, studded with occasional cobbles, long since worn and polished to a quarter of their original size. Two mutts of dubious origin yapped at them, only to quiet as the column progressed along the narrow lane. Then, suddenly, a large, snarling beast bounded into the roadway ahead.

Huge jaws revealed long, yellowed fangs. The dog slavered and the hackles rose on his back. Stiff-legged he advanced on his new quarry. Corporal Montez, at Griff's side, moved swiftly to the left and then darted toward the creature. One fast stroke, a pitiful yip and the aggressive animal lay kicking in a pool of its own blood. Montez returned to the formation, wiping a crimson smear from the blade of his knife.

"Good work, corporal," Griff whispered. "Let's keep moving, men."

"Looks like that's a likely place," Temple Ames told the soldier on his left. "Go on over there and break in a winder. We gotta have all the kerosene we can get."

A moment later, the smack and tinkle of breaking glass sounded through the plaza area reserved for merchants and market stalls. The slim form of the Juarista private disappeared through the opening in the sidewall of a low adobe building. He returned to the window a moment later, grinning broadly and displaying a wicker-covered jug.

"Kerosene," he whispered hoarsely.

"Good. Some a you fellers give him a hand. We're runnin' late."

For a moment, Temple became confused as to direction, then oriented himself on the Big Dipper and signaled his men to advance along a slightly wider street leading toward the north end of town. A sign tacked to a lamp post identified it as the road to Celaya. They reached the granary with a minute to spare.

"You two split up an' locate the guards. Don't do nothin', jest come back and let us know where they is."

"And then?" the corporal inquired.

Temple grinned. "Then we give 'em the surprise o' their lives."

Gordo Ruiz stood beside his patient mount, eyes fixed on the dark masses formed by the low adobe structures that housed the people of Irapuato. In the distance he heard a dog bark, answered by another across the small village. A rooster, disturbed by the racket, stretched its neck and uttered an annoyingly early salute to the dawn. In a house nearby, a man's deep voice cursed at the fowl. Gordo grinned and shook his head in sympathy.

These sounds had the familiarity of home to him. This could be the village in which he grew up. Intellectually he knew that the soldiers quartered here were the enemy, not the residents, yet he felt a moment's regret at bringing violence and death to the tidy little town. He roused himself to break the spell and went to inspect his men.

"Be ready. The attack will come at any moment now. Do not shoot unless you see an armed man or one in uniform. We are here only to hurt the soldiers and to destroy the traitor, Santos's, supplies."

"*Sí, serjento,*" a private whispered. "It is funny. This village seems so much like the one in which I was born."

"Get such foolishness out of your mind, Pablo," Gordo growled. "We are here to kill the enemy. Don't forget that," he admonished, though his own heart ached with similar sentiments. He walked on to the next man.

"You are supposed to be turned the other way, watching our rear. Do you wish to taste the provost's lash? Do your duty as a soldier and stop dreaming. Alicia will be there when you return to Léon."

"*Ay de mí!*" the soldier exclaimed in exasperation. "I do not always think of my woman, sergeant. I am only curious as to what is happening in the village."

187

"You will find out soon enough."

As though to emphasize the sergeant's words, shots blasted into the night from the direction of the barracks.

Crackling gunfire brought Lieutenant O'Bannion out of a troubled sleep with a start that had him halfway out of bed before his eyes opened. Quickly he rose and tugged on a pair of uniform trousers. Silly, he thought, as he reached for his pistol belt. Those white pants would make him a perfect target in the dark. He crossed the room to a window that looked out on the two buildings where his men were quartered.

As his eyes focused in the dim light, he saw a sentry spin away and fall to the ground, his body bent at an odd angle. From across the street he saw the flashes of several weapons being fired. He judged them, from the sound of the report, to be heavy .56 calibre Marchots or American .45-70 Springfields. That would mean troops from Mexico City. A sudden, wild thought struck his imagination.

For some time his growing disaffection with the methods employed by Santos and his followers had become a subject of discussion at headquarters. At last, General Santos had sent him here to this backwater, relieved from staff duties and assignment to the bodyguard company. A disciplinary action, he had been told. Well, for his own part, he wished for some means of disassociating himself from Santos and his bloody rebellion.

Perhaps, his racing thoughts suggested, this sudden attack presented some answer to his wishes. Disdaining a shirt, Filipe rushed into the street in time to see a skirmish line of well-trained soldiers cross the street. They bent low, to make smaller targets, and fired as they advanced. Behind them, in the flash of a revolver going off, he saw and recognized a big Anglo. It was a man he had seen not long ago in the streets of Guanajuato. Amazement registered a moment on Filipe's face, then a wide grin spread.

A spy. One of Juarez's men, he realized in the swiftness

of the unfolding battle. Here was a man who might help him. He recalled, also, that he had seen the familiar face of a friend at the festival in Guanajuato not two weeks ago. If this *gringo* was here, perhaps his former comrade in arms would not be far away. Quickly he stepped back into shadow, more conscious than before of the vulnerability of his white trousers. A moment later, a soldier loyal to General Santos came into view. Unseen by the attacking force, he took aim at the big *gringo* who led them. Without conscious command, O'Bannion found his revolver in his hand, the hammer back and muzzle aimed.

His shot blasted into the fury around him and he saw the ambusher jerk away like a puppet on a string. The dead soldier lay twitching in the dirt before him. For a moment, Filipe O'Bannion wondered at what he had done. Then he shrugged and stepped out to slip away in the night.

"Sure an' ye've tipped over a bucket of muck this time, O'Bannion," he told himself as he sought out the rear guard he knew had to be there. He intended first to surrender to them, then volunteer to join their cause. As a formerly loyal officer with a good record, he had little doubt that he would be welcomed.

"Figger that," Temple Ames muttered aloud. "Not more'n four guards on a place this size. Welp, boys, we've got us an easy task. You get into position to take 'em out quick. When we hear the shootin' from the other end of town, open up on 'em. This chile's gonna shake up any others around with a bit of noise. Don't let it worry you all that much when ya hear a bit of catter-wallin'."

Another long, nervous minute passed, then rifles cracked from the direction of the barracks. One sentry lounged at his post not twenty feet from where Temple and two of his men stood. When the soldier stiffened and came alert at the sound of gunfire, Temple slid a tomahawk from his belt and ran forward.

He threw back his head and opened his mouth wide. From deep in his throat came a hideous screech and yowl.

Momentarily paralyzed by the unfamiliar Sioux war cry, the guard stood stunned while Temple closed. The tomahawk flashed downward and connected with the unprotected top of the sentry's head.

It made a sound like an overripe melon as the steel blade cleaved through. Split from crown to jawbone, the dead trooper crumpled and fell into the dust. Temple cut loose with another savage screech and two soldiers sleeping in an alcove nearby leaped to their feet and began to run, their rifles forgotten in their terror.

Two shots ripped out into the night from his right and then silence descended on the warehouses and grain bins.

"The fightin's over, boys. Now let's get to work."

Within five minutes the grain had been thoroughly saturated with kerosene. One soldier found crates of ammunition, which Temple directed be dragged to safety beyond the area of the fire. Then he scraped a sulfureous lucifer match to life and touched off the first blaze.

Slowly the oily liquid began to flicker a pale yellow-orange. Then, as it caught better, blue tongues licked along the heaps of feed for horses and man alike. In seconds the storage area became an inferno.

"Time to be movin' on, lads. We'll link up with Major Stark and finish cleanin' out this rat's nest."

"They are holding up in there, *señor Mayor*," a sergeant told Griff. "We will lose too many men to make a direct assault. We need a way to drive them into the open."

Griff studied the thick walls of the adobe buildings used as billets by the rebel soldiers. If they had thought to bring along grenades, it would be a simple matter. He had decided against it because of the added weight. Now he regretted his decree. What he needed was something that, like grenades, would force the defenders to abandon the buildings. A figure moved in the darkness of a sidestreet and a trooper near Griff threw his rifle to his shoulder. Swiftly, Griff reached out and jerked the weapon down.

"No. That's Captain Ames. Temple, over here," he

called in a loud voice.

A second later, the gangly, ginger-haired mountain man joined him. "We got them grain stores burnin' nicely. Two gallons of kerosene left over."

"Good," Griff offered offhandedly. Then his fertile brain began to wrestle with an idea. "I wonder, Temple, we're meeting more resistance than expected. What we have to do is drive the rebels out of those buildings. Fire ought to do that, don't you think?" he asked rhetorically. "Without grenades, that's the next best thing. Have your men search around for some bottles. Any kind they can find. I think we can put that kerosene to use."

"Shore enough, Griff. I'll have one o' the boys tote it over here an' get right on scruffin' up some bottles."

"Good." Griff turned to an NCO. "Corporal, go to Sergeant Ruiz. Tell him I need him and his trumpeter up here on the double."

"Yes, major," the man answered smartly and disappeared into the darkness.

Bullets whined and moaned off buildings as the defenders put up a withering fire that kept heads low. A private, crouched near where Griff stood, grunted and toppled backward, a large, dark hole in his forehead. Two men dragged him away and took his place.

Better disciplined than their enemy, they took careful aim and fired at the flashes that appeared in the grilled-over windows of the adobe building. After three shots each, the hail of bullets slackened. At the corner of one barracks, a small door opened and Griff sensed movement.

"They're going to make a counterattack," he warned. "Get ready."

"Don't shoot!" Filipe O'Bannion called out in Spanish and English as he approached a group of men gathered at the edge of town. "I'm a friend."

"Come forward," Gordo Ruiz commanded.

As the newcomer approached, Ruiz kept him covered with his short-barreled carbine. The tall, slim figure

191

seemed vaguely familiar, and the sergeant had nearly put a name to him when O'Bannion stepped in close and his troubled look changed to a warm smile.

"As I live and breathe. Sergeant Ruiz? Is that really you?"

"*Tienente* O'Bannion? I thought you had gone over to the traitor or had been killed by him by now."

"Uh, well, I did throw in with Santos for a bit, sergeant. Only his ways weren't suited to a gentleman, nor fittin' for warfare. I'm surrendering to you and offering my services to President Juarez."

"If I didn't know you from the old days fighting the French, I'd shoot you down like a dog, lieutenant. No disrespect meant, sir. Welcome to the right side, if I may say so, sir."

"Thank you, sergeant. What's the situation?"

"You'll have to ask the major that, sir."

"Major who?"

"Stark, sir. A *gringo*, but a good man all the same. He's up by the barracks directing the fight."

"Yes, I saw him."

A corporal ran up and announced Griff's needs.

"Lieutenant, you can come with us, sir. We are going there now."

All the same, Gordo Ruiz had not been born under a cabbage leaf. He kept a watchful eye on the "reformed" lieutenant as he and the trumpeter hurried forward, with O'Bannion at his side. They had made a little more than a block when a sniper appeared on a balcony behind the trio. The clack of his closing breech alerted O'Bannion a moment before Ruiz reacted.

By the time the sergeant had turned, Filipe O'Bannion's fast reflexes had him pivoted around, his revolver in his hand. The lieutenant tripped the trigger and, before the hidden killer could fire a round, a ball sped on its way to smash into his jaw and blow away part of his teeth and a chunk of cheek. Shrieking, the man rose and flipped over the wrought-iron railing to smack noisily onto the cobbles below.

"Good shot, lieutenant."

"Thank you, Gordo. One less to fight for Santos, eh?"

A big grin replaced the frown of doubt that earlier creased Gordo Ruiz's face. "Come along, lieutenant, I think Major Stark will be glad to see you after all."

Ta-a-a-a ta-ti-ta-aa-ta-ti-ta! The haunting, brazen notes of the Diguello sounded across the momentarily silent portion of the village of Irapuato. As the dreadful cadence of the No Quarter drifted over the walls to the besieged followers of General Santos, Griffin Stark nodded to Sergeant Ruiz.

"*Atención*!" Ruiz shouted. "You men are doomed if you do not surrender. Come out or die. You can hear what we play. We give no quarter once the attack begins."

"*Tu madre chingar con los indios borrachos*!" a man shouted back.

Gordo gritted his teeth at the deadly insult. "This is your last warning. We give no quarter. Surrender or die."

"*Chinga tu madre*!" another besieged soldier snarled.

Gordo's temper and his manhood could stand no more. "*Mierda in la leche de tu madre, cabrón*!" the sergeant bellowed. "*En tu boca, tambien.*"

"I take it you didn't invite them to tea," Griff remarked casually.

"Not likely, major," Gordo replied. "They made insults about my mother and some drunken Indians. So I told them the worst insult in all Mexico."

"Which is?"

"That I shit in the milk of their mothers."

"It's graphic enough," the ex-Confederate allowed. "We'll give them two minutes. Then send forward the men with the bottles of kerosene."

"*Sí, señor Mayor.*"

Three minutes later, the small village of Irapuato became illuminated by the towering flames over the soldiers' quarters. The screams of the dying could be heard for a long way out of town. Riding between Griffin Stark

193

and Temple Ames, Lieutenant O'Bannion looked back sadly and commented in a low voice.

"Sure an' they weren't all such bad lads."

"They were willing to fight and die for Emilio Santos. Right up to the end," Griff told him.

"Aye, there's that."

"And here you are, asking to join us in fighting Santos. How do you explain that?"

"It's me Irish nature, that's the truth of it. I was deceived at first. Then when the general let women and children be tormented and murdered, an' he killed a priest, I saw that he was not the man for Mexico. I'll throw me lot with President Juarez."

"There's room for good infantry officers in Diaz's army, I'm sure."

"Oh, now that I hear ye've cavalry, I'll be wantin' to join."

Griff gave him a close look. "Do you think you can stay aboard a mount in combat?"

"Sure an' is there an Irishman born who isn't a natural on a horse?" O'Bannion defended himself. "Besides, I did me trainin' with the Lancers, I did. From me old friend, Gordo Ruiz, I hear me bunkmate Luis Hertado is with this army o' Porferio Diaz and in the cavalry to boot. It would do me heart good to serve with him again."

"Then that you shall do. From here on we press Santos until he cracks."

CHAPTER TWENTY-ONE

"And so, gentlemen," General Diaz announced to his staff late the next afternoon. "As of tomorrow, the cavalry joins us as an effective fighting unit. I trust each of you has consulted with Major Stark to learn the means of best employing this new arm to aid your infantry? If so, we can begin an immediate campaign against the traitor, Santos, and all who follow him. That is all."

Griff and Temple drifted away from the staff meeting, which had been held in the fragrant courtyard of the house that held Diaz's headquarters. They joined Captain Hertado and Lieutenant O'Bannion for a friendly glass of beer, then Griff rose and excused himself from the table. He walked over two blocks and stopped at a small inn that featured the best food in Léon.

There, Consuelo waited for him. She smiled radiantly as he approached the small table where she sat under the shade of an olive tree.

"You are late, *corozón*," she told him.

"General Diaz decided to be long-winded today."

"I have ordered a small basket of food to take with us."

"You have something special in mind?"

"Oh, no," she teased. "Only a short walk in the country, a bit of food and wine and then back here for dinner tonight. After all, I am the daughter of a *hildago*. My reputation must be considered."

"Before or after we make love?"

Consuelo giggled. "After, of course."

Hand-in-hand, Griff and Consuelo strolled through the trees outside town. Already the charcoalers had made deep inroads into the abundant supply of hardwood, so that only the softer, second growth of pines and cottonwood remained over most of the hillsides. They found a quiet, mossy spot beside a large pool and Consuelo laid out a blanket. She spread a hearty repast of roast chicken, beans still warm in a covered olla, corn tortillas, and a pungent cheese. They washed it all down with draughts of cold spring water and chilled white wine. The last bites found them looking soulfully into each other's eyes.

"I . . . I am still afraid to face most men, to talk with them or be alone with one. With you it is different, *mí carro* Griff."

"You are lovely. You deserve a better life than what has been forced on you. I sometimes feel ashamed of taking advantage of you."

"Oh, no! It is *I* who take advantage of you."

Unable to forebear longer, Griff took Consuelo in his arms. Their embrace grew tighter, their kisses more impassioned as :he moments fled. Birds chirped above and in the distance a hunting hawk cried defiance to the land below. The moss provided a gentle pad beneath the wool blanket. As their amorous clinch ended, Griff deftly undid the buttons and tie-strings of Consuelo's dress.

"There. There . . . and there," he announced with each further parting of the cloth. He slid the puffy sleeves off her creamy tan shoulders and exposed firm, young breasts, upthrust in eagerness. With a moan of pleasure he began to rain kisses upon them as Consuelo worked on the fastening of his belt.

In moments they had divested themselves of all clothing. They lay naked as innocents in Paradise, hands, eyes, and lips exploring each other with delirious abandon.

With loving determination, Griff massaged the swollen, moist mound, delicately parting the sparce coverage of silky black threads to manipulate the sensitive spots within its outer portals. His manhood swelled to magnificent proportions. Deftly, Consuelo took it in her small hand and began to manipulate it in a thrilling manner. They built each other to new heights of excitement. Their sighs and gasps blended with the joyful sounds of nature as the creatures of the forest gave voice to their own celebration. Vibrating with inner need, Consuelo at last cried out.

"Quickly, Griff. Take me. Make me yours again so that I won't be lonely. Hurry. Oh, hurry!"

With the eagerness of a proud stallion, Griff hastened to comply.

Griff, along with other commanders and the entire staff, was summoned to General Diaz's office late that evening. The general looked grim and his words soon darkened the minds of those in attendance.

"I have been informed through agents in Guanajuato that the traitor, former General Santos, has decided to make reprisals for the raid on his grain supply."

"Let him," an old campaigner on the staff snapped. "Then we will raid more of his food warehouses."

"Unfortunately," Diaz went on, ignoring the caustic remark, "we have already sent another small force out to attack the supply lines between Celaya and Guanajuato. Wagons are to be burned with all contents, drivers killed, livestock run off. It is too late to call them back."

"Why should we?" a staff major demanded.

"The nature of the reprisals is such—" General Diaz began, only to be shouted down.

"Let him do his worst!"

"It is nothing to us. He is a traitor and should be crushed!"

"Death to Santos! *Viva Mexico!*"

"Quiet!" the small, usually soft-voice general shouted.

Shamefaced, his officers silenced their tirade and looked askance at their leader.

"General Santos has announced that he will execute one

197

hundred men, women, and children for each such raid as that we pulled on Irapuato. One hundred have already been killed for the attack on those supplies and the deaths of his soldiers. For my own part, *amigos*, I do not want the blood of these innocents on my hands."

"You haven't much choice, general," Griffin Stark said into the shocked silence. "If you once give in to his tactics, he can have you run all the way back to Mexico City by threats of similar mass murders. The thing to do is hit him harder and faster, drive him back against a wall and force him to submit. That or strike directly at the city of Guanajuato and smash him in his lair."

"In the meanwhile he goes ahead butchering innocent women and children."

"He will slaughter a great many more if you do back down."

"What do you propose, Major Stark?"

"Let me take the company of Lancers, with Captain Hertado in command, naturally. We will pursue the raiders. If we can do nothing, we will determined where Santos's men have taken any hostages they might round up. We will strike there, free the hostages and kill every one of Santos's soldiers, except for one. Him we send back with a message so clear that even a fanatic like Emilio Santos will not miss the meaning."

"How is that, major?" General Diaz inquired mildly.

"There are a number of things I learned from the Sioux. Highly unpleasant things that can be done to a man. We might employ those, depending upon what we find at the end of our ride. Or perhaps let him witness the summary execution, for treason of course, of his comrades in arms, then give him a good fright by making him believe the same will happen to him. After that, give him a message and turn him loose. His own fear and humiliation will take him down a notch or two, I should think. It will also insure he is an effective messenger for our side. Should he fail to make his point, we convince him we will hunt him down and he will die horribly."

"That sounds a cruel thing, Major Stark," Colonel

Maldanado challenged.

"From what I know of the history of your country, colonel, it is a small thing compared to methods used as recently as 'sixty-four, against the French. I am not saying that you are savages, merely that the appearance of savagery will often weaken the will to resist on the part of many of your enemies, let alone a man already at your mercy." Griff smiled icily and waited for more reply.

When none came, he appealed directly to General Diaz. "Something must be done. If we strike, and apparently fearlessly, it will give Santos cause to consider. He can go on with this summary execution ploy for only so long. Before many more die, the entire populace would rise against him."

"You make an interesting point, Major Stark," the general returned. "Yes. I think it is important we do something. And we must act from a position of strength. Very well. Take the Lancers. Ride out and try to prevent the next raid. Failing that, make so horrible an example of the perpetrators of any retaliation, that the soldiers themselves will hesitate to carry out Emilio Santos's orders."

"Thank you, general. It will reap you many benefits. We will ride before nightfall."

CHAPTER TWENTY-TWO

Rolling hills, nearly devoid of vegetation, sped past as the Lancers swiftly headed for the Celaya road. After consultation with locals, Luis Hertado and Griffin Stark decided on saving time by going cross-country. Here and there the dark forms of cattle dotted the browning pastures. The men rode silently, each with his own thoughts.

Revenge for the murdered victims of Santos's retalliation rested foremost among their contemplations. It could happen, or similar atrocities had already happened, in their own villages. Poorly educated for the most part, these soldiers had no knowledge of the War Lords of faraway China. Yet periodically, since the first uprisings against the Spanish viceroy, hill bandits would become strong and begin to raid small settlements in one area of Mexico or another. Always, it seemed, the spoils went to the strong, while the weak toiled in vain.

Now they had a chance to exact payment for these past, or imagined future, offenses. Griff thought, too, of the ruthless and wanton destruction and murder performed by Sherman's troops on their march through Georgia and the wholesale depredations of the Recontruction occupation troops and their puppet government of recently liberated darkies. That such bestiality could be unleashed on any people, let alone his own family and friends, set his blood to steaming and dark thoughts of retribution whirled in his head.

He experienced considerable satisfaction then when the expedition reached the road between Celaya and Guanajuato in a little under half the time it would have taken by way of the old, convoluted Camino Real that wound through the valleys and over mountain passes.

His pleasure was short lived.

Two miles along the wide, rutted "King's Highway," the Lancer column came upon the ruins of freight wagons and the uniformed bodies of Emilio Santos's soldiers.

"Hit 'em at sunup, th' way this chile sees it," Temple Ames observed.

"Dead for a good four hours then. Where was the next target?' Griff asked of Luis Hertado.

"The group that hit this supply train was supposed to go on to a small garrison outside San Miguel de Allende and poison the water supply."

"Is there any chance of intercepting them?"

"Not with the lead they have," Luis responded.

Bloated vultures hovered in the sky above, soaring on wide-spread wings. They scolded the soldiers below in their loud voices, unhappy at being disturbed at their feast. Several of the Diaz troopers eyed them dubiously and crossed themselves to ward off the evil represented by these carrion-eaters.

"Where to now?" Temple inquired as he rubbed at a few strands of gray that had invaded his thick, ginger sideburns. His pale, nearly colorless gray eyes twinkled as if amused, and he judged these Mexicans to be better at fighting Injun-style than he had expected.

"We have to make a sweep of the small villages around here, find out if Santos has learned of this and ordered reprisals," Griff commanded. "We'll take a circular route and go to Celaya last."

Rather than divide the force, in the event of hostile activity by any of Santos's troops, Griff and Luis agreed the unit should remain intact. They had covered less than a mile toward the next village when a teenaged boy on a trotting burro hailed the column from behind. As the youth rode up. Griff could see that he had been beaten about the head and shoulders. He called out repeatedly until he reached the head of the small force.

"What brings you here to us?" Luis asked the lad.

"You are not the soldiers of General Santos?"

"No. We come from the capital to bring an end to this rebellion," Griff responded through Luis's interpretation.

"*Gracias a Dios*! You must ride quickly, then, and give us help."

"Where?"

"I am from Celaya. A little while ago soldiers of the rebel traitor, Santos, rode into town. They claimed that the people had attacked a shipment of goods headed for Guanajuato. Everyone was frightened. Some, like myself, tried to run away. Many were caught. The man in charge, a *Capitan* Rojas, said that we had aided the Juaristas and that an example would be made of our people. They caught me once and hit me with rifle butts. But I got away again. These soldiers . . . they . . . I am afraid they are going to kill everyone in the town."

Griff and Luis exchanged glances.

"*Bastardos*!" Filipe O'Bannion growled.

No debate was required to determine what to do. Griff turned his horse and started back down the column, with Luis and Temple at his sides. Sergeants quickly gave crisp orders and the soldiers reversed their formation, ready to ride out when the command came.

"At the gallop. Forward, HO!" Griff called.

Captain Rojas stalked through the Plaza de Armas in Celaya, snapping a riding crop against his left thigh. The huddled, frightened people looked at him with shock-slackened faces and dull eyes that reflected their resignation to the fate they fully expected to be visited upon them. It excited Rojas. His loins throbbed and he felt his manhood stiffen. He flicked his eyes back and forth, quickly focusing on this or that figure.

203

He rejected several candidates for various reasons, savoring the tingle of eager desire that rose in him at the wide variety he had to choose from. They all had a promise of secret delights, though some he knew would satisfy more than the others. He'd like to have them all. Too bad, he thought, that his new friend Arturo Treadwell had not come along.

After their first adventure together, in which Arturo had indeed found that he derived certain exquisite satisfaction from the small boy captive, they had journeyed out in the streets of Celaya. In the crush of poverty, they had found many willing, even eager, boys and girls to participate in their deviant pursuits. One thing, though, bothered Ignacio Rojas. On at least two of these occasions, he knew for certain that Arturo had cold bloodedly killed the little girl he had pleasured himself with. Such things, Ignacio thought, were of the *ojo malo*. He didn't want to mix into that sort of thing again. A vision of absolute loveliness suddenly jolted him out of his reflections.

"Now there's exactly what I want," he muttered aloud. He turned away, though his eyes lingered hungrily, as a sergeant came up to him.

"Everything is in readiness, *capitan*."

"Excellent. Have *Teniente* Duran begin making the selections. And, ah, sergeant, have him include that boy, and that one." Rojas nearly shivered with delight as he swung slowly around and pointed at the exceptionally beautiful boy of ten or so he had seen a moment before. "Especially that one is to be in the group. Take them aside from the others and get the firing squad ready. I will, naturally, want to inspect the choices before the executions begin."

"Yes, sir, captain." The sergeant departed at a trot, shouting orders to his subordinates as he hurried across the square.

In a few minutes, men, women, and children began to be pulled from the crowd of residents and taken over to the front of the church. Women, separated from their husbands and families, wailed pitiously. Smaller children cried and wiped grubby fists at their eyes. Here and there a man resisted and he was battered into unconsciousness by heavy rifle butts that thudded meatily into his flesh until he lay still.

"You are going to give them all a little lecture first, aren't you?" Chester Breathwaite asked as he walked up to Rojas.

Captain Rojas broke his fascinated gaze away from the angelic little boy long enough to acknowledge Breathwaite. "Oh, certainly. All about being an object lesson and so on. Then the killing begins. You have witnessed our method of firing squads before, have you not? Ah, yes, in Silao. Tell me, what do you think of our technique? Of *El Peridón*, the firing wall?"

"Efficient. Before that all I had seen was a single person shot at a stake. Twenty at a time is . . . impressive, to say the least."

Rojas uttered a snort of laughter. "But, ah, offends your Yanqui sensitivites, *verdad?*"

Breathwaite frowned slightly in consideration. "That's a good way of saying it, I think. It lacks a certain dignity that even the lowliest of peasants deserves in the face of death."

"This is a harsh country, *coronel*. There is little time for such refined sentiments. The *peons* must learn, swiftly and absolutely. Kill twenty, fifty, a hundred here today, maybe five hundred somewhere the next time. After that," Rojas said, shrugging elaborately. "Well, after that, then we may be spared the execution of more of our countrymen. You will excuse me now. I must look over the ones selected to serve as our example."

"Certainly, captain."

Rojas walked among the one hundred selected victims, his eyes noting one face after another, as he mentally sized up each for his potential as a fitting sacrifice. At last he came to the lovely boy he had seen earlier. Rojas squatted down to be on a level with the child.

"You don't want to die, do you, son," he said mildly, his pounding heart accelerating as he studied his prospective partner.

"Oh, no, general," the boy answered in a cherubic voice.

"Well then. All you must do is please me. It will be most enjoyable, you'll see. Come with me now and we will find a nice place where we can take pleasure together."

A look of utter disgust surged over the youthful features. The small boy worked up his mouth and spat a large glob of phlegm and saliva into Ignacio Rojas's face. *"Puto!"* he snarled in a soprano voice. *"Hijo de tu madre!"*

Stunned, Rojas remained squatting a moment while the slimy gobbet slid down his cheek. Almost absent-mindedly, he reached for a linen kerchief in his trousers' pocket and wiped away the offending matter. Then, red-faced, he rose and turned to a soldier nearby.

"See that this one is in the last group to die. I want him to watch the others and know what is in store for him. Find his parents, if you can. Put them in the place of some already chosen. Them we will kill first."

"Yes, captain."

Captain Rojas walked on until he found his second choice. Again he hunkered down and searched the smooth, child's face before him. "Boy," he began softly. "Would you rather be laying in my big, soft bed, waiting for me to come to you and do wonderful, tickling things with your body instead of out here facing a firing squad?"

A sly, knowing cast came to the youngster's slitted eyes but he smiled sweetly. "You mean like *punjeta* and other things?"

"Exactly. You do understand, I see."

"Oh, *sí*, captain. I would be most pleased. I am called Raul. I am ready to go with you right now." Raul reached out one small hand and had it enclosed in Rojas's large one. Together, they started walking across the plaza toward a small posada.

"I will be back to start the executions in one hour," Rojas told Lieutenant Duran. "Let them confess and have

206

the priest give them absolution. See that all are ready when I return."

Forty-seven men silently sat their horses behind the brow of a low hill that overlooked Celaya. On the opposite slope, Griff, Luis, and Temple crouched in a thicket of brush. They watched in rapt concentration as twenty local residents were separated from a group of a hundred or so and herded toward the wall of the church. Only the sobs of women and wails of children could be heard for some time. Then another voice, stronger, came to them.

"You people in Celaya have defied an edict of the most Excellent, Gen. Emilio Santos. Consorting and comforting an enemy is a deadly crime. In order that others might take example, the general has decreed that for such evil, one hundred of you must die. We have made our selections. There is no appeal and we do not care about the innocence of any involved. I am advised that those who are about to make their sacrifice have been shriven and are ready to face the ordeal with the Grace of God. That is good.

"Twenty of you will die at a time. The first are ready. Lisutenant Duran, will you take charge of the firing party, please?"

"*Sí, capitan.*"

"We don't have much time," Luis observed needlessly.

"I agree," Griff told him. "Let's get back. I want a convex, squadron-wing formation for the attack. Two ranks deep. Lances to the front. We'll hit the town at a full gallop. Drive straight through to the plaza. Don't let a Santos man escape alive. We'll hang any who surrender or are wounded after the place is mopped up."

Together, the three men walked back to the waiting troops. Brisk commands were given and the formation took shape and started forward at a walk.

A hundred yards from the small town of Celaya, Luis rose in his stirrups and canted his lance forward. A forest of slender poles rippled into place to either side.

"Trumpeter, sound the charge," he commanded.

Clear notes tumbled into the hot morning air.

"Yeeeee-aaaaah-whooooo!" Griff yelled from Luis's side.

Instantly the forty-seven mounts leaped forward and thundered into the streets of Celaya. Chickens squawked and fluttered out of the way. A pig grunted pugnaciously and waddled toward safety, only a step ahead of the sharp, thudding hoofs. Beyond in the plaza, Lieutenant Duran's voice could barely be heard over the tumult.

"Atención!"

The twenty soldiers selected for the firing squad drew themselves up rigidly.

"Carga!"

A score of rifles clattered noisily as the executioners loaded their weapons.

"A punto!"

The same rifles came to twenty shoulders.

A tremble of excitement rippled through Ignacio Ruiz as he waited for the final command to fire. He felt his phallus lengthening and firming as he saw a vision of little Raul, drowsy and unclothed lying in the big white bed, a sated smile on his face as he waited for the captain's return. Killing a hundred people wouldn't take long, Rojas speculated. He could be back with Raul in not much over half an hour.

Lieutenant Duran opened his mouth to shout the final word. In the split instant before the sound came, he felt a blinding pain in the side of his head. Then, his brains, bone, and flesh sprayed out in a gout of blood. The gory material spattered over the faces and shoulders of the firing squad. Blackness enveloped Duran and he fell, shuddering, to the cobbles of the plaza.

Although Lieutenant Duran did not hear the report of Griffin Stark's Starr revolver, the men of his firing squad did. They turned partway around in time to have their breasts pierced by swiftly moving lance points. Shots crackled along the curved line of uniformed soldiers trampling into the plaza, and more of the followers of

Emilio Santos went off to find God.

Startled and confused, Captain Rojas started a hasty retreat. Suddenly the angelic little boy who had refused him bounded away from the cluster of hostages and ran, screaming at the pervert officer.

"Puto! Bastardo! Hijo de un perro y una puerca!"

With his small fists he began to beat at the fleeing officer's broad back.

In the midst of the chaos in the plaza, Luis Hertado heard the boy's shrill voice calling the retreating captain a homosexual and a bastard, the son of a dog and a sow. In a flash he recognized an old and soundly disliked enemy, Captain Rojas. He veered his mount slightly and fell down on the perverse commander of this Santos contingent.

Too late, Ignacio Rojas looked behind him at the rumble of rapidly approaching hoofbeats. His eyes widened as he saw and recognized Luis Hertado. Then his face paled to a sickly gray-green. The long, pennant-bedecked lance in Hertado's right hand lowered its point in line with his back.

Frantically, Ignacio Rojas fumbled at the flap of his holster. At last he freed his revolver, a fraction of a second before Luis closed the gap. A burning shaft of hot agony speared through Rojas's body as the wide, flat blade of the lance entered under his solar plexus and surged upward, bringing blinding agony with its rapid progress. The lancer captain's momentum and strong arm lifted Rojas off his feet and left him writhing in the air at the end of the slightly bowed lance. His mouth worked in spasmodic contortions and at last a long, eerie shriek of utter misery ripped from his constricted throat.

With a sensation of absolute satisfaction at eliminating something vile and slimy from the world, Luis shook the reflexively jerking corpse from his lance and rode on. He took only time to wave jauntily at Griff Stark.

Griff returned the gesture and blasted down two more Santos soldiers. Beyond them, huddled against a cantina front, Griff saw a familiar and hated face.

Ex-Colonel Chester Breathwaite.

Instantly, Griff changed course and surged his mount toward the consortium agent. Blood lust rose in Griff's veins and his throat worked convulsively in an attempt to swallow the bile of hate that rose to choke him. Now he would have his chance. Breathwaite would not escape him now.

CHAPTER TWENTY-THREE

Shouting men on horseback suddenly filled the plaza, firing rifles into the chests and backs of the Santos soldiers. Chester Breathwaite had been standing to one side, by a small fountain that no longer spewed a pleasant spray of water into the air. When he saw the riders bearing down, it took little time to realize that they had to be troops dispatched by General Diaz to put down the rebellion. He had no intention of being caught up in a debacle of someone else's making. Immediately, he began to edge toward an available route of escape down a narrow side street.

Bullets smacked into the adobe walls and he heard the hideous screams of men as they died with the razor-edged blades of lances driven into their bodies. This, he decided, was far worse than Indian fighting. Covered by the trappings of civilization, the terrible edged weapons took on an aspect of greater savagery. At the moment of attack, he had been stricken immobile by a chilling sound from the past which for four long years had been only too familiar to him. It could mean only one thing, he decided.

Along with the force of Mexican army troops rode Griffin Stark. It added energy to his flight. As he neared the side street, he hazarded another glance backward.

Soldiers swarmed in from three directions, closing off all retreat, except the one alleyway toward which he ran. Then, looming large and menacing in the swirling clouds

211

of dust and powder smoke, he made out the broad-shouldered form of Griffin Stark, astride a sturdy horse of Mexican breed. The man he had sought to kill fired a Starr revolver with uncanny accuracy, downing one after another of the men in Captain Rojas's company. Stark looked up then and, for a moment, their eyes locked.

Recognition brought a black cloud of anger to Stark's face and he drove his mount forward in an effort to close with Breathwaite. The former colonel spun away from the grasping hands of a wounded soldier and ran toward his avenue of escape, heedless of the battle around him. Griffin Stark plunged after him.

Griff rounded the corner into the narrow street and saw no sign of Chester Breathwaite. It was as though no one had come that way at all. Then he heard a rattle of red clay roof tiles and fired instinctively as he looked upward.

Griff's bullet narrowly missed Breathwaite, as the portly ex-colonel struggled to maintain his hold on the slanted roof. The former Rebel colonel bolted upright and ran toward the far edge of the building. A wild leap took him to the next and Griff resumed the pursuit.

It took only a second to discover that Breathwaite had not fled further.

The wily consortium agent slid down the canted roof to the eaves and dropped into the walled garden of the house. Griff made a careful, final check of the area, reloaded his revolver with a new cylinder and entered the structure through widely flung, tall wooden doors, on which had been carved huge, smiling representations of the sun. Dim light and coolness enveloped him as he walked along the short, covered corridor toward the wrought-iron gates that gave access to the inner courtyard. In his left hand he held his Starr revolver, cocked and ready.

A bullet sent a shower of adobe and plaster dust into his face a split second before he heard the report of Breathwaite's weapon. The slug moaned away toward the front entrance and smacked noisily into the yellowed wood of an inner panel. Reflexively, Griff had ducked and triggered off a response. His ears rang from the detonation in such a confined area. From somewhere in the patio, he heard the squeak of a rusty hinge and rushed forward.

He saw nothing of Breathwaite. Across the tiled flooring of the garden, he noticed an open iron gate that gave access through the back wall to an alley beyond. He ran back through the house and retrieved his horse. A quick sprint brought him to the far corner of the block. He turned in the direction of Breathwaite's flight and raced for the alley.

As he rounded the crumbling edge of one building he could hear the distant sounds of continued fighting in the plaza. It took only an instant to discover Breathwaite had eluded him again. Griff started to change direction when he felt the hot sting of a bullet as it creased the outer side of his left thigh. The sound of the shot came right behind its passage. Blindly, Griff fired two rounds in the direction of the attack.

Another shot answered it and left the patter of retreating footsteps in its wake. Griff winced as he applied heels to his mount and urged the well-muscled Mexican horse on into the narrow alley.

Ahead of him he saw movement and strove to close the distance. Once more Breathwaite disappeared. A second later a fourth shot rang Griff's ears as the fleeing man fired at close range. A faulty powder charge set the ball on an erratic course. It struck the hat from Griff's head and veered to the left, shattering a large olla of water that sat on a small wrought-iron balcony above and to his right. Griff swung out of the saddle under the cover of a blast from his Starr.

Obediently, the war-trained horse followed him as he advanced toward the place where Breathwaite had holed up behind a low portion of crumbled wall. He had chosen in ignorance and haste and come against a dead end. Griff could hear Breathwaite's labored breathing, stentorian as an idling steam locomotive, as he covered the half block that separated them.

Breathwaite fired again, the report blending with the crack from Griff's Starr. Then, suddenly, the tainted Rebel leaped upward, snagged the edge of the decayed wall and swung his way over the top. Griff ran in pursuit.

On the opposite side, Chester Breathwaite encountered a dead officer, who had been loyal to Emilio Santos and two soldiers. One barely remained alive, the other sprawled grotesquely in the posture of his demise. The next second Griffin Stark's leg appeared over the weathered adobe blocks.

The moment Griff's head came into view, Breathwaite eared back the hammer of his Remington Model '60 Army revolver and squeezed the trigger. Only a loud click followed. Then he saw the long, slender blade in his opponent's hand.

More observant of combat rules, Griff had counted his shots. With an empty cylinder in his Starr, he had taken his finely made sword from its scabbard and pressed the chase. If he lost track of Breathwaite for a moment and time allowed, he decided, he would place his last preloaded cylinder in the revolver. Now his enemy stood, gape-mouthed, in the center of a ruined, roofless structure with an empty weapon in his hand.

Not for long. Chester Breathwaite darted to one side and bent over the corpse of the Santos officer. He came up with a short, heavy sabre, which he brandished with more than a little expertise.

"There's a lot you can tell me, Breathwaite. I want to take you back with me to answer for the crimes you've committed in the name of the consortium."

"I think I prefer not to go. Though there's nothing you could do about it. The consortium is untouchable. Too powerful for the likes of a landless, impoverished former Rebel like you. Too powerful even for the few in government who do not yet give allegiance to our cause."

"Big talk from a little man. You're trapped, Breathwaite. Give up and you will be treated fairly."

Suddenly the pudgy man leaped forward, striking out at Griff with the heavy sabre in his right fist.

Griff easily parried it with a flick of his shining blade. Metal rang in a shower of sparks when the swords met. At home with the familiar weapon, Breathwaite danced nimbly backward and struck again, this time in *second*.

A deft parry let his blade slide past Griff's body. The younger, stronger man lashed out at Breathwaite with a solid right fist that connected with the surprised former colonel's jaw. He staggered backward and Griff initiated his own offense.

Breathwaite tried to block a mid-line attack in *quartere* and disarm Griff with a *moulinet*. The "windmill" sabre defense went awry in mid-execution and again Griff stepped in and punched Breathwaite squarely in the mouth. Blood ran from split lips and the evil minion of the consortium staggered backward, out of range of this formidable opponent.

Swift as a Georgia thunderbolt, Griff followed up. Point, true edge, and face wove a dazzling pattern in the bright sunlight as Griff manipulated his richly engraved sword with deadly precision. Breathwaite gave ground reluctantly, his heavier, blunter weapon battering aside all attempts to pierce his vulnerable skin. Carefully Griff set him up for a deadly reverse stroke. In the span of a heartbeat, his opening came.

As the blade whistled toward Breathwaite's suddenly exposed abdomen, the wounded soldier at Griff's feet lashed out with strong, clawed fingers. He clasped them tightly around Griff's ankle and heaved with the last of his waning strength.

Off balance, Griff crashed to the ground even as his despoiler gave a mighty groan and convulsed himself into eternal blackness. In a flash of renewed energy and hope, Breathwaite leaped forward and drove the point of his sabre downward. It sliced through the muscle of Griff's right shoulder.

Hot rays of pain washed through Griff's body and he felt his strength ebbing. Quickly, before Breathwaite could compound his damage, Griff made a slash at his enemy's unprotected genitals.

A sudden jump backward saved Chester Breathwaite from harm similar to that of Arthur Treadwell. It also jerked his blade free. Released, Griff took advantage of the situation to surge into a sitting position and thrust again.

With the ease of a hot knife in butter, the long, gold-inlaid sword slid into Chester Breathwaite's belly. The ex-colonel's eyes widened into round pools of white and his lips twisted in reflex to unendurable pain. He dropped the sabre and reached for the cold steel that had brought such burning agony to his pierced abdomen.

As the blade sank to midway on the fuller, Griff gave his weapon a strong wrench and pulled it free. As he gained his feet, Chester Breathwaite sank to his knees.

"P-please . . . get help for me. I . . . I hurt," Breathwaite moaned pitifully.

"You'll answer questions, first. Tell me about the consortium."

Tears sprang to Chester Breathwaite's eyes. "Please. I'm on fire. G-give me some water."

"Talk," Griff demanded implacably.

"Th-they are big. The biggest organization the world has known. They'll kill me if I say anything."

"And I'll kill you if you don't. So, do you want to die now . . . slowly and painfully? Or do you want to take your chance on the future?"

Breathwaite struggled with his fears and the pain in his gut. His lips worked and he licked at them to restore moisture. "The men who . . . who make up the leadership of the consortium are from several nations. Bankers, for the most part. But they control more than banks. Steel mills, railroads, textile mills, and mines, they even own newspapers and control the telegraph company that sends stories to the tabloids and magazines. They are rich beyond all belief. Their power is absolute."

"Who are they? Give me some names."

"I . . . I don't know any of the top men," Breathwaite lied in an attempt to protect himself. "There was a Lord Johnathan Chancellor. He came out to Colorado to direct my activities there."

"He's dead. Do better than that." Roughly Griff emphasized his words by grinding a boot heel into Breathwaite's stomach.

The portly man wailed in agony and gasped for breath. "I . . . I'm telling you the truth. They are like a secret society. One only knows what one is told to do and those working for him."

"Where is their headquarters?"

"Some . . . somewhere in New York City. A bank owned by someone named Felder. And there's some involvement with the United States Fur Company. The fur business is dead, but someone maintains an office in the name of the old company. Please. That's all I know. Get me some help, please."

"Why is the consortium trying to kill Damien and Jennifer Carmichael and me?"

"I . . . don't know," Breathwaite told him truthfully. "They only told me there would be a big bonus if I arranged your death and that of the Carmichaels."

"You're lying, Breathwaite. You know a lot more than you're telling me."

"No! I swear it. You have to believe me."

"You must know something about the orders to murder us."

"Th-they were given by a man named Chambers. He's the general manager of the Rocky Mountain Railroad."

"Where is he located?"

"In St. Louis."

"What did he tell you?"

"That in addition to the bounty that had been put on your head by the Railroad Protective Association—which the consortium also owns—I would get an additional five thousand in gold if I saw to it that all three of you were turned in dead."

Griff recalled the bounty notice he had seen in Georgia. In it he had been branded as a brigand and terrorist, called a sympathizer with John Wilkes Booth. It had gone on to state that he was a known collaborator with the secret societies of the unreconstructed Rebels. Even now, Griff had no idea what that meant. But if these "secret societies" were enemies of the consortium, then he thought it might be well to learn more about them. Perhaps, even, join forces to wrestle with this financial and industrial monster. Breathwaite groaned and slumped back.

Griff glanced down and saw that the man had nearly lost consciousness. He bent and slapped Breathwaite's cheeks until some color returned. Then he pulled the nearly senseless man to his feet.

"Come on. You'll have to walk back to where I left my horse. I'll get help for you."

Within ten minutes, Griff had Breathwaite slumped in his saddle and led the sturdy mount back to the plaza. There the few followers of Emilio Santos who had surrendered or been captured due to wounds had been drawn up before a table, where Captain Hertado sat with two of his officers. When the Lancer commander looked up and saw Griff, he motioned him forward.

"This is the man you sought?"

"That's right, Luis."

"Well, then. We can try him with the rest."

"Try?"

"Of course. We have to have a trial before we hang them."

"I wanted to take Breathwaite back with me."

"Not possible, my friend."

"But—"

Luis raised a hand. "He has been involved in a conspiracy and open revolt against the government of Mexico. As a result, we alone have jurisdiction over him. Please, *amigo*, don't complicate matters at this point."

Griff glanced from his friend to the prisoner. After a long, silent moment of contemplation he shrugged. What the hell, he thought. He had learned all that Breathwaite would probably ever tell him. Wherever he went, the former Confederate colonel would hang anyway. Provided he outlived his wounds, of course. Griff handed the reins to his mount to a private standing at his side.

"Take him, Luis. He's all yours."

"You can't do this!" Breathwaite shrieked, fear of the rope giving him new alertness. "I'm an American. You can't let these peasants hang me," his wailing protest continued.

"*They* are Americans, too, Breathwaite," Griff told him icily. "Or haven't you noticed that Mexico is on the same continent with our country? As to letting them, it seems I haven't any choice. Besides, you won't tell me anything more."

"I can't. I can't tell you what I don't know," Breathwaite remained adamant.

"Well then, you might as well hang here as in Denver."

"No! *Please no.*"

The trial went swiftly.

Predictably, the verdict of the drumhead tribunal was guilty. Eleven ropes were prepared, and an equal number of horses stood in line under a hastily assembled crossbeam that rested in the limbs of the only two trees in the plaza. Most of the condemned had become resigned. They went to their places calmly, a few shedding tears. Not so Chester Breathwaite.

He bellowed and struggled as best his wound would allow. Griff had already been attended to by what passed for medical personnel and he stood grim-faced as his enemy passed by, dragged by three burly Mexican soldiers.

Breathwaite tried to kick his captors in their faces as they hoisted him into place, his hands tied behind his back. It did him no good. At a command, the nooses were fitted around the necks of those about to die. Captain Hertado stepped forward and read off the names given him, then concluded with the usual last words.

"Do any of you have anything to say before sentence is carried out?"

"*Viva Emilio Santos!*" one doomed soldier cried.

"*Viva le revolucion!*" shouted another.

"*Chinga tu madre!*" a more defiant one bellowed.

"Please . . . this is all a mistake . . . you . . ." Chester Breathwaite mumbled, his eyes darting from one face to another, fear making his pale body greasy with sweat.

"You can't do this to me. YOU CAN'T."

Leather quirts flailed horseflesh at a silent command. Eleven neighing steeds leaped forward and left their passengers dangling by the ropes around their necks.

Bones snapped with loud cracks on several, who started to convulse and void themselves. Due to his great weight, Chester Breathwaite's neck stretched to a grotesque length before a small pop signified the severing of his spinal column.

As darkness descended, Chester Breathwaite had a final vision of all the riches and power promised him by the consortium. He had kept faith with them, had not revealed the involvement of the Treadwell family or the actual extent of consortium activities. Why then had this happened to him? Then, with a great groan of absolute misery, his mind screamed its last thought.

"Why must it be me, God? OH WHY ME?"

CHAPTER TWENTY-FOUR

"Naturally," General Diaz remarked to Griffin Stark, three days after the battle at Celaya, "with the apprehension and execution of this Colonel Breathwaite, your involvement is technically ended. That I must agree with. There is, though, still the matter of the rebellious troops and that traitor, Santos. My sources of information indicate that his situation is deteriorating rapidly.

"Now is the time to strike a final, decisive blow against Guanajuato itself. I would be pleased, no, I would be delighted, if you would consent to lead the cavalry squadron in that engagement, sir."

Griff had been looking forward to taking up the search for his son. With Breathwaite dead, he saw his fight against the consortium at least in abeyance, if not concluded. The time would come when the men responsible for so much misery directed toward himself and the Carmichaels could be brought to justice. At the present, he wanted only to complete the task he had given himself two years before. Jeremy must be found and taken home. The way General Diaz had couched his order, the Confederate had little choice, though.

"General Diaz, had you ordered me to participate in this campaign, I might have reminded you that I am a citizen of the United States and a scout for that country's army. As such, it is illegal for me to aid the military services of any other nation." Griff paused and smiled. "A small technicality that you and I both overlooked earlier. It would be repehensible for me to renege on that arrangement at this late date. When you are ready to move against Santos, I will be honored to lead the cavalry."

"Remarkable. If all *gringos* were like you, Major Stark, then perhaps Mexico and the United States could become one vast nation. One in which neither people need fear the loss of their dignity and identity or the plundering of their resources." The general paused a moment and lowered his voice in a confidential manner. "That is a dream that I have harbored for a long while and sincerely believe needs fulfilling. It is inevitable that it will happen. In a hundred years, maybe not for two hundred, but it will be so. Either by friendly means or by conquest.

"We here in Mexico cannot forget the invasion of our land by your soldiers in 'Forty-seven. The occupation of our capitol is a mark of shame. Half of the land claimed by Mexico was taken from us. Many resent this. Yet, the time will come when it is necessary to the survival of both nations to become one. I can only pray that it will be accomplished through peaceful means."

"You are a visionary, General Diaz."

"No. Only a realist. Conditions change and people must change along with them. Without that there is no progress. All becomes stagnation, much like the utopian societies described by unrealistic philosophers in Europe today. The selfless world of pastoral coexistence with nature, described by Mills, is one of futility. The static, beehive nature of Marx's workers' state is a cruel fraud that can only end in disaster. No. Man must grow. Nations, likewise, must expand or they stagnate and die."

"How frivolous you make my former life seem," Griff replied in a tone of wonder. "We, the entire South, lived in a static world of cotillions, sow and harvest, work our slaves and enjoy our wealth. We did not expand our business interests beyond that which related to the products of our plantations. We did not provide adequate educational facilities, but relied on those of other places. We did not build industry, because we could afford to import manufactured goods from Europe or the North.

No wonder we lost the war. I must confess, I have gained much from coming here and in particular from you, general. Now, if you will excuse me, I must talk with my company commanders."

"Certainly, Major Stark. And, ah, remember. If ever you find it difficult to continue your life in your own country, there will always be a place for you in Mexico."

"Thank you, general."

Consuelo looked up from the bed. The scarlet rays of the setting sun highlighted her bronze complexion. Her eyes were hooded, the lids drooped with satiation, her lips swollen and bruised with love. She moved languidly and the sheet slid back to reveal one pink-tipped breast. Griff stared down at her with a mixture of desire and pity. What he must say would hurt. He had waited for as long as he could to broach the subject. He had, in fact, put it off until after all arrangements had been made for the upcoming engagement. He even avoided it until the next day, after his meeting with Diaz. With regret, he realized he could delay no longer.

"Connie. This is the last time we will be able to be together. After the attack on Guanajuato, I am heading back to Chihuahua to try to find some trace of my son. We—"

"Don't say it, *corazón*. It has been a happy time. I have learned how to be a woman again. How to give freely and receive in return. For that I thank you from the depths of my soul. I have but nineteen years, yet, I seemed to be a woman wearied by too much life. You have made me young again. After we have achieved victory in Guanajuato, I, too, will seek another goal."

"*We* are not fighting in Guanajuato. You must stay behind."

"Oh, no. That cannot be. I will have my revenge on Colonel Cardoza. It is, ah, necessary."

"Not so much as to risk your life. Santos still has a lot of men loyal to him. The campaign could be long and bloody. I would not like to see you harmed."

Fire flashed in Consuelo's eyes. "There is little you can do about it. If I am forced to remain, I will follow after the army. If I am locked up, I can charm my captors into releasing me and again I will follow along. One way or another, I intend to use my little knife on that pig in a man's trousers."

"I can't let that happen, Connie. It would unalterably change you. And not for the better."

"*Mierda!* What am I that I must be cosseted like some delicate girl before her debut? Have I not risked all spying for General Diaz and President Juarez? I deserve my own revenge. I will have it!"

Their disagreement rapidly turned into a violent argument. Consuelo resorted to tears. Griff became more stubborn and demanding. At last it dissolved into hugs and kisses as they made up and shared another long, delightful hour of love. Then, poignantly, Griff took his leave and headed for the barracks where his men had been quartered. Only a day remained before departure to Guanajuato.

"Soldiers of Mexico!" General Diaz addressed his assembled troops. A division of infantry had been drawn up, along with artillary, the squadron of cavalry commanded by Griffin Stark, and auxiliary units of Indian bowmen, slingers, and *macheteros*, men who wielded the deadly jungle knives with chilling proficiency.

"Do not forget that you are the sons of men who fought to liberate our fatherland from Spain. Many of you struggled to throw out the French. Our present task will be no less demanding, no less dangerous, and no less important to the history of Mexico. Every citizen's eyes are on you. I can only ask that you do your duty. By doing so, you will cover yourselves with glory! *Viva Mexico!*"

With a grand shout, the huge expeditionary force wheeled right and rode out of Léon, on their way to close the account of General Santos. Ahead of the trotting infantry rode Griffin Stark and his neophyte cavalry.

CHAPTER TWENTY-FIVE

Like the swift tide of the Apocalypse, the horsemen of
Griffin Stark's cavalry swept over the fields outside
Guanajuato. Three lines of infantry rose to resist them.
Unused to the new tactic, the first two files broke in terror
before the thundering hoofs and glittering lances of the
advancing force. From behind the charging men, artillery
boomed and the ground spouted geysers of mud and grass.
For his own part, Griff would have preferred the cannon
duel to have come before, but this was a military tenet of
the Mexican army that dated back to Gen. Antonio Lopez de
Santa Anna.

It showed courage and resolution to charge under the
firing guns, Griff had been told. It was only another
impetuous exhibition of *macho*, Griff privately reminded
himself. It was also, he believed, only a bit short of
suicidal. Unknown to Griff, a better reason existed for him
to feel anxious over this method of attack. In the midst of
his men, disguised as a sergeant, Consuelo Alvarez rode a
sturdy animal, her hair hidden under the shako of a
Lancer and her hands steady on the reins, despite the
horrors of an artillery barrage.

A short round suddenly burst among his galloping
squadron.

Three horses and their riders vaulted into the air,
cartwheeled heels-over-heads and crashed to the earth with
piercing screams from the injured men and animals.

Enough of this, Griff thought angrily. He shouted to his trumpeter, and the signal sounded to swing to the flanks, exposing the infantry running behind to the direct fire of the enemy. He saved his cavalry for their vital task of routing the opposition and sending them fleeing from the field.

"Echelons left and right," he bawled over the growing rattle of musketry and rumble of cannon. "A and C Companies to the right and left flanks, B Company follow me!"

"Diaz is attacking me!" Emilio Santos shouted in a tone of wonder. "It cannot be!"

"I'm afraid it is, Excellency," Arthur Treadwell drawled. "And I, for one, am making preparations to depart by the most expedient means. It is not the province of the consortium to endanger its senior members. Therefore, I am afraid that our association is, ah, terminated as of now."

"What about the support you promised? What about the supplies, men, and arms? Where is this flow of information? We should have known in advance." Confused, now that he had been confronted by a superior force and vastly more capable commander, Santos could only protest like a pouting child, denied his promised sugar treat.

Treadwell laughed cruelly. "Forget that, general. Let's be honest with each other. You failed. Your own innate incompetence caused you to make irreconcilable errors. The consortium does not subsidize weakness, failure, or stupidity. We have been withdrawing our support and contingents of volunteers for a week, since you reverted to type and ordered the mass executions."

"*Pendejo!* Traitors! You and your consortium. You are all traitors. Backstabbing filth. You cannot do this to me. I am Gen. Emilio Santos! I will have your balls hanging on my office door for this."

" 'Fraid you can't have those. They're all I have left, you

226

know. You have failed, Santos. You are all washed up. The consortium is cutting its losses and leaving you to the tender mercies of your own people."

General Santos looked desperately around him. Only he and the arrogant *gringo puto* occupied the room. Anger suffused his face. They *had* to back him. Once Diaz had been put out of the way, what matter would it make? The road to Mexico City then lay open. He could not let this happen. His hand went toward the pistol stuck into the wide red sash around his large belly.

"If I go down to ruin, then you shall stay and go with me."

"Sorry, general. I'm compelled by my superior intelligence to decline the honor." Arthur Treadwell drew a nickle-plated revolver from under his coat. The small .32 calibre weapon barked twice and two ring finger-sized holes appeared in Emilio Santos's swelling stomach. He grunted softly and sat back in the big chair behind his desk. Tears filled his eyes and he moved his hands feebly, unable to complete his own try for a gun and robbed of energy to cry out an alarm.

"Good-bye, general. Too bad we couldn't conclude our transaction successfully." Arthur Treadwell used a concealed side entrance to exit from the building.

Outside, he encountered pandemonium as the Diaz forces pressed even closer to the city. Quickly he hurried in the direction of the underground drainage system.

What an impossible position, Colonel Cardoza thought frantically. Most of their recruits and auxiliary forces had deserted. Worse, where was General Santos? Somehow, at the height of the attack by Diaz and his army, the task of commanding the defenses had devolved on him. Every messenger who rushed up to report had news of yet another disaster.

To the south and west, the defenses had crumbled and the invading soldiers had rolled up even the elite units sent to fill the gaps. Artillery rounds were landing in the military compound north of town in the foothills. He received word that the Juarista cannons had been limbered up and moved to within five hundred yards of the town. There could be no counter attacks. He hadn't enough troops to man the city.

Such an action would be suicide for the men involved. It would also accomplish nothing toward stemming the advance. How had Diaz conceived of cavalry? A brilliant tactical advantage and far too effective. Wherever they went, they created panic. The armies of Europe and the United States did well with such troops. For some unknown reason, Mexico had abandoned the use of regular cavalry after the time of Santa Anna. Consequently they had no proper training in combating lightning attacks by mounted troops. No time for philosophising, Cardoza reminded himself roughly. The dreams of Emilio Santos crumbled about his ears and he, alone, appeared left to deal with it.

"General Diaz's compliments, Major Stark," a messenger rattled off along with a snappy salute. "The infantry are moving into the streets of the town. You are to bring your cavalry around to the east and press the last defenders there to create a diversion while General Diaz and the main force strike at their rear."

"Thank you, corporal." Quickly Griff issued the appropriate orders and the squadron wheeled to the right and struck off toward the last pocket of resistance. Immediately behind the commander rode Consuelo Alvarez, still dressed in the uniform of a lancer sergeant.

Consuelo had no way of knowing that the target of her hatred commanded the remaining soldiers fighting against the Diaz forces. She pressed on, reacting to the commands a bit slowly, but not enough to generate comment. In her heart burned the desire to make sure Cardoza paid in full. She would, she vowed, see to it that he did.

The volume of gunfire increased as the cavalry neared

the eastern edge of Guanajuato. A few small field pieces brazenly defied the attackers. With the arrival of the cavalry, two companies of infantry surged up from their concealment among the rocks on the hillside and dashed toward the handful of defenders who made a valiant, desperate last stand.

Bullets split the air like tearing canvas and cracked close by to nearly every head. Griff directed his mounted doom with pitiless efficiency. To each volley that offered a challenge to fight, he answered with ringing steel, flashing lances, and the blaze of nearly two hundred rifles.

"Over there," he shouted. "To the right. There's about thirty of them."

A Santos soldier reared upward at that moment and let go a shot that cut skin from the neck of the horse that bore Griff into battle. It neighed out its pain and began to crowhop. Years of experience came into play as Griff quickly quelled the animal's frantic gyrations. He reversed his course and swung the Starr in line with his attacker.

A .44 ball spat from the muzzle of Griff's revolver and punched a neat hole in the rebel's upper lip. Blood and fluids sprayed out when a small flap of skin and bone popped upward at the back of the sniper's head.

A short distance beyond, in the midst of the melee, Griff saw the flashes of an officer's uniform and the gold insignia of a colonel. He put spurs to his mount and forced his way through the struggling forms of fighting men. At almost the same second, Consuelo spotted the hated features of Colonel Cardoza. She, too, urged her horse in that direction.

Lieutenant O'Bannion rode at her side. He had been prevailed upon to provide her with the disguise that had brought her this far, and he felt morally obligated to do all he could to protect her. Two of the defenders swung in their direction and the Irish-Mexican officer fired at the nearest, punching a large hole in the man's chest. From ahead of them, Griff blasted the other with his Starr. The trio forged their way past the twitching bodies and closed in on Colonel Cardoza.

In the distance, bells began to ring in the city's many churches. Here and there, men ceased fighting and began to cheer. Some fired their weapons into the air and even embraced the common soldiers of the other side. Joyously they celebrated the end of the battle. Not so, Ramon Cardoza.

Fully aware that defeat brought with it only death before a firing squad, or worse, at the end of a rope, he abandoned the small detachment he had rallied a few minutes earlier and sought to escape into the city. Instantly, Griff, Consuelo, and O'Bannion raced after him.

The chase led to the headquarters of Emilio Santos. Soldiers of both sides stood in mingled lots outside this imposing structure. Too awed to enter without the urging of an officer, they talked in low voices and nervously eyed the windows. When Cardoza burst past their throng and threw himself through the tall main doors, a shout rose from the gathering. A few moments later, three figures, in the uniform of Diaz's army, pounded up and flung themselves out of their saddles.

Swiftly, Griffin Stark led the way up the three steps to the entrance. At his heels came Consuelo Alvarez, her tall Lancer's cap missing, long black hair flying. At her side ran Filipe O'Bannion.

Inside, wounded men moaned and cried out in pain as the scant medical personnel attempted to tend their many injuries. Down a long corridor, the form of Colonel Cardoza disappeared into a room. The trio of pursuers streamed after him.

"It's Santos's office," Filipe declared as they neared the doorway through which Cardoza had run.

"Two rats in one nest," Griff jibed.

Cautiously, they entered, crouched low, revolvers cocked and ready.

Wood splintered from the tall doors as two shots roared from inside. Slivers of wood bit into Griff's cheek and forehead and he flattened himself on the floor. Ahead of him he could see the form of Emilio Santos, blood staining the wide expanse of his shirt. He held an antiquated Colt Dragoon in one hand and grunted with the effort of pulling back the hammer.

"I . . . will get . . . you . . . all!" he panted out. "The people will rally to my cause. I . . . I . . . am . . . Emilio Santos. I am the ruler of all Mexico!"

The former hill bandit, turned general, had his tirade ended by a .44 slug that struck the center of his forehead and bulged both his eyes, as blood squirted from his nose and ears. Griff evaluated the accuracy of his shot and looked at once for Ramon Cardoza.

After firing a single shot at the intruders, the wily colonel had bolted from the room through a side door. A quick search assured Griff that his quarry had eluded him. Disappointment burned in his chest. He had made it a point to locate and capture the man so that he could bring him back to Léon. At least Consuelo would have the satisfaction of witnessing Cardoza's execution. Conscious of the others in the room, he turned to inform them that the chase had to continue.

Griff's jaw went slack when he saw Consuelo standing beside Filipe O'Bannion. "Con-Consuelo . . . what the hell are you doing here? You were . . . supposed to . . ." Griff turned partway back toward the corpse of Emilio Santos. "What kind of crazy people are you, anyway?"

The lovely girl merely bobbed her head and gave him a winning, winsome smile. O'Bannion felt compelled to stammer out an explanation.

"I . . . I couldn't h-help it, Griff. Sure an' she bewitched me. I—"

"Never mind. Any idea where he might have gone?" he asked Consuelo.

"Yes. He will not get far."

Grimly, Consuelo led the way to her former workplace. The front door stood open and most of the inmates had rushed into the streets to greet the liberating army. Consuelo walked boldly down one corridor, opening each door as she progressed. At last she came to one that had been securely locked.

"There. He'll be inside."

Griff and Filipe made ready, weapons cocked and tightly held. At a nod from Griff, Filipe kicked open the door. Both fired blindly into the room and dived through the opening, thumbs cocking back the hammers of their smoking revolvers. Heedless of any danger, Consuelo dashed between them, a blazing French LeMatt 8mm revolver in one hand.

"No! Please," Colonel Cardoza begged when he recognized the furious girl who faced him across the room.

Cardoza cowered behind a rumpled bed, his face ashen and his hands empty. "I only did what I had to do. It would have gone far worse for your family had I not interfered. You have to believe that," he babbled.

"You are a pig and the son of a pig and a goat," Consuelo spat as she advanced on him. "I am going to cut off your *cojones* and stuff them down your miserable throat. I will take your prick and feed it to the birds. You filth. You unspeakable monster."

Suddenly she began to cry. Sensing his only opportunity, Cardoza reacted swiftly. He leaped across the bed and snatched the LeMatt pistol from Consuelo's grasp. She gasped in surprise and recoiled.

A look of gloating distorted Cardoza's face as he aimed the 8mm revolver at Consuelo's heaving bosom. Then a lightning bolt of pain flashed across his twisted features and he opened his mouth in a soundless scream.

Consuelo's shoulders bunched and her left arm jerked forcefully upward. An expression of utter joyfulness lighted her face as she yanked once more.

Now Cardoza found voice.

He shrieked and wailed, moaned and begged for mercy while Consuelo continued to draw the keen-edged knife higher through his abdomen. She had thrust it in low, only an inch above the base of his thick penis, and proceeded to slice through his bladder, large intestine, and one lobe of his liver. As she persisted in her ruinous course, the wound began to gape.

Blood and fluids poured out in a river, followed by coils of grayish, purple-blotched intestines. They slithered toward the floor with a serpent's liquid hiss. As they did, escaping gasses made flatulent sounds as they bubbled out of the violated cavity.

At last it ended, with the blade pressed against the solid dome of Cardoza's diaphragm. Splattered with gore from nose to ankle, Consuelo relaxed her pressure and his emptied husk fell away. Dead, staring eyes gazed upward at the ceiling and Roman Cardoza moved no more. Choking, Consuelo turned away and began to vomit.

"Not the best way to go," Filipe O'Bannion observed as he struggled to retain the contents of his own stomach.

"I hope," Griff managed after a difficult swallow, "that she's never that angry at me. Come on. We have a lot yet to do."

CHAPTER TWENTY-SIX

Rounding up the remainder of Emilio Santos's rebellious troops took two long, arduous weeks. Many of the brave soldiers of Porferio Diaz died in the brief, hard-fought battles. Always, at the center of action, Griffin Stark led his cavalry in flashes of brilliant strategy that often gave him pangs of haunting memory. In them, he saw the slender, dashing figure of James Ewell Brown Stuart, his wide-brimmed gray hat and long black feather plume flying in the breeze as he directed his brave boys against the Yankees. Frequently Griff used the same maneuvers to vanquish the unschooled troops of the would-be master of Mexico.

Without their leader, though, resistance quickly crumbled. At the end of the protracted campaign, Griff and Temple, who had sustained severe wounds during the storming of Guanajuato, both received the Order of Merit from a grateful Benito Juarez, with the smiling approval of General Diaz. The day following, they took a coach to Aguascalientes and the train on to Chihuahua. Intelligence operatives of the president of Mexico had brought word that Apache tribesmen, raiding in Mexico, were seen to have a light-skinned boy with white hair along with them. More could be learned from a *Señor* Alfredo Sanchez in the desert city.

On a hot, June afternoon, Griff and Temple sat at a table in an expensive cafe-saloon a block off the plaza in

Chihuahua, talking earnestly with Sanchez. Temple's wounds had healed nicely and he experienced only a mild pain and an infernal itching that drove him near to distraction. Grumpily he scratched at the bandage around his ribs, complaining that he would be better off without it.

"This chile's had horses roll on him before an' it didn't take no yards of cotton cloth to hold him together," he grumbled during a lull in the conversation. "'Tweren't fer that knife slash along the ribs, I'd be for takin' this off."

Griffin Stark and Alfredo Sanchez chuckled sympathetically. "Why, Temple," the Confederate said mildly, "I figured a tough mountain man like you would never notice a little thing like that."

"It's the li'l things that bothers the most. Like fleas. You ever notice how one tiny, bitty flea can ruin a feller's whole day?"

"You've a point, *Señor* Ames," Alfredo agreed. Then he returned to the subject. "I could have not been more than two houses from the big Mescalero who led the raid. Beside him rode a small boy, oh, not more than eleven or so years of age. His skin was browned, like the Apaches, only his hair shined in the sunlight like so much silver. A true *rubio, Señores*. So blond it was white. I swear this on the grave of my sainted mother."

"You say he was small," Griff pressed. "Could he have been younger than you thought?"

"Oh, yes, *Señor* Stark. He was thick in the shoulders and the muscles made ridges on his belly, but he had not too many years, I think. He had scars, from wounds I would say, and big black eyes that burned hatred for the people of the village. He was every bit an Apache."

Icy fingers clutched Griff's heart. Could Jeremy have become so thoroughly an Indian that he willingly participated in raids against helpless villagers? Did he now relish the wanton slaughter of women and children? Was it, the welcome thought came, even Jeremy that Alfredo Sanchez described? Movement at the entranceway attracted the attention of the idlers along the bar.

It wasn't often that an unescorted woman entered the premises. At least not one who could own to being a lady. Like the regular patrons, Griff looked up to appraise the new arrival. Instantly his jaw sagged.

"Griff? Oh, Griff is it really you?" a sweet, musical voice he knew only so well asked.

"Jennifer? I thought . . . I didn't . . . how did you come to be here?" the ex-major inquired as he rose and crossed the room to her side.

Tears filled Jennifer Carmichael's vivid green eyes and she abandoned her poise to rush into Griff's outstretched arms. "Griff, I thought I would never find you. I've been searching for weeks now. No one knew of you or what had happened. I'm sorry, darling, but I couldn't go off to St. Joseph like Damien wanted me to. I had to find you."

"And now you have." Deep-seated joy welled up in Griff's breast and he squeezed Jennifer in a hug that went far beyond fierce. "You shouldn't have done this," he admonished.

Jennifer dried the moisture from her eyes and tried to look demure and contrite. "That's what Damien said you would say. A-aren't you glad to see me?"

"Of course I am. But who came with you?"

"No one." She caught her breath, waiting for the expected eruption. It came in an instant.

"What! You should never travel alone, my dearest. Especially not into Mexico. How? Oh, the letter I wrote to Damien."

"Yes. When I knew you had been here in Chihuahua I had to come. I didn't know it was such a large place. So many people. And so few who speak English. But I kept trying. And now I have found you."

"Only to lose me again, I'm afraid. I've been talking with a man who has seen a white boy riding with Apaches. It could be Jeremy. The Indians, the Mescalero band of Apaches, Sanchez says, raided a village northwest of here only five days ago. If Temple and I hurry, we can get on their trail."

"Oh . . . I . . . it's so important to you to find your son and . . . it would be small of me to object. Only—"

"We've just found each other, is that it?"

Jennifer nodded. "Yes," she admitted in a small voice.

"There's the rest of today."

Her decision made, Jennifer firmed her jaw and gazed intently into Griff's eyes, as though to compel his agreement by force of will. "Well then, we'll need lots of rest tonight if we leave in the morning."

"Jen . . . Jen, *we* are not going together. You must return to the United States. Temple and I will check out this possibility and then head back."

"Nonsense. I've come this far alone. Do you think I would be any less safe in the company of two brave men? I'm coming along and that's the end of it."

"Jen, I—"

"Not a word, Griffin Stark. I love you and you love me. We are meant to be together, *in all things.*" She smiled sweetly and brushed at a stray lock of her dark hair. Then she turned slightly away from him. "So. That's all settled. Now let's find a decent place and have something to eat. I have so much to tell you."

Griffin Stark remained silent. He knew it would be useless to argue with this strong-willed young woman who meant so much to him. If he was to find his son, Jennifer Carmichael would be at his side when he did. He sighed resignedly and mentally began to make new arrangements for the search for Jeremy Stark.

THE NEWEST ADVENTURES AND ESCAPADES OF BOLT
by Cort Martin

#11: THE LAST BORDELLO   (1224, $2.25)

A working girl in Angel's camp doesn't stand a chance—unless Jared Bolt takes up arms to bring a little peace to the town . . . and discovers that the trouble is caused by a woman who used to do the same!

#12: THE HANGTOWN HARLOTS   (1275, $2.25)

When the miners come to town, the local girls are used to having wild parties, but events are turning ugly . . . and murderous. Jared Bolt knows the trade of tricking better than anyone, though, and is always the first to come to a lady in need . . .

#13: MONTANA MISTRESS   (1316, $2.25)

Roland Cameron owns the local bank, the sheriff, and the town—and he thinks he owns the sensuous saloon singer, Charity, as well. But the moment Bolt and Charity eye each other there's fire—especially gunfire!

#14: VIRGINIA CITY VIRGIN   (1360, $2.25)

When Katie's bawdy house holds a high stakes raffle, Bolt figures to take a chance. It's winner take all—and the prize is a budding nineteen year old virgin! But there's a passle of gun-toting folks who'd rather see Bolt in a coffin than in the virgin's bed!

#15: BORDELLO BACKSHOOTER   (1411, $2.25)

Nobody has ever seen the face of curvaceous Cherry Bonner, the mysterious madam of the bawdiest bordello in Cheyenne. When Bolt keeps a pimp with big ideas and a terrible temper from having his way with Cherry, gunfire flares and a gambling man would bet on murder: Bolt's!

#16: HARDCASE HUSSY   (1513, $2.25)

Traveling to set up his next bordello, Bolt is surrounded by six prime ladies of the evening. But just as Bolt is about to explore this lovely terrain, their stagecoach is ambushed by the murdering Beeler gang, bucking to be in Bolt's position!

Available wherever paperbacks are sold, or order direct from the Publisher. Send cover price plus 50¢ per copy for mailing and handling to Zebra Books, 475 Park Avenue South, New York, N.Y. 10016. DO NOT SEND CASH.